For Kym,

Who also loves Christmas.
xxx

Also by Kiltie Jackson

A Rock 'n' Roll Lovestyle
An Artisan Lovestyle
An Incidental Lovestyle
A Timeless Lovestyle

Waiting Since Forever

Radio Ha Ha!

ACKNOWLEDGMENTS

When I set out on this writing journey five years ago, I honestly didn't think I'd still be at it seven books later. And yet, here we are, another book is being sent out into the world. I hope it brings joy and smiles to many.

These words do not get put together, however, without the support of many wonderful people. Space allows me to only mention a mere handful but that does not mean you are not important to me if your name is not mentioned.

To get the (snow)ball rolling, my best friend in the Universe – Kym. The support you give is appreciated more than I'll ever be able to tell you. You are the best wing-woman a gal could have.

My BFF – Stuart James Dunne. A great author who generously shares his success in order to help others do well. Every author needs a BFF like this; I'm so glad you're mine!

My parents who continue to keep reading and telling me I'm great even though my dad would be happier if a few wizards and warlocks were to pop up.

The excellent Facebook book groups who are so generous with their support for authors regardless of status within the writing community – you love us all and we love you for it. If you're looking to join an online book group, then I heartily recommend The Fiction Café Book Group, Chick-Lit & Prosecco and TBC – The Book Club. Great bookish places with fabulously friendly members.

To everyone in my own little Facebook group – The Kiltie Jackson Speakeasy – thank you for all the love and support you give and the time you take to participate throughout the day. I'm not naming members this time because you are all special and I don't want anyone to feel left out

i

because I adore each and every one of you. (By the way, new members are always welcome.)

I have to give a MASSIVE thank you to two people without whom this book wouldn't make it beyond my keyboard – John Husdpith, my Editor Extraordinaire and Berni Stevens who creates the most stunning covers. I'm so happy you're on my team.

An extra special mention goes out to all the fantastic bloggers who willing read, review and who help to spread the word. Thank you so much for the time you give. You make the book community a great place to be.

The following people are my crew and they make sure I don't give up when it all gets too much: Mark Fearn, the best Beta-Reader ever, Sue Baker, Sumaira Wilson, Dee Groocock, Zoe-Lee O'Farrell for the wonderful blog tours, Anita Faulkner, Julie Caplin, Rosie Travers, Ritu Kaur, Jaimie Admans and Isabella May. I could list so many more but that means we'd be here for rather a long time.

For my Mr Mogs – the darling man who has to live with someone whose head is only ever half in the room as her imagination runs riot while brewing new stories to tell. Thank you for loving me and dealing with it. Love you to the end of eternity… and a day! xx

And finally, to absolutely the most important people of all – all you wonderful readers. Thank you for taking the time to read my work, for leaving reviews, for telling your friends and for always waiting impatiently for the next offering… and letting me know this! You encourage me to keep going and that means everything. From the bottom of my heart, I thank you.

Until the next time,

Kiltie xx

<u>1</u>

November 30th

Polly Snowflake walked along the pavement looking for a good spot to cross the road. Three days of constant rain had left puddles the size of small swimming pools along the side of the kerb and as the long jump had never been a sport in which she'd excelled, finding a crossing point was proving to be a nuisance. Okay, she could make her way down to the traffic lights but they were at the other end of the high street and a good bit away from where she needed to be. It would also add ten minutes to her journey and give her troll of a boss, Edith, yet another excuse to moan and complain.

She looked along the road again and saw an upcoming break in the traffic. If she could traverse the large, muddy expanse of water at her feet, she could be back inside The Calderly Top Gift & Wrapping Emporium within a few moments and her ears would be safe from Edith's wrath.

Just as she decided to chance it, there was a sharp thump

against her right shoulder blade and time moved into the slowest of motions as her feet gave way on the wet ground, the air around her let out a whooshing sound and the dirty, murky water of the roadside puddle splashed high as she landed face first and flat out in it. The mud-filled droplets hung suspended above her for a fraction of a second before giving in to gravity and coming down to land on her back, her neck and in her hair.

'OI, YOU STUPID-ARSED MORON! GET BACK HERE!' a voice somewhere over her head was yelling as her first wave of shock found itself rapidly pushed aside by a flood of mortification and she quickly tried to get back up on her feet.

'Here, take it easy. Grab my hand.'

A pair of small, brown shiny brogues appeared in her eyeline and a hand came down from above to hover close by. A hand which she gratefully grabbed hold of and allowed to pull her upright. An arm around the small of her back guided her onto the pavement once more.

'Are you okay? Apart from being soaking wet and your gorgeous coat now looking rather the worse for wear, that is.'

Her coat!

Polly looked down and tears blurred her vision. Her beautiful pale cream coat was now a sodden, black, sopping mess.

'Oh no! No, no, no!'

'Look, come with me, we'll get it sorted.'

With the arm still around her back and the other under her elbow, she allowed her rescuer to guide her along the street.

'I can't believe that idiot didn't stop to help you.'

'What… what happened? I was standing by the roadside—'

'—when some asswipe walked right into you because

he was too busy looking at his mobile phone! I don't think he even realised what he'd done because I didn't see him look up when I shouted at him.'

'Oh, I see.'

By now, Polly was beginning to shiver and she could feel her teeth trying hard to chatter. She clenched her jaw in an attempt to stop them.

'Here we are. The stairwell is a bit narrow so I'll go first and you follow behind.'

Her rescuer pulled the solid wooden door open and held it for her. Just as it clicked closed, it suddenly dawned on Polly that she'd allowed some unknown man to assume control of her predicament and he was now taking her goodness only knew where.

She tried to assess him, as he walked up the stairs in front of her. He didn't look very tall, was slight of stature and had short brown hair. She could see his scalp through the fine, soft fuzz. He was wearing jeans and a cable-knit type jumper with a shirt collar peeping out the top. In truth, from the back, he didn't look like any kind of serial killer but then, what exactly did serial killers look like?

When she reached the top of the stairs, she walked through a second door – a glass one this time – and found herself in an open, airy reception area. Directly in front of her was a large wooden desk, the kind you would find in the study of a stately home, with the leather top writing area, solid front and, most likely, drawers on either side of the seating well. Upon it sat a computer and a small telephone switchboard.

'Come, sit down and take that wet coat off. Let's see if we can rescue it for you. ANDY!'

She was led over to a large green leather Chesterfield sofa and she dropped her bags onto it as her coat was unbuttoned and eased off her shoulders. While the familiarity of her rescuer was perhaps a step too far, her

3

own fingers tingled with icy numbness and she knew she wouldn't have been able to undo it herself.

'I have to say, this coat is beautiful. The cashmere is exquisite.'

'Thank you. It was my grandmother's. She fell in love with it the first time she saw it and asked the shop to put it aside for her – as they used to do in the days before credit cards. It took her forty-three weeks to pay for it. She was wearing it for the first time when she met the man who would become my grandfather. He always said it was the coat which first grabbed his attention and then he realised it was all the more beautiful because of the girl who was wearing it.'

'Aw, that's lovely. So, even more reason to get it seen to. ANDY!'

'Okay, okay, I'm here! I'm here!'

A man who looked to be of a similar age to herself, jumped down the three small steps from the mezzanine floor directly opposite where Polly was standing.

'Andy, could you take this lovely coat down to Kelly, please, and see if he can work his magic on it. Explain to him that the wearer was pushed into a puddle on the road so he knows that there may be oil in the dirt.'

'Will do.'

'And on your way back, pop into Dottie's and pick up some hot chocolates – this young lady needs to be warmed up inside as well as out.'

'On it!'

Before Polly could say anything, Andy had gathered up her coat and was out the door.

'Please, sit down, you poor thing. You're still shaking.'

He picked up an elegantly-draped-over-the-arm-of-the-sofa throw and carefully placed it around her shoulders. Polly pulled the edges together in front of her and the softness of the wool suggested it was cashmere.

4

'Now then, I suppose I should introduce myself since I've just taken the liberty of de-coating you. I'm Monty, Monty Watkins.'

The hand which had pulled her from the puddle reappeared in her eyeline once again. She smiled as she looked up and put her own hand in it.

'Polly Snowflake.'

'Wow! Now there's a surname! How much grief have you had through the years over that one?'

Polly let out a bark of a laugh at Monty's refreshing forthrightness.

'More than you can possibly imagine.'

'I'll bet. Now, don't you worry about your coat – Kelly is one of the best dry-cleaners in the business and I'm in no doubt that it'll come back as good as new.'

'Thank you for sorting it. And for rescuing me. I'm very grateful.'

She smiled up at the kind face looking down on her. Everything about Monty was petite. His hands were as small as his feet, he was as slender in the front as he was from the back and his brown eyes twinkled behind his small, rimless glasses. The receding hairline was less noticeable due to his uber-short haircut.

'Now,' he shot a sharp look at the reception desk before returning his full attention to her, 'when Andy gets back, we'll sort you out with another coat but, in the meantime, if you want to slip your shoes and socks off, I'll go and get you a basin of hot water so you can warm up your feet.'

'Look, there's no need to go to such trouble—'

'Oh, but there is. You've had a nasty fall – luckily, you don't appear to be hurt in any way and thank *goodness* there was no traffic when it happened – but you need a little time to recover and I want to be sure you don't go into shock. You need to be patched up before I would feel comfortable sending you back out into the cold, cruel world.'

Polly chuckled at his dramatic statement. She sensed he'd probably had as much of a fright as she had and focusing on her needs was Monty's way of dealing with it.

'Then I thank you for your courtesy and assistance, kind sir.'

Monty gave her a full-on grin and was in the process of performing a sweeping bow when the door at the bottom of the stairs slammed and footsteps resembling a herd of small elephants could be heard running up them.

'Ah, this'll be—'

The glass door at the top of the stairs was flung open and the tallest, widest, and most truly-gorgeous man she had ever set eyes on, walked in.

'—my twin brother, Maxwell.'

2

'Twin brother?'

'Yup, twin brother. I know, I know, we look like the characters from the Arnie film, Twins, except I like to think I'm a bit better looking than Danny DeVito!'

Polly didn't know what to say. Monty was totally on the money when he said they resembled the characters from the movie. Maxwell, however, was infinitely hotter than Arnold Schwarzenegger although he definitely shared his solidly built physique. She decided the best course of action would be to play along.

'I quite agree, Monty, you are decidedly better looking than Danny DeVi— hang on,' she looked at the two men in front of her and then looked around the room until she saw the discrete logo on the wall above the reception desk, 'Monty and Maxwell? As in, Monty Maxwell? Monty Maxwell, the growing-more-famous-by-the-day men's clothing designer?'

The interlinking double "M" motif that she'd seen in department stores and fashion magazines was also adorning the reception wall.

'He's Monty Maxwell, I'm just Maxwell, his brother.'

'Oh, right.'

She couldn't work out what was making her head swim more – the realisation that she was sitting in the presence of fashion designing greatness or the deep timbered rasp of Maxwell Watkin's voice. Maybe she could get away with blaming the sensation on late-onset shock.

'When we were younger, Maxwell could never find clothes to fit because of his height and width. All the XXXL's were too short in the arms, tight across the shoulders and like small tents down the front. They were made for men with girth, not men with height and width. He inspired me to begin designing outfits for taller and bigger men. There was a gap in the market and I went for it. He was also my first model – and why not, he is rather gorgeous if I say so myself – so it seemed only right to include him in the naming of the company.'

Maxwell turned a stunning shade of red at his brother's words and Polly moved her attention to her feet so that he wouldn't see her smiling at his discomfort.

'And do you both design? Is it a family business? Sorry, I know you're a big deal in the fashion world but I'm not really up on men's fashion.'

'No, we're not,' Maxwell rumbled above her, 'I'm an arboriculturist.'

'An abori-what?'

'It's a posh term for a tree-surgeon, Polly. He's just showing off.'

'It's a bit more than that, Monty, as you well know.'

'Yeah, yeah, whatever!'

Polly smiled at the banter between the brothers. At first, she'd thought Monty was pulling her leg about them being twins but despite the differences in their stature, she could see several similarities – the shape and colour of their eyes, the small dimples in their cheeks when they smiled and the same high, sharp cheekbones.

Just then, the phone on the reception desk began to ring and Monty looked around in annoyance.

'KAREN? ARE YOU HERE? KAREN?'

When he received no reply and the phone continued to ring, he let out a tut of annoyance and strode over to answer it.

'As my brother didn't see fit to introduce us properly, I'll do the honours. Maxwell Watkins.'

He held out his hand and it was all Polly could do not to melt at his feet. He'd hunkered down as he spoke so he was eye-level with her and the tone of his voice was deep and warm. If pushed to describe it, she'd have said it was like warm honey being poured over glass shards—

Whoa!

What the hell?

Warm honey over glass shards?

What was wrong with her?

A good-looking man… okay, a drop-dead gorgeous man… speaks to her and she turns into a Barbara Cartland novel? Time to back it up, sister!

She pulled in a deep breath, sat up a little straighter, and put her hand in his. She forced herself to ignore the tingling sensation making its way up her arm.

'Hi, I'm Polly. Your brother kindly rescued me when some oaf on his mobile thought I should have an early bath in a puddle at the side of the road.'

'Oh no, what a moron!'

'I believe your brother thought the same.'

Maxwell smiled and she could see Monty's own smile in it.

'Tell me, I don't want to be rude, but are you really twins?'

'Yes, we really are.'

She didn't get a chance to reply as Andy returned at that

moment and thrust a large hot chocolate under her nose. Monty ended the phone call and came back to join them.

'Andy, where's Karen?'

'Ah… err… she popped out on an errand.'

Polly noticed the man's growing discomfort under Monty's gaze.

'When did she "pop out", Andy?'

'Urm… I'm not quite sure…'

'Andy, does Karen pay the wages around here?'

'Err, no.'

'So, I'll ask again – when did Karen go out?'

Andy's shoulders dropped as he replied in a miserable tone, 'Just after you left to go to the accountants.'

Monty looked at his watch. 'So, she's been away for nearly two hours?'

'Yes.'

'Grrr!' he growled, 'That does it! That girl is fired! I've had enough of her lazy ways.'

He spun back round to face Polly again.

'Right, I said I'd sort you out with a bowl of water for your feet – Andy, would you mind boiling the kettle and bringing a basin of nice warm water and a couple of towels back for Polly. While you're doing that, I'll go up to the stockroom to sort out some outerwear as I can't send her on her way in just a thin top. Maxwell, are you okay to keep our guest company for a few minutes?'

'I'm sorry, Monty, I'm double parked and need to rescue the truck before I get done. I only popped in to let you know I'll be bringing your Christmas tree over later this afternoon.'

'Oh, right.'

'Monty, I'll be fine on my own for a couple of minutes.'

Polly gave him an embarrassed smile – she didn't need to be babysat; she was a grown woman after all.

'Okay, I won't be long.'

A few seconds later, she was sitting alone in the reception and she let out a long breath. Well, that had all been a bit hectic. She took some deep breaths to soothe the butterflies in her stomach and several sips of the rather delicious hot chocolate to warm her insides. She was just beginning to feel a bit more like herself when the phone on the reception desk rang again. She looked about but there was no sign of Andy or Monty. She stayed on the sofa, hoping someone would appear to take the call but after the fourth ring and with no other sign of life in the vicinity, she jumped to her feet and squelched across to the desk. As luck would have it, the switchboard was a model she was familiar with and she grabbed the handset.

'Good morning, Monty Maxwell's office, how may I help you?'

She listened to the caller while rummaging in the desk drawers to find a pad and pen to jot down a message.

Five minutes later, she had three messages to pass on to Monty when he came back down the steps carrying a hanger inside a long, zipped-up, suit-cover.

'Here you go, try this on for size.'

He put the hanger on the old-style hat and coat stand by the side of the sofa, unzipped it and brought out a stunning dark-red coat. From the front, it looked fairly ordinary – single-breasted, a Peter Pan collar with black embroidered stitching around it and a slight flare from the waist down. When he turned it around, however, the back was something else entirely. Across the shoulders to the waist, it had small, sewn-up, box pleats. A martingale sat on the waist with the same black embroidery as the collar and below it, the box pleats all opened up to allow the skirt of the coat to swing. As if that wasn't enough, the pleats came down to end with a small fish-tail at the bottom.

'Oh, Monty, this is amazing. What a beautiful, beautiful coat. It is gorgeous.'

'I thought you might like it. Go on, try it to see if it fits.'

'Did you design this?' Polly asked as she slipped her arms into the sleeves.

'I did. I've been humming and hawing about trying my hand in woman's fashion but haven't been brave enough to take the plunge. This is a sample garment. If you don't mind wearing it for a few days until Kelly has cleaned yours, I would really appreciate your feedback on it. You know, is it comfortable to wear? Or too tight in places? Not practical? That sort of thing. Ladies' fashion would be a whole new step for me so your input would be great.'

Polly pulled the coat together in front of her and fastened the buttons. It was soft to the touch and the fit was almost perfect. It was a touch longer than she was used to but if she wore her boots with the higher heels when she had it on, the length would be less of a problem.

'I'd be happy to wear it and "sample" it for you, Monty, as long as you're happy about me doing so. It feels like you're putting a lot of trust in me and we barely know each other.'

'You strike me as a good sort, Polly. Besides, I do have your grandmother's coat as collateral if my instincts turn out to be wrong.'

'I can assure you they are not. I feel immensely flattered. Oh, and while you were sorting this out, the phone rang again – I took some messages for you.' She pointed to the three pages sitting neatly on the reception desk. 'I hope you don't mind.'

'Mind? Of course, I don't mind. Thank you so very much.'

He walked over to read them as Andy arrived and walked slowly down the steps in order not to spill the water in the bowl he was carrying.

Polly had undone the buttons on the coat and was carefully slipping it off when Monty came back across.

'This message,' he held a piece of paper in his hand, 'is really important. It's regarding a fabric order which is vital for my next collection. Had you not taken the call, and I'd missed it, it would have been a disaster. Would you be at all offended if I offered you a job as my receptionist or office person or whatever name you would be comfortable calling yourself?'

'Aw, Monty, you're very kind but I'm afraid I already have a jo— Oh shit! Edith! She's going to kill me! How long have I been here?'

A quick look at her wristwatch told Polly it had been fifty-five minutes since Edith had sent her out to buy more sticky tape as her stationery suppliers had forgotten to include it in the weekly order.

She bent down and pulled back on the shoes she'd been in the process of removing.

'Polly, you can't go out with your feet all wet like that, you'll catch your death!'

'Monty, I'll be even more dead when Edith sees how long I've been away for.'

'Surely, she'll understand once you explain what's happened?'

'No, she won't. She is an evil little troll who, I am convinced, worships at the shrine of Krampus. I have to go now! Thank you so much for all your help today, you're my Christmas angel. I'll bring your coat back in a few days.'

With those words, she pulled the red coat back on, gathered up her handbag along with the plastic carrier containing the sticky tape, and after giving Monty a quick kiss on the cheek and wishing a hurried farewell to Andy, Polly rushed out the door.

<u>3</u>

'WHERE HAVE YOU BEEN? How long does it take to buy some tape?'

Polly had barely put her toe over the threshold of the doorway when her boss launched her verbal attack.

'I had an accident—'

'You liar!' Edith's narrowed eyes looked her up and down and a thunderous look came across her face. 'YOU WENT SHOPPING! YOU WENT SHOPPING ON WORKING TIME! HOW DARE YOU!'

The next thing Polly knew, Edith had grabbed her arm and was dragging her through to the stockroom at the back of the shop.

'Let go of me!'

She tried to pull herself free but Edith's grip was surprisingly strong for such a small woman. She wriggled her arm again but was still unable to break away from Edith's grasp. Worried that any further attempt to get loose might damage Monty's coat, she gave up and allowed her employer to woman-handle her through the shop.

Once the door had slammed closed behind them, Edith

let rip.

'You ungrateful wretch! I send you out on an errand and you think it's okay to go and buy yourself a new coat! That is completely unacceptable!'

'Edith,' Polly spoke quietly in the hope it might calm the older women down as she now looked like an advert for a heart attack, 'I did not buy a new coat—'

'Is that the coat you were wearing when you went out?'

'No, it's not. I—'

'So, if it's not the coat you had on when you went out, you must have bought a new one.'

'Edith, I didn't—'

'What, you're telling me you just so happen to carry a spare coat in your handbag in the event that you might fancy a change?'

'No, I—'

'I don't want to hear any excuses. The time will be docked from your wages and you can stay behind after hours tonight and tidy up this stock room as a punishment.'

'I beg your pardon?'

Polly wasn't sure she'd heard correctly. Was Edith really talking to her as though she was a misbehaving schoolgirl? Did she honestly think she had the right to "punish" her?

'You heard me! As punishment for your bad behaviour, you'll stay late tonight and clean this room.'

'Oh, no I won't! You don't get to talk to me like that. I don't know who you think you are but you do not have the right to speak to me in that manner.'

'You WERE my employee but not anymore. You're fired.'

'That's where you're wrong, Edith. You're not firing me – I quit! Just like every other member of staff who's ever worked for you.'

The woman's face changed from thunderous to shocked

in the blink of an eye.

'Yes, Edith, your reputation precedes you. I didn't think the stories were true but it turns out they are. You're just a miserable, nasty old hag and I wish you all the luck in the world in finding another assistant but don't hold your breath because I don't think there are any idiots left in this village for you to terrorise!'

She stepped closer to Edith and the woman shrank back in fear as Polly's arm moved towards her. It then snaked past her ear, over her shoulder and picked up the lunch bag sitting on the shelf behind her. She was walking out of the store room when Edith's shrill tones assaulted her ears once more.

'Oi, what about my sticky tape?'

Polly stopped, looked over her shoulder and replied, 'Go and get your own, I'm not your errand girl!' before letting the store room door close behind her.

As she stormed along the pavement, chuntering to herself about the bad luck that had led to her losing her grandmother's coat and her job within the space of two hours, Polly became aware that her feet were still squelching away inside her shoes. Which were now also going to be ruined.

'Right! Home, shower, coffee and a good think is what I need to do now!'

She made her way to the pedestrian crossing and began the trudge up the steep hill, feeling her temper ease away with each water-logged footstep. When she reached the top and turned into her lane, she stopped to look across the valley. She'd lived here eight months now and hadn't yet tired of the stunning view across this part of the Peak District. This time last year, she'd thought nothing could ever make her leave London; now she knew nothing could ever make her go back. Calderly Top had soothed her troubled soul when she'd arrived on the back of her ex-husband's deceit and for that alone, she loved the place.

Her eyes moved away from the view and came to rest upon her home. An old, four-bedroomed, grey sandstone detached house standing in its own four acres of land. This had been her main reason for moving out of the capital – being able to live in a beautiful house with its own space over being crammed into a two-bedroom flat with a shared postage stamp of a lawn. Okay, the downside was that she hadn't known anyone when she arrived here and was still working on fitting in but she'd always enjoyed her own company, so being alone now wasn't a problem. These things took time.

A gust of wind blew past, making her shiver.

'Home, shower, coffee, and a think,' she muttered again as she walked down the lane to her gate. She smiled at how deceiving the house looked from this angle. Four small windows along the top and three equally small windows and a front door at the far end along the bottom. It looked old and dark and had almost had her doing a U-turn when she first came to view the property. It was only the knowledge of what was hidden inside, which the online photographs had promised, that had got her through the front door which she'd just closed behind her. The ruined shoes were kicked off and she grabbed an old pair of socks from her garden boots to slip over her wet feet before running up the stairs.

As always, Polly stopped to pause when she stepped onto the gallery which led to her bedroom at the far end of the house. The lounge area below had been opened up and the outside wall replaced with vast floor to ceiling windows that looked out over the adjoining fields and hills. The previous owner's son had been an architect and modernising the family home had been his first project.

He'd done a great job in bringing a new lease of life to the old building without losing any of its olde-worlde charm.

Further shivers ran up her body and without any further ado, Polly made her way towards her bedroom and the hot, hot shower which awaited her.

4

'Hey, Bailey, coming up for a snuggle?'

The long-haired grey and white tabby cat gave a little mewl as he jumped onto the sofa and burrowed up close to Polly's side. She hadn't had a pet before she'd arrived here at Bailey House and there had been no intention of getting one either. That was until the day she'd gone out into the garden after a particularly nasty storm and found a wet, bedraggled, grey mass underneath one of the bushes. She'd brought it indoors, dried it off, fed it and then taken it to the vet to be checked over whereupon she'd learnt the cat was a "he", roughly four years old and not microchipped. The vet had advised he was in fairly good shape, so not a stray or a feral, and surmised he'd most likely been a pet who'd been dumped as he hadn't seen him before and he was the only small animal vet in the immediate vicinity so knew most of the cats and dogs in the area. This information had made Polly's blood boil and she'd vowed that she'd give this poor little man the kind of life he deserved. He'd come back home with her then, all newly named – Bailey after her house – freshly chipped and vet-registered and had turned out to be the snuggliest, cuddliest cat she'd ever come across and she now adored the very bones of him. She moved her coffee mug to her right hand and let her left hand gently rub his head while she thought on what to do next. Her encounter with Edith had left her feeling a little raw. In all her working days – and she'd worked all of her adult life – she'd never come across anyone so nasty. Sure, the odd bitchy woman or grouchy man had crossed her path, but Edith was a whole new level of horrible altogether.

Her thoughts went back to the offer Monty had made – had he really meant it? Or had it just been said as a joke in a moment of slight despair at his receptionist's absence? Office management was her line of work but there hadn't been anything of that nature available when she'd signed up with the two employment agencies who covered the area. Was her perceived "bad luck" actually a stroke of good luck in disguise? And, more to the point, would her skills be suitable for working in a fashion house? All of her experience to date had been gathered within the City walls of London. Sure, she'd be able to get him a good deal on his insurance but other than that…

'Excuse me a moment, beautiful boy, I need to move.'

She patted Bailey's head gently and, carefully extracting herself so as not to disturb him too much, she went to pick up her handbag from where she'd dumped it just inside the front door. As Polly went to unzip it, she noticed the splash marks on the cream leather so took it through to the kitchen to wipe them off before reaching inside to retrieve her mobile phone. It would seem that the phone's bad habit of falling down to the bottom of her bag may have, on this occasion, saved its life as it was damage-free and good to go when she pulled it out.

One quick swipe and a few finger-taps later, she had pulled up the Monty Maxwell media page. She sat down at the kitchen table to read through the information but found that it didn't tell her much more than she'd already learnt from the man himself that morning. She returned to her search engine and looked for other articles which may have been written. Half an hour later, the only other thing she'd learnt was that Monty was a strong advocate for the LGBTQ movement and had spoken at several rallies. That was it.

She returned to the sofa and snuggled up to Bailey again.

'Okay, wise one, give me your thoughts – do I go back to see Monty and ask if he was serious about the job offer or do I stay at home with you, curl up here on the sofa where we can watch crappy films and eat our weight in chocolate muffins?'

Bailey opened one green eye to look at her, stood up, stretched, turned around and then lay back down again, pulling his big fluffy tail over his face.

'Oh, I see, like that is it? Well, fine! For that, I'm going to get myself dressed in something more professional than a pair of joggies and a sweatshirt and I'm going back into town to find myself some form of employment!'

Polly stood outside the solid wooden door that led up to Monty's office and looked at her watch. She couldn't believe it was only just after one o'clock – so much had happened this morning in such a short space of time. She'd really expected it to be later than that.

She was about to push the door open when she hesitated – what if Karen, the errant receptionist, had returned? How could she ask Monty about the job if the woman was sitting right there? That would be awkward.

Polly walked along the pavement, trying to think of an

excuse for being there if Karen was back in situ. As she walked, a sweet smell began to curl around her nose and she looked up to find herself outside a small café with the name "Dottie's" written in gold curves across the window.

That was it!

She could buy Monty and Andy a hot chocolate as a thank you for taking care of her. If Karen was there, she could leave without causing any embarrassment and if she wasn't… well, there was nothing to lose in questioning Monty about the validity of his offer.

A few minutes later, she pushed the wooden door open, taking care not to jolt the cardboard cup-holder in her hands. As she made her way up the stairs and the reception desk came into view, she was relieved to see the seat behind it was still vacant. This did not mean that Karen wasn't in the building but did suggest that she may not be.

After doing a small juggle with the glass door which opened outwards, Polly gently placed the cupholder on the wooden desk and looked around. The reception area was empty and all was quiet. She unbuttoned her borrowed coat and moved towards the steps that led up to the area behind the reception and which had two long wooden tables running along either side. The room went back further than she'd first realised and she was now able to hear the quiet murmur of voices towards the rear.

'Hello? Monty, are you there?' Polly called out as she walked towards an open door on the back wall.

'Polly! You've come back to me!'

Monty burst through the door, rushed towards her with open arms and grabbed her in a bear hug.

'Oops, sorry, no longer considered appropriate. My apologies.'

He quickly let her go and stepped back to put some space between them.

'Hey, not a problem, Monty. It was a lovely welcome.

I've brought you and Andy some hot chocolate to say thank you for looking after me this morning. I rushed away so suddenly that I feel I didn't show my gratitude towards you adequately enough.'

'Oh, you did, you did. You don't need to worry about that. Are you on your lunch break now? We could pop out and grab a sandwich.'

'I'm not on my lunch break,' Polly paused for a moment. Here goes nothing, she thought. 'I no longer have a job.'

'You were fired? For having an accident?'

'More like I quit after my employer tried to treat me like a twelve-year-old.'

'Does that mean you can come and work for me now?'

'If the offer still stands? If you really meant it, that is…'

'Of course I meant it! I would be thrilled to have you on board.'

'But you know nothing of my experience. Don't you want to check my CV and take up some references?'

'Polly, you gorgeous girl, I will most likely do those things but the fact you already know how to work that horrible brat of a switchboard is good enough for me. Why don't we have a sit down, you tell me what you can do and we'll work something out?'

Monty led her down to the sofa in the reception, brought over the hot chocolates and listened while she brought him up to speed on her office management experience and her previous places of employment.

'Well, Ms Snowflake, if anything, I would say you are over-qualified for the role I am offering but you are welcome to take it on board and do with it as you wish. The less admin I have to bother myself with, the happier I am. My priorities are designing and creating so if you are able to deal with all the other things which are not in those categories, we'll rub along very nicely.'

'I think I can help to keep you admin-free,' Polly said, 'When would you like me to start?'

'Right now, this minute, if that's okay with you?'

She stood and removed her coat – *his* coat.

'I'm already on it!'

Monty smiled with joy and she found herself returning it. She already knew she was going to enjoy being here and learning about the fashion world was an added bonus. Something different to add to her experience.

'Oh, Polly…'

'Yes, boss?'

'Your first job will be to sack Karen whenever she deigns to show her face again.'

'Oh, right. Okay!'

Hmm, maybe not such a great start after all!

5

The slam of the door at the bottom of the stairs made Polly look up from the pile of paperwork she'd found stashed in the larger of the desk drawers. She had to look twice to ensure her eyes were not deceiving her and that a huge Christmas tree really was making its way up the stairs. As it drew closer, she spotted two solid arms encased in red check, wrapped around its middle. That was when she recalled the earlier conversation between Monty and Maxwell about the tree being delivered this afternoon.

She jumped up and ran to the glass door, holding it open for Maxwell to stagger through.

'Cheers, thanks for that,' he puffed, as he made his way to the far corner and leant the tree carefully up against the wall.

'I can't believe you've just carried that up on your own! It's massive!'

'Oh, it was nothing. Not when you're used to lugging the things around.'

'But it's taller than you. It's huge!' Polly eyed up the brute in the corner.

'Not by much. It's a seven-footer, I'm six-foot, seven inches.'

'It's still a beast though.'

'It's a beauty. I hand-picked it myself. And, as Monty called me when he left earlier to tell me you now work here and are in charge of the office, you will have the pleasure of decorating it. Don't say I'm not good to you.'

The wide grin on his face slowly faded as the colour in Polly's cheeks rapidly drained away.

'Polly? Are you okay? Come, quick, sit down.'

Maxwell guided her over to the Chesterfield and she perched on the edge.

'I… I… I can't decorate it,' she whispered.

'Why ever not?'

Maxwell had knelt on the floor by her feet and was looking straight at her.

'I can't… I don't… I don't do Christmas.'

'I'm sorry? You don't do Christmas? Everyone does Christm— oh!' He stopped suddenly. 'My apologies. I wasn't thinking. I forgot that other faiths have different times and different types of celebration. Please, forgive me.'

'No, it's okay, it's nothing like that. It's not a faith thing.'

'Okaaaaaay, then may I ask why? If it's not too pushy. Tell me if it is. Tell me to mind my own nosy business if you want.'

The gentle smile that accompanied his words soothed the quaking sensation that had risen up in her stomach.

'My father died on Christmas Day when I was fifteen. I haven't "done" Christmas since then. Christmas ceased to exist for me, as a cause for celebration, twenty years ago.'

'Oh no, I'm so sorry to hear that.'

'It's alright. I don't talk about it – I don't want to bring other people down with my tale of sorrow.'

'Have you ever spoken about it? To anyone?'

The small tilt of Maxwell's head to the side, suggesting that he was genuinely interested in her answer, gave Polly the courage to speak truthfully.

'My best friend knows but we never talk about it. Like I said, folks don't want to hear sad stories when they're looking forward to partying and having fun.'

'Well, I don't mind hearing it, if you're of a mind to share. It's possible that, after twenty years, it's time to get it out there. And then maybe, just maybe, you might be able to begin enjoying the season of goodwill again – even if it's just a little bit. What do you say? Sometimes it's easier to talk to a stranger than to folks you know. Both of my big fat ears are here for you, if you want them.'

These words elicited a small chuckle which Polly would never have believed possible, for whenever she thought back to that awful Christmas Day, everything around her would go black and she'd be filled with a heavy sense of dread. She couldn't help looking at Maxwell's ears and yes, they were a bit big but only because he was. They were perfectly proportioned to his head and definitely not fat.

'Are you sure you want to hear it?'

'If you feel you can share it, then I'm more than ready to listen.'

For a minute or so, there was silence as Polly tried to dredge up the words that would adequately explain that day and how her family had broken apart because of it. She appreciated Maxwell's patience as he sat quietly beside her, waiting for her to speak and not pushing her to do so.

'My father loved Christmas. Adored it! With the surname Snowflake, how could he not? He threw himself into all the festivities and was like a big kid when the first day of December arrived. Every year, without fail, he'd be up in the loft sorting out the tree and decorations. My mum and I would wait below for him to pass down the items he wanted out that year. I should interject at this point that my dad could not pass a Christmas-themed shop without going inside and making a purchase. It could be the hottest day in July and if my dad found a Christmas shop, he'd be right in the door, humming along to the festive music while making a decision on what to buy. The result was that we had a LOT of Christmas stuff in that loft for him to choose from.'

'He sounds like my kind of guy. I'm totally on board with anyone who loves Christmas that much.'

Polly smiled before continuing.

'He really did make December feel very special and exciting. That year was no different. I'm an only child but it was always fun. My mum would be baking in the kitchen, making mince pies, shortbread, Stollen and many other Christmas goodies. The Christmas cake had, of course, been made a few months earlier.'

'Well, of course. The cake needs plenty of time to be watered and matured.'

'You get it!'

'My mum makes her own cake every year so I completely get it.'

'So, when the big day arrived, everything was as it had always been. We opened the pressies first thing in the morning, had mince pies for breakfast and then it was all hands on deck for the Christmas dinner which we always sat down to eat after the Queen's Speech. Nothing was different. Nothing changed from our usual routine. It was perfect. At six-thirty, Mum and I headed into the kitchen to put together a light supper. That's when we'd cut the cake, make a pot of tea and a plate of turkey sandwiches. We left Dad in his chair watching a repeat of a Morecambe and Wise Christmas Special. He loved those guys so much.

They always made him laugh. You know, a real full-on belly laugh that came all the way up from his boots. We could hear him in the kitchen.'

Polly stopped. The memory was so vivid, even now, and she could no longer see the reception area in front of her – her eyes were filled with the sight of the kitchen at home, her mother smiling as she took the mince pies out from warming up in the oven.

She took a breath and continued.

'My mum was smiling at the sound of Dad's laughter. She always said his joy was contagious. That was the last time I saw her smiling so freely. A moment later there was a crash from the front room and we both ran in to find Dad collapsed on the chair, his wine glass smashed on the floor. When the ambulance arrived, they told us there was nothing they could do, he was already dead. He'd had a stroke. A massive stroke that wiped him out in a matter of seconds. We couldn't understand it – he wasn't overweight, kept reasonably fit, didn't smoke or drink in excess. The doctors thought he'd most likely had a ruptured aneurysm. Anyway, when the following Christmas came round, neither Mum nor I felt like celebrating it. The next year was no different either. Dad had been Mum's world and part of her died with him. When it was my eighteenth Christmas, I was home alone. Dad had taken out a really hefty life insurance policy and Mum used some of it to buy an apartment in Spain with her sister. For the last eighteen years, they've spent every Christmas out there together. They go out in October and return in March.'

'You don't go with them?'

'No, I'm not a lover of the heat and even though I no longer do the actual Christmas thing, I do still love the winter season. Well, maybe not the rain but frosty mornings and cold foggy nights float my boat. If we get a decent snowfall, I'm in my element.'

'Well, being here in the Peak District should bring you a few of those in the next couple of months or so.'

'One of the reasons I moved here.' Polly gave Maxwell a smile. 'Anyway, to bring my tale of woe to a conclusion, I've managed to avoid all things Christmassy pretty well since then. When I worked on the reception desk in my old London job, the office manager preferred to decorate the tree and the office herself. When I was promoted to office manager, I delegated the task to the receptionists.'

'But, what about boyfriends and the like? Surely, they must have tried to get you involved with the season of goodwill?'

'My ex-husband didn't have much time for Christmas.'

'Ex-husband?'

'Definitely a story I'm not yet ready to talk about.'

'Fair enough.'

They sat in silence for a few moments and Polly had just become aware that Maxwell was holding her hand when he suddenly said, 'Your father died laughing…'

'What?'

She jumped up from the sofa and spun round to look at him. She caught a glimpse of her stricken face in the window behind him.

'What did you just say?'

'Oh, my goodness, I am SO sorry. I have this problem where my brain comes up with things and I'm speaking them before taking the time to assess if they're appropriate. I—'

Polly raised a hand like she was stopping traffic.

'Cease your prattling!'

In the sudden silence, she walked over to the desk, placed her hands flat upon it and let her head drop down between her shoulders. She took some deep breaths. How dare he… how dare he… how dare he say such a thing…

A moment passed and her shoulders began to shake. A moaning sound began to grow and forced its way up through her stomach, through her chest, filling every part of her being until it reached her lips where it exploded out… in a gust of laughter. Deep, deep, long, side-aching laughter. Laughter that had her bent double over the desk as it held her up. Laughter that caused tears to spring from her eyes and escape down her cheeks.

'Polly, oh my—'

She heard Maxwell jump to his feet to approach her and she raised her hand again to make him stop. Still laughing, she turned slowly round to face him.

'Died laughing… oh my, died laughing… oh… oh…'

This continued for about another minute in which time, Maxwell had retrieved the box of tissues from the unit behind the reception desk and handed them over to her. Once she'd wiped the tears and snot from her face, and had made an attempt to tidy herself up, Polly was finally able to look at Maxwell.

'Thank you. Thank you so much.'

'Huh? For what? For being so rudely flippant?'

'No, for making me see something that I've missed for the last twenty years. My dad died laughing. It's absolutely true. He did.' She took a deep breath to try and quell the giggles that were threatening to begin. 'And, what's more, he wouldn't have wanted to go any other way. He loved to laugh. He was always smiling and constantly cracking jokes. Some really awful jokes at times but he just loved being surrounded by joy. He was a man full of joy. Leaving this earth while laughing at the antics of his favourite comedians would have been the perfect death as far as he was concerned. I've always been so busy mourning his loss and how it affected me that I never took the time to think of it from his perspective. So, thank you. Thank you, Maxwell, for showing me the other side of the coin.'

'Well, it's not often my stupid gob gets praised so, I'm going to take it! You're very welcome. Does this now mean you're going to begin celebrating Christmas again? I think it's what he would have wanted. From your description, I think your dad would be most upset that his death had robbed you of the joy for the season, especially when it was a time that he loved so much. Maybe now you can move forward and honour his memory by revelling in some Yuletide celebrations.'

'That's a lovely idea, Maxwell, but after all these years, I don't know that I can. I'm rather out of practice. I've spent more years of my life ignoring Christmas than I have celebrating it.'

'Then I will help you. I love Christmas and have got no problem taking you under my wing and refuelling your joy and topping up your Christmas spirit once again. We'll begin tomorrow, when I will return to help you decorate the tree beast. And I'm afraid that I won't take no for an answer.'

6

December 1st

'Blooming heck, Andy, how many more boxes are there?'

'This is just a selection of what's stashed away in the loft,'Andy said, 'These are the heavier boxes but you're welcome to go and have a look to see what else is up there. You're in complete charge of decorating the reception and office space so feel free to do it as you like.'

'Erm, doesn't Monty prefer it to be all minimal and tasteful? You know, like one would expect the office of a fashion house to look like.'

'The first thing you need to know about Monty is that he doesn't wear the cliché of how fashion designers are supposed to be. He's really down to earth, has no ego whatsoever and only throws tantrums when collection time is approaching. And those are usually down to stress and he just needs to vent. Once he's exploded, all is calm again so don't ever take them at anything more than face-value.'

'What's the second thing?'

'Sorry?'

'You said that was the first thing I needed to know, what else is there?'

'Ah, yes! He loves Christmas. Adores it! So minimal is the last thing he would want or expect. Go to town in here. Make it feel like Santa's grotto and he'll love you for ever.'

'I've got it. He definitely shares the same love of the festive season as his twin brother – which I'm still getting my head around, by the way – and when it comes to Christmas, less is definitely not better.'

'In a nutshell, honey.'

'Have you worked for him a long time then?'

'Err, no. But I have worked *with* him since we both left college.'

'Oh, I thought he…'

'It's okay. We're equal partners but he's the creative genius in the partnership so I'm happy to let him get on with ruling the roost.'

'I see. What do you do then? If it's okay to ask?'

'Sure it is. I'm his soundboard. He'll come up with designs and then we'll discuss them, going over what parts work and what parts don't. I give him input on fabrics, I keep my ear to the ground on what's new, what's old and what's making a comeback. I help to design the sets for photoshoots and collection launches. There's a lot more to this business than just designing and sewing, you know.'

He gave her a little wink, letting her know that he wasn't mocking her lack of knowledge.

'You should also know, to avoid any issues, that we're also partners outside of the business too.'

'Wow! You work and live together – don't you find that claustrophobic?'

'Not at all. Because I already know how his day has been, when we get home, I can ensure we focus our free time on doing things that are not work related. This keeps everything fresh and alive. It works well.'

'That's great.'

'What about you? Is there a Mr Polly at home? Or a Mrs Polly? I'm very open-minded about these things, you know.'

Polly laughed along with Andy.

'No, there's neither. There was a Mr Polly until eighteen months ago but I don't talk about him as he's nothing more than an oxygen thief.'

'Fair enough. Well, I had best get on and finish getting everything ready for London.'

'London?'

'Oh, didn't Monty tell you? We're off down to the smoke later this afternoon. We've got a two-day photo session lined up – getting everything ready for next year's winter collection – so we'll be out of the office for the next two days. Two days which you now have off.'

'Oh what? But I've only just been here a day – I can't be taking time off already.'

'Yes, you can because when things get really hairy around here, you'll be expected to muck in and that can often mean working the occasional Saturday or staying late during the week to make sure everything is ready on time. If you'd been here last week, you'd have had all that to contend with.'

'Right. But what about the phones?'

'We have them redirected to the London office and get a temp in to cover them.'

'Can I ask, please, why does Monty have two offices? Why doesn't he have a full set-up in London like the other designer establishments?'

'The shop in Bond Street has an office above it but he loves being here at home. He's a Derbyshire lad, born and bred. When he was starting out, we lived in London for a time and he did enjoy the lifestyle that came with this occupation but after a time, it began to wane. There really is too much of a good thing. Once he'd had his breakthrough and established himself, he was straight back here. This building belonged to his grandfather who was a lawyer. When he passed on, it was left to the twins as they'd spent a lot of time here as kids and were rather attached to the place. They agreed it was the perfect place to set up in. A few structural alterations were made – nothing drastic, just some walls removed to open up the space – and here we are. We both prefer being in the Peaks, we're happier here.'

'As an escapee from London myself, I can understand that.'

'A fellow conformer? Nice! Now, I really must get on. I might be Monty's other half but that doesn't mean I don't get it in the neck if we're not ready to go when we're supposed to be. I suppose that's the third thing you need to know about Monty – punctuality is his weak point. He's a stickler for it and lateness stresses him out – both personally and professionally. Which means I have to go.'

'Sure. If there's anything I can do to help you, just shout. It's what I'm here for. Feel free to pass over anything you believe I could be getting on with.'

'Thank you, Polly, much appreciated. I can see you're going to be the perfect addition to our little team.'

'Yes! Get in there!'

Polly finally won the battle and managed to get the large filing drawer back inside the desk. Her first task yesterday, after Monty had given her the job, had been to go through all the drawers and clear out anything which looked like it belonged to her predecessor. The box with Karen's name on it had been filled with makeup, straighteners, various nail varnishes and nail products including an electric file, a plethora of moisturisers – both hand and body – and a selection of clothing. The three pairs of tights she'd also found were the only items Polly had felt were necessary; it was, after all, always good to have a spare set or two to hand in case of emergencies.

When Karen had deigned to return to the office late in the afternoon, she hadn't been happy to see Polly sitting in her place. She'd been even less happy when informed that she no longer had a job. A vicious rant had followed which Polly ignored until the girl had eventually run out of steam. When she then became upset at her lack of employment, Polly had given her directions to The Gift and Wrapping Emporium while advising her there was an opening there if she was quick. Edith would soon strip the laziness out of the girl and perhaps she'd be more grateful in future.

'Right, all washed and clean. Now I can put you lot back in.'

She turned to the files piled up on the floor by the desk and began slotting them into the crumb and scum-free drawers. She didn't know when they'd last been emptied out and washed but she felt all the better for having done it herself. It also helped to put off the time when she'd have to begin decorating the beast in the corner.

Polly glanced at the clock. Three-thirty. She really hoped Maxwell would keep his promise of coming to help as there was no way she'd be able to get the tree into the metal stand on her own. There was also the issue of reaching up to decorate the top branches. Maxwell would be able to get to those without any problem – she'd be up and down the ladder like a Jack in the Box if she had to do it on her own.

As the last file was dropped into place, a sigh slipped from her lips when she saw she had nothing further to do. She'd procrastinated long enough. It was time to check out the boxes Andy had left for her and see what they contained. She took the scissors from the top drawer and used them to slit open the tape holding the containers closed.

She was busy laying out the decorations in different areas of the reception when she heard the oak door slam and heavy footsteps coming up the stairs. She was not so happy, however, when her heart began to beat a little faster and she became aware of how much she'd been looking forward to seeing Maxwell again. When he walked in the door and threw a wide smile in her direction, Polly felt a little lightheaded and had to draw in a sharp breath to steady herself.

'Hey! How are you today? Have you started without me?'

He pointed at the various piles of decorations lying around.

'Hi, Maxwell, I'm great, thank you, and no, I haven't started without you. Andy brought all these boxes down and I was just going through them to see what we've got to work with. The piles, if you look closely, are the colours on offer. So, are you a colour-coded kind of chap who likes things to be traditional and matching, alternative and matching, or do you prefer to just throw everything at the tree with wild abandon?'

'Err… I'm a bloke who never gives it that much thought. Here, have a hot chocolate and let's take a moment to consider our options before we begin.'

He thrust one of Dottie's cardboard cups at her and then placed his phone on the desk, swiping through it until the sound of Slade's "Merry Christmas, Everybody" filled the air.

'Christmas songs? Already?'

'I thought it would help us get in the mood. Do you have a favourite tune? I can put it on…'

'No, no, you're good. I just haven't heard them for a long time.'

'But they're everywhere at Christmas, how do you avoid them?'

'I tune them out. Make a point of not listening. I'll either put in my earphones and play something loudly, pull down my hat to muffle the sound or hum something in my head that drowns out the noise.'

'Wow! You really are hard-core non-Christmas, aren't you?'

'I did warn you.'

'Yes, well, I was giving it some thought last night and I've decided – with your permission of course – that, with my help and expert Christmas input, you will have fallen back in love with Christmas by Christmas Day.'

'Oh, you think so, do you?'

'Yes, I do.'

'And how do you plan to achieve this Christmas miracle?'

'Ah, you have to trust me and agree to it before I reveal anything more.'

Polly looked at Maxwell, kneeling on the floor in front of her. He'd already twisted some tinsel around his neck like a scarf and had found a pair of reindeer antlers which now adorned his head. He was smiling up at her, his dark-chocolate brown eyes twinkling with excitement, and he made her think of her father. This is exactly the kind of thing he would do. Would it really hurt to put her faith in a man whose joy for the season was as on par as her dad's?

'Okay, you're on! I'll trust you. I'll trust you to do your best to have me fall back in love with Christmas by the twenty-fifth of December. So, will you now share your plans with me?'

'Fantastic. Unfortunately, I can only share part of my plan.'

'Really! And that is what, exactly?'

'Every day, for twenty-four days, we will do a Christmas activity. It will be a Living Advent Calendar.'

'A Living Advent Calendar? Is there even such a thing?'

'I dunno but there is now and you're it!'

'And what will these activities consist of?'

'Aw come on, you know I can't tell you that. The whole point of an advent calendar is the surprise when you open the door. I can tell you, however, that today's surprise is decorating the tree. Since we're already here for that, it seemed a good place to start. Now, where's the stand to put it in? Let's get this party started!'

Polly looked at Maxwell with a mixture of shock and amazement. Twenty-four days? Twenty-four days of this, let's be honest, rather gorgeous man, taking her through goodness only knew what sort of Christmas tasks… She couldn't decide if she was thrilled or horrified by the idea.

However, as she'd already blindly agreed, there was nothing she could do now.

Twenty-four days to fall back in love with Christmas? Bloody hell!

<u>7</u>

December 2ⁿᵈ

Polly shuffled her handbag and carrier bag into one hand as she unlocked the front door of the office. It had just gone nine-thirty in the morning and Maxwell was coming over at ten to help her hang the beautiful pine and tartan swags they'd found last night when putting the empty boxes and unused tree decorations back in the loft. She'd also come across a number of small fibre optic trees which she planned to place around the work spaces so that Monty would see something Christmassy every time he turned around. He'd been so kind to her that Polly wanted to do this for him as another way of saying thank you. Just because she was a bit "Bah humbug" at this time of the year didn't mean she had to make it so for others. Besides, she was now on a mission to try and get the Christmas spirit flowing inside her again. Although, after twenty years, she figured the pipes might be a bit clogged up and rusty but at least she was willing to make the effort.

She dumped the bags on the reception desk and went over to turn on the tree lights. After shrugging off her coat and hanging it up, she turned round and her breath caught in her throat. The tree lights were now twinkling on and off and in that instant, she was thrown back to the Christmas two years before her father had died. She'd come home from school to find her dad at home and the Christmas tree all decorated. She'd been disappointed that he hadn't waited for her to help him but he'd appeased her by telling her he'd saved the honour of switching on the lights for her. At the time, she'd been pretty mardy about it and had flicked the switch with relatively poor grace. Her dad had pulled her into his side in a big hug, forcing her to stand beside him and admire his handiwork. As her scowling face took in the pretty baubles she so liked to hang already sitting in place, the static lights began to twinkle. On and off they flashed, like little diamonds playing peek-a-boo between the pine scented branches. At first it didn't register what she was seeing but when the penny did finally drop, she'd let out a squeal of joy while throwing her arms around her dad's neck, peppering kisses all over his face. She'd been nagging him to try the new LED lights that she'd seen the last few years in gorgeous shop displays but he'd been suspicious of them and their safety. When she'd asked why they now had some, he'd simply told her that he hadn't seen any stories of houses burning down because of them and so they must be okay to use.

Polly found herself smiling at the memory as she looked at the tree in front of her. She cast a critical eye over it and decided that between them, she and Maxwell hadn't done too bad a job. The traditional red and gold was warming and the warm-white lights were perfect. She'd just turned away to go and put the kettle on when she heard the door downstairs bang closed and Maxwell coming up the stairs. She knew his footsteps by now – after all, when you're six-foot-seven, a quiet entrance up wooden stairs is not easy.

'Hey, good morning. How are you on this fine day?'

His shiny happy greeting sent her tummy into a fizz and it took a quick tightening of the same tummy muscles that allowed her to reply in what she hoped was a normal tone.

'Hi, Maxwell, I'm great, thanks. Yourself?'

'All good here too, thank you. I must say, that tree looks pretty good.'

'I was just thinking that myself.'

'Oh, really? Are you becoming imbued with the Christmas spirit? Is my work here done already?'

'Er, no! Good try. I'm afraid it's going to take more than a twinkly tree to do that, no matter how pretty it is.'

'I'm glad to hear it.'

'You are?'

'Sure! Such an easy conquest would have been no fun. And it would certainly have made today's *advent*-ure less exciting. Hey, did you see what I did there? *Advent*-ure! Get it?'

'Yes, I got it!' she responded in a dry tone but with a smile on her face. 'Now, before we start on the swags, can I interest you in a coffee and a mincemeat muffin?'

'Mincemeat muffins? Wow, I've never heard of those before. Where did you get them?'

'Out of my oven at eight o'clock this morning.'

She walked over to her desk and drew the plastic storage tub out of the carrier bag. When she popped the lid off, the spicy, fruity smell wafted out and reminded her once again of how much she'd loved her mince pies when she'd been a kid. Unwilling to take yet another trip down memory lane this morning, she passed the tub to Maxwell.

'It's a new recipe that I found on the internet last night. You are my guinea pig – I don't know what they'll be like. I'll brew up a coffee so we have something to wash the taste away if they're really nasty.'

'I have a question.' Maxwell's voice called through to her in the kitchen as she filled the kettle and switched it on.

'What?' she called back.

'Why did you have mincemeat in your home if you don't do Christmas?'

'I didn't but we have these great things called twenty-four-hour supermarkets which have shelves and shelves of all sorts of goodies…'

'Ha ha! Think you're funny, do you?'

'I have my moments!' She stuck her head out the kitchen door and grinned at him.

'So, do you do much baking or were you struck by some Christmas inspiration?'

Polly picked up the tray with the coffee jug, mugs, milk and sugar on and replied as she carried it out.

'I love baking. My grandmother taught me when I was little and it has always stayed with me. I faltered for a few years in my teens – partly from being a teenager and thinking baking was lame and then with my dad… – anyway, I found my way back to it in my early twenties and it's been my hobby ever since.'

'So, you're pretty good at it?'

'Good enough, I think. I took a stall at a number of the local farmer's markets over the summer and sold everything I had each time.'

'Wow! That's quite impressive. You didn't fancy doing the Christmas markets? You'd probably go down a storm at those too.'

She gave Maxwell a look and waited for him to realise what he'd said.

'What?'

She raised her eyebrows.

'Why didn't you— Oh, I'm an idiot!' He palm-slapped his forehead. 'Christmas markets! Of course, you're going to avoid those like the plague! I'm sorry. Have I told you about this problem I have with my brain and my mouth?'

'Yes,' she laughed, 'no need to go there again. And it's a pretty obvious question to ask.'

'With an even more obvious answer. I'm such a numpty!'

'Look, it's fine. But for your lack of thought, you have to go first on the muffin tasting.'

'Fair enough but let it be known that, if I keel over and die, it was all for a good cause.'

Polly gave an eye-roll.

'I don't think they'll be that bad.'

She waited while Maxwell took a large bite from the muffin he'd picked out of the box and watched his face as he ate it. She was relieved to see a look of pleasure cross it and by the time he'd swallowed his mouthful, she already knew the muffins were a success.

'Oh, Polly! This is delicious. It's something I'd never have thought of and yet tastes so good.'

'A winner, then?'

'Definitely! When you do your Christmas stalls next year, these have to be on the menu.'

'Wow, that's confidence. You think I'll be so enamoured with Christmas by next year, that I'll be doing the Christmas markets?'

'By the time I'm done, you most certainly will be!'

8

'Where are we going?'
    'I'm not telling you.'
    'Oh, go on! Please?'
    'Nope!'
    'Pretty please?'
    'Nope!'
    'Pretty, pretty please with Christmas bells on?'
    'Still nope but I like your style!'
    'Hmph! You're no fun!'
Polly threw herself back in the passenger seat of Maxwell's truck and pretended to have a strop on. She saw him look at her from the corner of her eye and they both burst out laughing.

'Look, I've already told you, advent days are surprises. You will only find out what each day brings on the day and when I deem it appropriate for you to know.'

'So, you're not even going to tell me *where* we're going? I don't have to know everything, just where you're taking me.'

'It's not far, just trust me.'

'Fine!'

Maxwell grinned again as she turned her head to look out at the passing scenery. They were now deep in the heart of the Peak District and the passing signs gave names of places she'd either never heard of or were on her list to visit at some point. Eventually, they pulled off the main road and followed a single-lane tarmac road down towards a vast woodland area. At the bottom of the hill, they turned onto a rough track that led them deep into the forest where they finally came to a stop in a clearing.

'Here we are, day two of your advent calendar.'

'A forest?'

'Trust me,' Maxwell said again.

He smiled at her as he alighted from the cab. She copied his actions and, as she closed the cab door behind her, the sounds of the forest surrounded her. The birds in the trees, the wind ruffling the boughs and... a strange sound that she couldn't put a name to.

'What is that noise?'

'Come, all is about to be revealed.'

He led her along a footpath into another, much larger, clearing with a big wooden barn and to the side, a pen containing a herd of reindeer.

'Oh!'

Polly's hands flew up to her mouth as she let out a gasp of happy surprise. She turned to look at Maxwell in delight.

'You've brought me to see reindeer?'

'Well, they are rather Christmassy, I think you would agree.'

'Hey, Maxwell, how are you? Nice to see you again, it's been a while.'

'Hi, Nick, your trees are all nice and healthy now – you don't need me.'

'That's true but you are allowed to visit just because you like us.'

'I know. It's just been really busy, I'm sorry.'

'I'm only pulling your leg. I know what it's like. How are the kids? Not with you today?'

Polly's head swung round to look at Maxwell. He had kids? He hadn't mentioned that? But then, what did she know of him? They'd only met two days ago and most of their time had been spent talking about her! Oh, dear Lord! He must think she's a right self-centered cow! She'd hardly asked him any personal questions at all. Note to self, she thought, ask more questions.

'No, they're still at school although only a couple more weeks until they finish.'

'I'll bet they're already excited.'

'You'd better believe it. Anyway, I've brought Polly here to meet your lovely babies. She's a bit of a Christmas sceptic and I'm trying to bring her round to my way of thinking. Polly, this is Nick. He and his wife, Chrissy, run this little reindeer retreat.'

'Retreat?'

'Well, it's more like a farm but as none of our herd are for consumption, it's not a term we find appropriate. Basically, we look after rescue reindeer and are part of a breeding programme.'

'May I ask why?'

'Because they're gorgeous animals that also need looking after. And it's something which is a little bit different. Would you like to meet them?'

'Oh, yes please. I would love to.'

'Then follow me.'

As they walked behind Nick, going around the pen to the gate on the opposite side, Polly whispered to Maxwell.

'Nick and Chrissy? Seriously?'

'Yup, seriously. Quite apt I think.'

Before she could reply, Nick stopped at the gate and turned to them.

'Polly, a few rules. Firstly, deer are curious animals so will most likely come over to you. Please don't approach them. Secondly, you can pet and stroke them but should you wish to do so, raise your hand very slowly in front of them and keep it loose. Do not make a fist or a flat, straight hand when you go to touch them as they may think it's threatening. Thirdly, I'll give you a pot of treats to feed to them but you need to keep your hand flat for that.'

'Like feeding a horse?'

'Exactly. Now, may I ask you to wash your hands before we go in?'

A few minutes later, they were standing inside the pen. To begin with, the deer didn't pay any attention to them but after a minute or two, Polly noticed that a few had raised their heads and were watching them. Finally, a couple began to move towards them and more followed.

'Is it correct that the male deer lose their antlers in the winter and it's really the ladies who are pulling Santa's sleigh?' she whispered.

'Mostly that would be the case although young male deer can retain their antlers for longer and the shedding cycle, as it's called, can also be delayed in neutered males. Also, a little point of fact – reindeer are the only members of the deer species where both the males and the females have antlers. All other deer – it's only the males.'

'Okay. I didn't know that.'

At that moment, one of the deer came right up to her and Polly was too busy fussing and petting to ask any further questions.

When her pot of food had been all doled out, Nick turned and asked, 'Would you like to have a trip out on the sleigh?'

'A sleigh-ride?'

'Yes.'

'Oh, that would be amazing. But, there's no snow.'

'Come with me.'

They walked through the pen towards the barn and Nick led them over to the far corner where her eye was caught by the sight of a beautiful red and gold sleigh. It had two double seats, one behind the other, glorious metal scrollwork picked out in gold and the back seat even had a roll-top. It looked just like Santa's sleigh.

'If you look closer, underneath the runners, you will see they're raised up off the ground by wheels hidden behind the solid metal skirt panels. We hide them so the children feel they're getting the real deal.'

'Hey, that's clever. And considerate. And are the deer okay about pulling it?'

'Yes, they are. It's good for them as it prevents boredom and it gives them a good workout too.'

'How many do you have pulling it?'

'This is a small sleigh so only four but some of the larger sleighs require eight. Just like Santa Claus.'

It didn't take Nick long to put four deer into harnesses and attach them to the sleigh. He went over to a nearby cupboard and came back with some soft blankets.

'It's not cold out there but when these guys pick up speed, it gets pretty chilly. It is an open sleigh you know.'

He grinned at Polly as he helped her up. Maxwell got in beside her and Nick took the front pew. A few minutes later, they were trotting along through the forest.

'Having fun?'

'Maxwell, this is great. Thank you. I have to say, I never thought I'd be doing this in the middle of Derbyshire, let me tell you. Sleigh rides are something you think of when snow is involved.'

'These guys come into their own when the snow arrives. What Nick hasn't mentioned is that the reindeer assist when small outlying villages are snowed in if we get really bad winter weather. They're used then to get supplies in and bring anyone who needs rescuing out.'

'Oh, I would never have thought of that. It's great to know that they are useful as well as totally gorgeous. I—'

The rest of her sentence was lost as the sleigh turned onto a long straight and the reindeer really took off. She grabbed a hold of Maxwell's hand under the blanket as she laughed in delight at the wind blowing her hair behind her. For the next twenty minutes, she pushed everything from her mind and let herself simply enjoy the moment and the experience. By the time they pulled back up in front of the barn, she was giddy with joy.

Nick helped her back down from the sleigh and held her hand for a moment until her legs stopped wobbling.

'Fun?'

'Nick, it was wonderful. I loved every second of it. Thank you so much.'

'It was my pleasure. Now, I must love you and leave you. It's almost feeding time and I need to cool these guys off before I put them back in. I hope we meet again.'

'I hope we do too. I would love to come again.'

'Well, we're open all year round and visitors are always welcome.'

Once they'd said their goodbyes, Polly more skipped than walked back to the truck.

'Oh, that was so much fun. I can't believe I've had a sleigh ride and petted reindeer and fed them… Thank you for this, Maxwell, thank you.'

'Are you feeling the spirit of the season yet?'

'No, but I am feeling full of the joy of having been on a sleigh-ride.'

Maxwell laughed.

'Tough crowd I see! Looks like I'll have to try harder.'

'You still have twenty-two days. Who knows, you might just get a Christmas miracle!'

They bantered back and forth until they turned off the

woodland track and onto the main road.

'Nick mentioned you have children?'

'Yes, a girl and a boy. She's eight going on eighteen, as they seem to do these days, and he's six.'

'Cute age.'

'It is. They're still innocent and this time of the year is so magical for them.'

'Is that why you're so into Christmas?'

'I've always loved Christmas but the kids make it even more special. There's something about seeing it through their eyes. Everything is a wonder for them.'

'That's lovely.'

There was silence for a few minutes until Maxwell broke it.

'I'm divorced. Three years. In case you were wondering.'

'Oh, right.'

'Were you?'

'What?'

'Wondering.'

'A little, I suppose. I kind of guessed you had to be single in some way because no wife would be happy with her husband running around the hills with another woman.'

'You mentioned an ex-husband – been divorced long?'

'Eighteen months.'

'Mine was very amicable. Helen and I were great friends who got married and then realised we should have stayed as friends. There was no malice or anger and we're back to being great friends again. We have joint custody and see each other most days when picking up and dropping off the kids.'

'That's good to hear. And great for the kids to have such stability. Too many end up being damaged and hurt by the divorce process.'

'For sure. What about you?'

'What about me?'

'Do you keep in touch with your ex?'

'Hell no! I'd harpoon the bastard if he ever crossed my path again.'

'Is that something you keep about your person?'

'I'm sorry?'

'A harpoon? Do you have one in your bag? It's a big bag after all.'

Polly laughed at his silliness.

'No, I don't. But if I knew he was in the vicinity, I'd make a point of finding one.'

'Wanna talk about it?'

'I'd rather not. I'm in a good mood and would like it to stay that way, thank you.'

'Fair enough. Now, where am I dropping you off? At home?'

'Actually, back at the office would be perfect. I need to pick up a few bits from the supermarket.'

'I'm happy to wait for you to do that and then drop you home.'

'Thank you but I'll be fine. I enjoy the walk – I think of it as my daily exercise.'

'Well, if you're baking stuff like those muffins, I can understand the need to.'

'Is that a hint that you'd like some more?'

'I didn't say that…'

'Your look of assumed innocence doesn't fool me, Maxwell Watkins! Good try though!'

They were still chucking like children as Maxwell pulled up outside the office as she'd asked.

'Monty's still in London tomorrow – is that correct?'

'Yes, he is.'

'Which means you have another free day?'

'I do.'

'Then I will meet you back here at ten tomorrow. Wear

comfortable shoes.'

'Any clues?'

'Are you going to ask that every time?'

'Might do. Just to see if you crack!'

'Well, it's not going to happen.'

'We'll see!'

Polly leant across and placed a quick kiss on Maxwell's cheek. As she did so, she smelt a hint of sandalwood and pine. His aftershave. So subtle, she had to get right up close to smell it. She liked that. She couldn't abide strong aftershaves or perfumes and often found the wearers to be as overbearing as the scent they drowned themselves in. With a last smile, she stepped out of the truck, closed the door and stood waving until it disappeared around the corner. When it was out of sight, Polly turned towards the road crossing, lost in thought as she wondered what to make of Maxwell and his sudden appearance in her life.

9

December 3rd

Polly was locking up the office door when there was a toot behind her. She turned to see Maxwell waving at her. She grinned in return while hurrying towards him, anxious to get out of the sharp wind that felt like little needles pricking her skin.

'Oh my, it's bitter out there,' she said, pulling the truck door closed and fumbling to put on her seatbelt.

'Yeah, they were saying on the weather forecast that temperatures will drop over this weekend.'

'I saw that and it's why I popped into the office – I wanted to set the heating to come on a few times to ensure the pipes don't burst. I don't think Monty would thank me if his stock was ruined in a flood.'

'No, but he will definitely thank you for being so conscientious as to think of it.'

'Oh, I doubt he would notice. And so he shouldn't. The whole point of my role as office manager is to make sure things run smoothly for the boss so he may concentrate on his own role.'

'I assure you, Monty will notice.'

Maxwell smiled at her before indicating to pull back out into the traffic.

'So, where are we going?'

'That would be telling!'

'That's right, it would be. So…'

'Not telling.'

'Well, are we nearly there yet?'

Maxwell burst out laughing. 'New tactics, eh? Still not going to happen.'

'It was worth a try.' She returned his smile before asking, 'Tell me, what are you going to do next week when Monty and Andy are back?'

'What do you mean?'

'I'll be back in the office. I can't just take the day off so you can work on making me fall back in love with Christmas again.'

'Don't you worry – I have plenty of evening events too. You having these two days off was a bonus as far as I'm concerned.'

Maxwell grinned at her again and pointed towards the dashboard.

'You can put the radio on if you like.'

'Thanks, but I'm okay. I'm happy to admire the scenery while being chauffeured about.'

They'd taken the road out on the opposite side of town from the day before and were soon driving through small hamlets and villages.

'I haven't seen much of the Peak District yet, since I moved up, but I can't help noticing that the older cottages and buildings are built of different coloured stone. I would have expected them to be all quite similar.'

'Ah, over the centuries, there have been many quarries

in this area and each location produced different kinds of stone. Some are grey-ish in colour, some sandy and some even have a pink-ish hue. It all comes down to what they're made up of – clay-based, sandstone or limestone. Many of the villages would have been home to the quarry workers so the cottages would have been built from the local stone. Hence the variations you have noticed.'

'I see. Thank you for explaining. It's nice to see the variety. It's keeping me occupied while you whisk me away to some unknown location.'

'Good to hear. I won't need to dig out the colouring books and crayons that I brought along!'

Polly gave a very un-ladylike snort of amusement and then turned to look back out at the hills undulating across the skyline. Despite mulling over this new friendship that was developing, she was still no further in assessing what the likely outcome could be. Was Maxwell just being friendly and no more? Did he think there was a chance of it developing into something more? Equally, what was her own role? Was she simply happy to have some company – male or female? How did she feel about Maxwell herself?

She sneaked a sidelong glance towards him. His profile was as strong and chiselled as his front view. His hair, a lovely rich chestnut colour, was longer than Monty's and it had a soft curl just beginning to show. The creases at the corners of his eyes told her that he smiled often. Something she was beginning to learn for herself.

'You okay there?'

Polly sat up straight with a start.

'Yes, why?'

'You were very quiet.'

'Just thinking.'

'Anything you fancy sharing?'

Hell no! She most certainly did not!

'Just wondering what it's like to be a twin. As an only

child, I grew up wishing I had a sibling. Did you ever wish for the opposite? Or were you always happy being one of two?'

There was silence for a few seconds and she could see that Maxwell was thinking about his answer. She liked that. It made her feel she would hear something more honest rather than a trite off-the-tongue retort.

'We had our moments, I suppose like most siblings would but, all in all, we rubbed along together quite well. I think the fact that we're both quite different characters helped. I was always the outdoorsy type, Monty preferred to read, watch old movies and draw. As such, we didn't encroach upon each other's space and there was rarely any ever vying for the same toys.'

'And, I'm guessing that, unlike sisters, no arguing over borrowed clothes.'

This put her on the receiving end of another wide grin.

'Definitely not.'

'I suppose Monty would have had a problem with your jeans and jumpers. There's a limit to how many times you can roll up a hem or a cuff.'

'Actually, up to when we hit thirteen, we were the same height although I always had a stockier build. I did wish, on the odd occasion, that I had his slimmer physique. Being built like a wrestler meant the school bullies used to think they could have a go at me. I'm not a fighter so that wasn't much fun.'

'What did you do? Report them?'

'No. I just made sure I kicked their ass good and hard at the first outing and they would mostly leave me alone after that.'

'Not exactly PC though...'

'Not now it's not but back then... things were different.'

'True, I suppose they were, although we don't always

see that.'

'No. Anyway, once the height thing kicked in, it all changed. It's one thing picking on the kid who's twice your width but when he's almost double your height too? Nah, even the stupidest bully knew when to leave well alone.'

'I'll bet you were popular with the sports teachers though, if you were the outdoor type. I'm guessing you liked sports.'

'I did although they weren't my forte. My preference lay more in camping, hiking through the hills and swimming in the lakes. My grandparents had a farm with a large woodland area on it. I used to disappear there every weekend I could, take my little tent and camp out, just being at one with the trees and wildlife.'

'Is that why you became a tree doctor?'

This was met with another laugh.

'Yes, it's why I became a tree doctor. I'm at my happiest when surrounded by the towering leafy giants. They have, for me anyway, a lovely calming effect and I always feel at peace when in that environment.'

'May I ask exactly what it is you do? I'm guessing it's not lopping the tops off conifers for Mr Jones because his neighbour, Mr Smith, is complaining about them.'

'Not any more although I started out on that level but as I gained more experience and knowledge, I moved into a consulting role. Like, for example, many of Joe Public thinks it is wrong to cut down any tree and they should all be preserved. However, it's not that straightforward. Sometimes, tree-thinning is necessary because the older, taller trees have become so dense, they block out the sunlight for the younger, smaller trees below. This can cause the younger trees to become weak and make them more susceptible to disease and infestation. Thinning also looks at removing younger trees which are inferior or weak. This ensures the genetic make-up of the species is safe. In addition to this, if the leafy, overhead canopy is thinned out, the rain can reach the forest floor which keeps it healthy for low-lying flora and fauna.'

'Do you then decide which trees should be felled and which should be preserved?'

'I do. I will also inspect trees where the landowner is concerned about disease and look at ways of remedying the situation.'

'You really are a tree doctor, then.'

'I suppose I am.'

'So, is there less work in the winter? Is that why you have time free to waste on me?'

'Right, first up – time spent with you is not a waste. I am performing a valuable service for society.'

'By making me fall in love with Christmas?'

'Yes, absolutely. Also, the winter period is when it's best for tree management. The trees are bare so no nests to disturb when felling. Also, the ground is nice and hard meaning the heavy machinery causes less damage as the soil doesn't get churned up. The reason I have been able to take this time out is because I've already done my consulting with my clients on what needs to be done. They've been waiting for temperatures to drop so they can move in and get on with it. Next week will be busier for me as I need to attend a few sites to ensure the fellers know what's what.'

'I never realised that.'

'Few people do unless they're nature buffs.'

'What about the modelling? Are you still doing that for Monty?'

'Yes, but I now only do the bi-yearly collection catalogue which is sent out throughout the industry.'

'But, aren't you still the face of Monty Maxwell?'

'Until the end of next year.'

'Why then?'

'I'm getting on and I'm a bit weathered and squidgy around the edges these days.'

'But isn't that the new thing – older models to show we're not an age-discriminate society anymore?'

'Probably but I don't want to do it any longer. The kids are growing up, becoming more aware of what's going on around them and I'd rather they knew their dad as a tree doctor than a supermodel. It's…' he paused for a moment, 'It's about values, you know? I'm not decrying the fashion industry but I feel it puts the wrong message out there and I would rather my children focus on the values of the need to preserve nature over what dress or shirt is so last season. I want them to save the planet, not worry about the clothes they're going to wear to decorate it. I need to help them set their moral compass and I feel a tree doctor is better suited for the task.'

Polly nodded at his words. She knew exactly what Maxwell was saying and she couldn't disagree with any of it.

'I get it. I hear you. I just have one last question.'

'Okay.'

'Are we there yet?'

10

Polly looked through the windscreen as Maxwell, laughing, pulled into a parking space.

'Yes, we're there now. Or here, if you prefer.'

"Here" was a large, grey stone building to one side and a number of small outbuildings to the other. Directly in front of them was a steep drop down to a river which was flowing with some speed, judging by the rushing sound that rose up to greet her as she got out of the truck.

She walked over to the wall and looked down to see the fast-moving water tumbling and gushing over the rocks and stones, causing splashes of white as it went by. A waterwheel was attached to the building and she was thrilled at the sight of it moving round.

'Is this an old mill?' she asked Maxwell, who'd come round to stand beside her.

'Yes, it is. There's a number of them along the River Derwent and they played a vital role during the Industrial Revolution. These days, most of the buildings have been transformed into shopping outlets and antique malls. This one, however, is a craft centre. Here, you can walk around and see all manner of hand-crafts being performed and the goods can be purchased. If you're looking for a unique gift for someone, this is a great place to start.'

'How fascinating. And those buildings over there,' she pointed to outbuildings, 'are they also part of the craft centre?'

'They are indeed and that's where we're heading first.'

Maxwell pushed himself off the wall with his hip and began walking towards the outbuildings. With a last glance at the hypnotic rotation of the waterwheel, Polly did the same and followed him.

They walked round the side and when they turned the corner, she saw that one of the buildings had its doors thrown wide open. As they drew closer, she saw a man wearing a pair of dark goggles, a thick, full-length leather apron and long heavy-duty gloves that extended up his arms to his elbows. They reminded her of the gauntlets worn by people who worked with birds of prey. However, when she saw what he was actually doing, her eyes lit up with surprise and delight.

'He's a glass-blower!'

'He is indeed. It's also why he's in this outbuilding – furnaces and hot glass close to combustible items like wools, cloth and wood is not recommended.'

'Oh, look at these, they're gorgeous.'

Her eye had been caught by a simple white, twig-style tree which had a number of glass ornaments hanging from its branches. The myriad shapes and colours swung gently in the breeze and were polished so well, they managed to glint even in the dullness of the day.

She turned to watch the craftsman at work and marvelled at the way he was able to manipulate the hot, molten blob of glass into an object of beauty. She was fascinated by the way he rolled, spun, added and cut with implements that wouldn't look out of place in a torture chamber to eventually produce a vase that was simply stunning. Once he'd carefully lifted it with a long, hooked pole and placed it inside a large kiln, he took off his goggles and smiled in their direction.

'Hey, Maxwell, how are you? Haven't seen you for a while.'

'Hi, Chester, I'm well, thank you. How are you keeping? Still full of hot air I see!'

The two men laughed before Maxwell beckoned her forward and introduced her to the glassblower.

'Polly, this is Chester. Chester, meet Polly.'

She shook hands with the craftsman and was surprised to find his hands quite soft. She'd expected them to be callused given the nature of what he did but clearly his gloves provided excellent protection.

'Chester, for her own reasons, Polly isn't the biggest fan of Christmas and I'm trying to help her find her way back to loving it again. I thought making her own tree bauble might help her along the way. Do you think you could help with this?'

'It would be my pleasure.'

'What? No way. I couldn't possibly go near that thing.'

She pointed to the long, hollow pole that Chester had been working with when they'd arrived.

'No fear, Polly, you won't have to. For smaller items like tree baubles, I use a Bunsen burner and glass rods although there will be a little rolling involved which you will have the pleasure of doing. Now then, what shape do you prefer?'

He pointed towards the tree and the baubles she'd been admiring.

'This one,' she replied, touching one that looked like a long, diamond, droplet.

'And your favourite colour?'

'Red.'

'Okay. We're going to make a clear bauble with a red centre. Sound good?'

'Sounds amazing.'

A few minutes later she was kitted out with her own leather apron, goggles and gloves. Chester sat her on a high stool next to a wooden work bench and stood beside her, talking her through the various tools and explaining how they were going to create her bauble.

'First of all, you take this tool, which is called a mandrel, and hold it in your non-dominant hand.'

He passed her a long, thin metal rod with a wooden handle.

'Now we light the Bunsen…'

For the next twenty-five minutes, Polly learnt how to melt the glass, pull it, push it, colour it, roll it and manipulate it until, finally, she had created her very own glass bauble with a gorgeous scarlet centre.

'Now, I'm just going to add the final touch.'

Chester took it from her, added some green glass and finished the top off with a small bow and a loop through which she could thread some twine for hanging it.

'Ta-da! All done!'

'Oh, it's stunning. I love it.'

She went to touch it and was startled when Chester quickly pulled it from her reach.

'Oh, no, don't touch. The glass is still exceptionally hot and it would be more than a little painful if you got burnt. You need to leave this with me to finish off which means placing it here in my kiln and letting it cook and cool over the next twenty-four hours.'

'Twenty-four hours? I thought I could take it home with me today.'

Polly was a little surprised by how disappointed she felt. It was only a Christmas ornament after all.

'I'm afraid not. If you leave your name and address with

me, I'll get it posted out.'

After taking her details, and admiring her surname, Chester turned to Maxwell who'd been patiently leaning up against the wall on the other side of the bench contentedly watching the tutorial.

'Have you been into the centre yet?'

'No, we're going there now.'

'Good. Polly, I hope you like the craft centre, it's really quite interesting. Pop in to see me before you leave, please.'

He shook their hands as Polly said, 'Thank you, Chester, for sharing your craft with me. I really enjoyed it.'

'You're quite welcome.'

'You looked like you had fun there.'

'Oh, I did! I never would have thought I'd ever create my own tree bauble.'

'Do you have a tree at home you can put it on?'

'No, I don't. Putting aside the whole "I don't do Christmas" thing, I have a cat and after doing some reading online, it would seem that Christmas and pets are not a good combination. They can really hurt themselves on things like tinsel, and beads, and baubles – unless they're shatter-proof – and real trees are quite toxic due to the oils in the pine needles or fertilisers in the soils if they're planted ones. Also, the needles can get in their eyes if they climb them, jab their paws or get stuck in their throat if ingested. On top of that, there's the risk of the flex on the tree lights being chewed. So, even if I was the greatest lover of Christmas on the planet, I still wouldn't have a tree.'

'Oh, that's a pity. What will you do with your bauble then?'

'Why, put it on the office tree where I can see it every day.'

'Cool.'

He held the door open for her to walk inside the mill building and she was immediately assaulted by a plethora of smells. The sweet smell of vanilla mingled with the dusty aroma of wood which vied with the tantalising scent of warm chocolate. These won out over the other, underlying, less obvious smells which permeated the air.

They walked round and Polly was astounded by the number of different crafts on display. There was a candlemaker creating all sorts of glorious shapes from the warm wax; a chocolate carver sculpting penguins, polar bears, elves, fairies and Santas from large, solid chunks of chocolate; a flower-stand where the florist was showing two ladies how to put together their Christmas table centrepiece and an embroidery stand displaying gorgeous handmade stockings for hanging on Christmas Eve along with table-runners, napkins and other various Christmas-themed items.

They headed down the stairs to the basement where the café was situated and next to that, an artisan baker who made your cakes as you watched. She had a number of small, personal-sized cakes that included a traditional Victoria sponge, lemon drizzle loaf, carrot cake or coffee and walnut. You gave her your order and then, while eating a sandwich or having a coffee, she would create and bake your cake. The personal-size meant they cooked in no time at all and twenty-five minutes later, you could be tucking into your favourite delight.

'Shall we be quite decadent and order a couple of cakes to cook while we have some lunch? I know for a fact the Victoria sponge is delicious.'

'Well, it is Christmas so it would be rude not to, although carrot cake is my downfall. As soon as I saw that on the list, I knew I was a goner.'

Polly smiled up at Maxwell, happy that he was a willing participant in her calorific downfall.

They placed their order and then went round to the café. Soon, they were seated and tucking into the open sandwiches that the café specialised in.

'So, what do you think of this place?'

She swallowed her mouthful and took a sip of tea before replying.

'A little gem. What a great idea to create a space where all these crafts can come together and be seen. I love how they "work" in front of you so you can see how they do it. I'm not the best with a needle and thread yet the embroidery lady made it look so easy.'

'Any favourites?'

'The lace stall. How on earth she knew what rod to put where and which pin to move… it was hypnotic watching her hands move around and she never once hesitated. If I were to try that, it would all be a jumbled mess within five minutes. It was also nice to see the lace being made in the old, traditional manner. With modern technology, it's a shame to see these old skills fading away.'

'Yes, I agree. That's why I think this place does so well – it helps to bring together the old skills which are being lost. My favourite place, and also that of my daughter, is on the top floor. We'll head up there after lunch.'

"After lunch" was forty minutes and a cake-filled tummy later. Polly didn't mind walking up the three flights of stairs as it was an opportunity to feel less guilty about the gooey-gorgeousness of her carrot cake that had melted in her mouth. Maxwell had offered her a taste of his Victoria sponge and it had been as light as the proverbial feather. He'd also "Mmmm-ed" his satisfaction on the bite of carrot cake she'd offered in return.

As she walked up the last flight of stairs, Polly realised

this was where the woody smell was coming from, for over in the far corner, she saw the largest workshop in the entire building and around it were various wood carvings in all shapes and sizes.

They walked across and she saw that this was the only stand on this floor. When she felt the sawdust underfoot, she realised why. In a few more steps, she was surrounded by the carvings which, when viewed close-up, were truly exquisite. The attention to detail was perfect, right down to the tiny little spores on the flower head, the gossamer effect of the fairy wings and the delicate spider's web inside the cave of the sleeping gnome.

On one side of the stand, the carvings were all modern with planes, trains and automobiles in many guises and sizes. On the other side, it was like walking into a woodland wonderland. All kinds of wild birds and animals nestled alongside wooden flowers, trees, fairies, elves, Santas and gnomes. She couldn't miss the almost life-sized eagle with its vast wings spread out and the beady eyes searching beneath for some unfortunate beast to consume. The carving of the feathers begged her to touch them and she couldn't resist doing so, trailing her fingers ever so gently across the wood and revelling in the feel of the contours beneath them.

'Now, isn't this worth climbing three flights of stairs for?'

'It really is. I didn't think I could be more impressed with this place but now I find that I am.'

'Come and meet Deric, he's lovely.'

The introductions were quickly made and she was surprised by how soft-spoken the wood turner was. As she listened to him talking to Maxwell, Polly came to realise that he was a gentle man and this was why he was able to replicate in such detail – he was sensitive by nature and that same sensitivity flowed into his work.

The conversation took a business turn so she walked away to let Maxwell and Deric discuss this privately and went to look again at the animals around her. It was while she was mooching that an idea began to form in her mind. She glanced around her and figured it would be more than feasible.

'Polly, I've got some wood down in the truck which I need to drop off at the service lift for Deric. Are you okay to wait here or do you want to come back to the truck with me?'

'I'm more than happy to stay here till you've done what you need to do. Come and get me when you're finished.'

'Okay, will do. I won't be long.'

'No problem, take all the time you need. I'm in no rush.'

Polly worked on trying to appear nonchalant while inside she was jumping for joy at this stroke of luck. She loitered close to the open stairwell and watched Maxwell walk down. As soon as she was sure he was out of the way, she scurried over to talk to Deric.

<u>11</u>

December 4th

Polly turned onto her side and let her eyes settle on the beautiful sunny morning outside. When she'd first moved into Bailey House, she'd closed the bedroom curtains religiously every night. The floor to ceiling wall of windows had freaked her out but it hadn't taken her long to grow used to them and now she loved these few early moments each morning when she took some time to lie and absorb all that Mother Nature had to offer right outside her window.

She felt the bed dip slightly as Bailey jumped up. She turned onto her back again so he could take up his preferred position where he stretched along the side of her with his head on her shoulder and purred in her ear. She wrapped her arm around him and thought back to the previous evening…

'Thank you again for a really lovely day.'

'It was my pleasure. I'm glad you enjoyed it. I'm sure glass blowing isn't for everyone but I got the feeling you wouldn't mind it.'

'You were right. I think it's good to try new things and something unusual like that was definitely good.'

She lifted the lid of the cardboard box on her lap, carefully moved aside the tissue paper and admired the surprise Chester had placed inside. While they'd been in the centre, he'd created a small lead window ornament for her to take home that day. He'd explained that as he used bits of cut glass held together by the soft metal, it meant no cooking was required and she could have a memento of the day until her own creation arrived. He'd used mostly red with a smattering of green and clear glass so it would match her bauble. She could take it into the office on Monday to place on the tree there but after Christmas, she was taking it home and would find somewhere for it to hang all year round. It was far too pretty to only see the light of day one month out of twelve.

As they drove back into town, Maxwell asked, 'So, where can I drop you tonight? Am I allowed to take you home yet or are you still being cautious?'

'Sorry? Cautious?'

'I thought that was why you had me drop you at the office last night and why I've picked you up from there the last two days. It's not a problem – I'm absolutely okay with it and I completely understand why.'

'It's not that at all – I really did need to go to the supermarket last night. And, as extreme as it might sound, I love walking up the steep hill to home as much as I hate it.'

'Huh?'

'I hate the walk up while I'm doing it but when I reach

72

the top, I'm chuffed that I did it and I love it for being there to make me. If that makes any sense.'

'I think I get it. So, you go up the steep hill – I'm guessing the one out of town?'

'That's right and then it's a sharp left down again.'

'Sharp left at the top? Do you live in Top Peak Lane? Did you buy Bailey House?'

She looked at Maxwell in surprise.

'Yes, I did! You know it?'

'Sure. My mum is good friends with Dorothy. She didn't want to sell but after her husband passed away and with her kids all gone, it was too much for her. Mind you, she hung onto it long enough. We were beginning to think she would never let it go.'

'What do you mean?'

'There were a number of offers before you that were all declined.'

'You mean the offers from the developers who wanted to flatten the house and build a housing estate on the land?'

'Those would be the ones. She told you?'

'Yes, she did. I was severely grilled on the subject and I had to promise many times over that I wouldn't sell to developers.'

'Good. Although, is it not a bit big for one person? Don't you feel you rattle around in the place?'

'When I lived in London, my ex and I once had a terraced house with neighbours on each side. You could hear them sneeze and they could hear you change your mind. In London, every square inch comes with a premium price tag so the room sizes are the compromises you make for a nice postcode – you know, residing on a street where you can walk out of your front door and no one is shooting up heroin outside your gate. So, I am now loving all the space around me. I can stretch out my arms and not touch the walls. I have a wonderfully large kitchen, complete with an island that, in itself, is the same dimensions as my entire London kitchen, and where I can bake my cakes with ease and pleasure. I have a glorious garden that is quiet and I can hear the birds chirrup and the wind rustling through the trees. Occasionally, a car horn from the road will interrupt but with it being up the hill and me being down, traffic noise is not a problem. And as for the land that came with it – I'm just letting it be. For now, the wildlife can have it as long as I get to wake up to the view every morning.'

As she'd been talking, Maxwell had driven her home and was pulling into her driveway when she stopped.

'It sounds to me like you've fallen in love with the place.'

'I have. I had the old annexe updated and modernised over the summer and from March next year, it will be a holiday let. It's far enough away from the house not to be a problem but will bring in a nice little income so the property kind of earns its keep. I might consider allowing camping on one of the fields – I'm not sure yet.'

'You should meet my mum; she'll be able to give you some pointers there.'

'Oh?'

'Yeah. You know I mentioned my grandparents had a farm, well, when they passed on, neither of my parents were inclined to become farmers so they transformed it into a holiday park.'

'Oh, that wouldn't happen to be the one about three miles up the road, would it?'

'Yes, that's it. They have a dozen on-site chalets which they rent out. They also have a couple of fields which they permit campers to pitch on through the summer.'

'Well, that's good to know. Thank you, I'll keep that in mind.'

She was just getting out of the truck when she stopped

and turned.

'Would you like to come in for a coffee? It seems rude not to offer since you've driven me around all day.'

'I would love to but I need to go and pick up the kids. They're with me this weekend. My folks, however, are babysitting tomorrow night so I'll be here to pick you up at six o'clock if that works for you?'

'Six is fine if you're sure that's okay. I don't want to be intruding on your family time.'

'You're not. Mum doesn't get called on that often for babysitting duties so she's happy to do it.'

'Then I'll see you at six. Do I need to wear anything in particular – walking shoes or whatever?'

'Just wear what you're comfortable in.'

She'd stood watching him as he turned around and drove away, giving a little wave when he tooted at the gate.

'Right then, Bailey, I need your manly input here.' She dragged her appreciation of the outside view away and looked down at her cat. 'What on earth does "wear what you're comfortable in" interpret into? Because a dress and heels are what I'm "comfortable in" when eating in a restaurant but not if I'm hiking over a cold frosty field.'

She let out a small sigh when instead of providing her with the answer she required, Bailey gave a little snuffle, licked her ear and began emitting small, squeaky snores.

'Hmm, fat lot of good you are. Well, if you're not going to help me, then I'm getting up.'

She eased the fluffball off her arm, got up and headed into the bathroom. When she returned, he'd moved down into the bed and had curled up on the warm spot she'd vacated, clearly having no regard for the wardrobe dilemma she was facing.

12

Polly was sitting on her sofa, looking out of the window to the hills beyond the fields. and debating if she fancied going for a walk. She'd done her housework and was all caught up on the weekly television drama she liked to watch. It was almost noon and she had five more hours of nothingness to fill before she had to get ready to go out. Once again, her stomach gave a little flip when she thought of Maxwell and she knew her head would begin to create all sorts of weird and wonderful scenarios unless she gave it something else to think on and while a brisk walk in the fresh air would be good for her physical being, it wouldn't be enough to distract her mental being so she grabbed her laptop and typed "Christmas cupcakes" in the search engine. Burying herself up to her elbows in flour and butter was a much better way of passing the time.

She'd only just opened up the first recipe on the screen when there was a knock at the door. For a few seconds she sat wondering who it could be in that sort of dazed moment you have when the doorbell rings but you're not expecting visitors but then moved the laptop and got off the sofa.

'I'm telling you, Bailey, if it's yet another estate agent asking me if I'm interested in selling, all hell is going to break loose,' she muttered, as she shoved her feet into her slippers. She'd had a few of those over the months since she'd moved in and was now heartily sick of it.

She opened the door, all set to give the rant of her life… and stopped short.

'Oh, err… hi! Err… hello.'

'Hi, Polly, erm… I'm really, really sorry to bother you but I… I mean, *we* were hoping you could help us out.'

Polly looked at Maxwell standing sheepishly on her doorstep and just behind him were two small faces displaying signs of recent tears.

'Come in, come in.'

She stepped back and opened the door further to let Maxwell and his children in.

'Just through there.'

She closed the door and ushered them into the lounge.

'What's wrong? How can I help?'

'The kids have been given a school project to make a Christmas gingerbread house. We got this kit off the internet and the plan was to build it today but we couldn't get it to work and then it broke. They need to take the finished articles in on Monday.'

'I see. And because I like to bake—'

'—I thought you might be able to help us fix it. If it's not too much trouble.'

She looked down at the two children who hadn't yet said a word. The girl was blonde and had startling blue eyes but the boy was the spit of his dad. Polly figured the girl must take after her mother. They looked up at her shyly and she couldn't miss the hope on their faces. She knelt down and looked at them both.

'Do you know, I was only just looking for a baking project on my laptop. I think making a gingerbread house would be the perfect one. Why don't you take off those coats and scarfs and let me see what we need to do to fix this?'

She stood quickly and turned away to move her computer, giving herself a moment to swallow down the lump in her throat that had suddenly appeared when two big smiles had come her way.

'You too, Maxwell. Coat off. This is going to be a team effort. Now, this way to the kitchen.'

Once the children had been enveloped in big aprons, placed upon the bar stools around the kitchen island and introductions made – Alanna for the little lady and Taylor, the mini-Maxwell – Polly took out the contents of the carrier bag Maxwell had presented to her.

'Ah, I can see the problem. It appears that the sides of the house and the roof have been mislabelled. If you look closely, you'll see this biscuit is a little thicker than this one. That's because it needs to be stronger to take the weight of the roof biscuit sitting on it. Because of the wrong labels, you've used the thinner roof biscuits as the house walls and that's why they broke when you put the roof on. It is not your fault, it's just one of those things.'

'Can you fix it?' asked Alanna, shyly.

'Nope, I'm afraid I can't.'

In one quick swoop, Polly swept all the gingerbread biscuits into the bin. Two pairs of brown eyes and one pair of blue looked at her in shock.

'What I can do, however, is help you to bake new, better, biscuits that will look so much classier than this!'

She pointed at the picture on the box and pulled a silly face of disgust which had the children giggling as she'd intended.

'Right, so first, we need to get a recipe, sort out the ingredients and get them weighed. Think you can help with that?'

Two little heads nodded vigorously and one big head smiled at her appreciatively while mouthing, "thank you", above them. She gave Maxwell a small nod as she passed by to retrieve her laptop.

'Okay, these will now go in the oven for ten to fifteen minutes and then we need to leave them for a few hours to cool before we can decorate them.'

'Why do they need to cool?'

Polly looked at Taylor and smiled.

'If you try to put the icing on when the biscuit is hot, it'll melt and fall off again. Your house would look more like a monster house than a gingerbread house.'

'Cool! I want a monster house!'

She laughed.

'I think your school project stated a gingerbread house but we can maybe do a monster house another time. Now, why don't you both go into the lounge and see if there's something to watch on the television while your daddy and I clear up in here.'

The children ran off and Maxwell turned to face her.

'Polly, I really am sorry for dropping this on you and am deeply grateful to you for helping. I appreciate it very much.'

'It's fine. No problem. In fact, I've rather enjoyed it.'

'What? You've enjoyed doing something Christmassy?'

'No!' She flicked him with the tea towel. 'I've enjoyed showing your children how to bake.'

'They enjoyed it too. Helen, their mother, doesn't bake and my mum is a great cook but a rubbish baker. The yearly Christmas cake is the limit of her baking prowess and that only works because my grandmother's recipe is foolproof!'

'That's a shame. Kids love doing things that are messy. If the messy thing also produces something tasty afterwards… double win!'

She pulled the rolling pin towards her and Maxwell quickly stepped away with his hands in the air.

'Hey, what are you planning to do with that?' he asked in mock fright.

'Giving the children a special surprise. You see, if you do this…' she placed some boiled sweets in a sandwich bag and bashed them with the rolling pin until they were crushed into little pieces, '…and then do this…' she opened the oven door, pulled out the trays with the biscuits and sprinkled the crushed sugar pieces into the gaps they'd cut out, '…it makes the house look like it has glass windows.'

She pushed the trays back in and stood up.

'Wow! The kids will love that.'

'I know.'

They shared a smile, finished the washing up and when the biscuits had been safely transferred onto the wire rack to cool, walked into the lounge to see what Alanna and Taylor were watching.

'You two okay?'

'Yes, Dad.'

The children were sitting on the sofa watching a cartoon on the television. Bailey was happily ensconced between them, enjoying the petting they were both giving him.

'Polly?'

'Yes, Taylor?'

'Why haven't you put up your Christmas tree yet?'

Polly felt Maxwell stiffen by her side.

'Because Christmas trees can be dangerous for cats and I don't want to risk Bailey hurting himself.'

'Can't you tell him not to touch it?'

'I could tell him but he may not understand. It's just

safer if I don't have one.'

'You could have other decorations though.'

She looked at Alanna who'd turned around to peer at her over the top of the sofa and kept her eyes firmly away from Maxwell who she just *knew* was trying to keep a straight face.

'Do you think so? Such as?'

'Well, your balcony bit up there,' Alanna pointed up at the gallery above, 'you could wrap some lights and ribbons around the top of it. They wouldn't hurt Bailey. Your vases there,' she pointed to the large pieces of glassware on either side of the fireplace, 'could be filled with baubles and some battery fairy lights. We went to the big shop with Grandma last week and they had loads of good stuff. Why don't we go there now and help you to choose things that would be safe for Bailey? Dad, you could take us, couldn't you? In your truck?'

'Yes, I would be more than happy to help Polly pick up some Christmas decorations.'

'Wouldn't you rather watch television until your biscuits are ready?'

'Polly, you were very nice and helped to fix our gingerbread project so we don't mind missing the cartoons to help you decorate. Besides, we really like the big shop and I would love to go there again. Wouldn't you, Taylor?'

Alanna gave her little brother a hefty nudge.

'Oh yes, it's great fun.'

'You're enjoying this, aren't you?' she muttered through gritted teeth to Maxwell while keeping a smile on her face for the children.

'You had better believe it!'

'Okay, you guys win. Give me five minutes to get changed.'

'You have to admit, it looks fabulous.'

Polly looked around her lounge and despite all her misgivings, had to agree with Maxwell – it did look good if also extremely festive. She wasn't so sure about the last item they were working on but the children had enjoyed putting it together for her and it would be churlish of her to be a Scrooge about it all.

'Who's going to put the star on the tree?'

'I think Polly should do that – it's her tree after all.'

Alanna held out the gold-painted, wooden star and Polly placed it on top of the wooden tree which now also sported other wooden baubles along with a little wooden rocking horse, some wooden nutcrackers, snowmen and a Santa Claus. The tree also had integrated lights so there had been absolutely no reason not to buy it when the kids had found it. Especially as the label had screamed in large print, "PET SAFE".

Once the star was in place, the lights were switched on and she couldn't stop herself from smiling when the children ooh'd in delight.

'Dad, I'm hungry.'

'Oh, my goodness, look at the time. I need to get you to Grandma's quickly if Polly and I are to get out tonight.'

Polly looked at her watch and saw it was almost five-thirty.

'Or, I have another suggestion. How about we all have dinner here and afterwards, finish decorating your gingerbread house? The biscuits are perfectly cold now.'

'YAY! Yes, please, Polly!'

Maxwell turned to face her, his back to the children.

'Are you sure? You've had us all day.'

'I'm perfectly sure. I've had lots of fun.' She moved away and went to where Alanna and Taylor were sitting putting the empty boxes back in the carrier bags.

'I'm hoping everyone likes spaghetti Bolognese

because I took a pot out of the freezer to defrost before we went out which means I'm going to need some big tummies to eat it all up. Think you guys can do that for me?'

'YES!'

After checking the children were properly strapped into their car seats, Maxwell turned to Polly and took the carefully packaged gingerbread house from her and placed it in the footwell at the front of the truck. He pulled the passenger seat forward to hold it in place and prevent it from sliding about.

'I can't thank you enough for this, Polly. You really saved the day. I am sorry, though, about all the decorations. You can take them down again when we've gone, I won't tell the kids.'

'Oh, I won't do that. They're up now and with them all being Bailey safe, I have no good reason to take them down. I will make every effort to suppress my inner humbug and enjoy them for what they are. And please stop thanking me, you've already done some really lovely things for me in the few days I've known you; the least I could do was help you out. I've had a lovely day, although I'm sure it wasn't the advent surprise you were planning.'

'It most certainly wasn't.'

'Are you going to tell me what should have been behind "door number four"?'

'No! I can use it for another day instead.'

'Spoilsport.'

'That would be me! Now, I promise that you WILL get tomorrow to yourself and I will pick you up at five. This time you need to wear walking boots or shoes and wrap up warm.'

With that, he gave her a kiss on the cheek, got into the truck and set off at a slow pace which Polly realised was to ensure the gingerbread house made it home in one piece.

When the truck was out of sight, she went back inside, locked up and, after a final look at her bright, sparkly lounge, walked round switching all the twinkles off.

It had been a busy day. Lots of fun but busy and the only place she wanted to be now was in her bed, Bailey by her side and a book in her hand.

She would definitely, however, be switching all the twinkles on again tomorrow.

13

December 5th

'We need to talk!'

'Polly, it's Sunday morning and not yet ten o'clock! Can't this wait a few more hours?'

'No, Ritchie, it can't wait. I've met someone and I don't know what to do.'

'Woah! Stop right there! Did you just say you've met someone?'

'Yes!'

'Okay, NOW you have my attention but before you say anything else, I need to pee and make coffee. So, I'm going to hang up, sort those things out and call you back. DO. NOT. GO. AWAY!'

Polly placed her laptop back on the coffee table and went into her own kitchen to sort out a coffee for herself. She made it extra strong because, by golly, she needed it!

She was back in position, ready for her best friend in the whole world to return her call once he'd done what he needed to do but that she didn't want, or need, to see.

Her laptop pinged and she quickly pulled it towards her.

'Right, I'm back. I have a large coffee and more in the pot. Tell me everything and speak clearly.'

Polly filled Ritchie in on all that had occurred since they'd chatted last week.

'Hang on, did you just say Maxwell Watkins? As in, THIS Maxwell Watkins?'

Ritchie held his phone up to the screen and she saw he'd pulled up a picture of Maxwell from his earlier modelling days.

'Yes, that's him although he's older now and not as fresh-faced.'

'But still so handsome you could happily lick whipped cream off his naked body?'

'You know I prefer Nutella but yes, still that handsome.'

'And he's made you his Christmas project? Trying to bring the love of Christmas back into your withered little soul?'

'That would be correct.'

'So, how many dates have there been?'

'Ritchie, use your noodle – if there are twenty-four days on an advent calendar and today is the fifth of December…'

'Today will be date number five!'

'Yes! Although it's the sixth day since we met.'

'Which means you've fallen in love in less than a week.'

'Hey, who said anything about love?'

'You've spent the whole of the last three days with him. Is he the last thing you're now thinking of when you go to sleep?'

'Err, yes.'

'Is he the first thing you think of when you wake up?'

'He was this morning.'

'What time did you wake up this morning?'

'Just after six…'

'Honey, the Love Train may not have arrived at the terminus but I can assure you it has already departed from the station and is hurtling its way there.'

'But… I don't want to fall in love.'

'Then stop seeing him.'

'I don't want to do that either.'

'How bad is it, sweetcheeks?'

'This bad!'

She picked up the laptop and turned it around, walking about the lounge so Ritchie could see the Christmas decorations. She finally brought it to rest upon the Christmas tree.

'OOOO! EMMMM! GEEEEE! Is that a Christmas tree, Polly?'

She turned the screen back to face her.

'Yes, it is.'

'Twenty years, Polly! For twenty years you refused to have anything to do with Christmas and yet, after a mere five days, this bloke – albeit drop-dead gorgeous bloke with a butt you could—'

'Ritchie!'

'Fine! My point is that I've spent most of my adult life trying to bring you back to Christmas life to no avail. Maxwell Watkins turns up and you're banging on Santa's grotto within five days. Can you see the point I'm making? This man is Prince Charming to your Snow White. He's woken you up. He's somehow reaching the part of you that you've had bricked up for two decades. I don't know how he's managed it but I'm thrilled that he has.'

'You think I should keep on seeing him?'

'I think you should do what makes you happy and despite the horrendously early hour of the day—'

'Ritchie, it's after nine!'

'Like I said, horrendously early hour of the day, you are

87

shining nearly as brightly as the star on your Bailey-friendly tree. You are positively glowing. So, my advice, for what it is worth, is to go with the flow. Take each advent day as it comes and see where it leads you.'

Polly paused for a moment to think over Ritchie's words.

'You really think I'm glowing?'

'Yes, you are sparkling like the little special snowflake that you are. Now, can I go back to bed? It was a late night and as thrilled as I am with your news, I need some more sleep.'

'Sure, off you go. Call me back later when you're more alert and tell me all your news.'

'Nothing to tell that compares to yours. Besides, you'll be too busy getting ready to go out by the time I feel like I belong to the human race again. I'll call you through the week. I want to hear what your latest surprises have been. Maybe I can pass them onto Scott and they'll inspire him to make more of an effort.'

'I thought you guys were going well.'

'Oh, we are, but after what you've just told me, I think we need to up our game. Anyway, till next time. Love you.'

'Love you too.'

After making kissy faces at each other, Polly closed the laptop and stared at the tree twinkling in front of her, thinking of Maxwell and wondering how it was all going to turn out.

14

'Do you mind if I leave the truck here and we walk into town?'

'No, not at all.'

'Thanks. It's going to be busy and parking will be a nightmare. I had thought about using the parking bay behind the office but getting out afterwards will be a pain.'

Polly fastened the buttons and ran her hands down the front of the borrowed red coat, enjoying the feel of the soft cashmere under her skin before pulling on her cream gloves and winding the matching scarf around her neck. She popped her head back into the lounge to check she'd switched off all the twinkling lights and then followed Maxwell out the front door.

'Where are we off to tonight? Somewhere in town, I'm guessing, if we can walk there.'

'Oh, so subtle and yet… just not subtle enough!'

'It was worth a try.'

When they reached the gate, she turned left as Maxwell turned right.

'Oh, we're not taking the main road?'

He turned to smile at her.

'There's a lane at the bottom of the hill which takes you right into the centre of the town. It's perfect for where we're going tonight. Didn't you know about it?'

'Yes, I know the lane but I don't feel comfortable using it on my own in the dark. I used it a couple of times in the summer though when the nights were lighter.'

'Good point. I'd like to say you'd be safe here but I think everywhere carries an element of risk these days. As there are two of us, however, I think we should be safe.'

'That and the fact you're built like a brick outhouse!'

'Sure, there is that.'

They talked as they walked but when they turned towards the footpath into town, Polly stopped, quite stunned by the picture in front of her.

'Oh, wow! How beautiful is that?'

She'd never seen the lane at night and so the big, old-fashioned, cast-iron Victorian streetlamps, now lit up, were a complete surprise. The large trees, although naked of leaves, reached across to come together above their heads, creating an intertwined roof which the stars peeked through. A light mist hung in the air, trapped in the enclosed space, making it look quite ethereal.

'It is rather pretty, isn't it?'

'It makes me think of the fantasy books I read as a child. Old lampposts, mist and big trees.'

'You don't mean the Narnia books, do you?'

'Yes! I do.'

They were so busy talking about their favourite books as children, that they were walking past the office door before Polly realised where they were.

'Gosh, the town's pretty busy tonight. It's not usually like this on a Sunday, is it?'

'No, but tonight's a bit special.'

'Why?'

'You'll see. Here… this is a good spot to stand.'

Maxwell led her to the edge of the pavement and stood behind her. She looked along the road and saw people all jostling and shuffling to take up similar positions. Somebody bumped against her and she felt Maxwell's hand take hold of her elbow. She was glad because she had no desire to fall onto the road in front of a car—

Hang on!

It was then that Polly became aware that no cars had gone by since they'd been standing there and some members of the crowd were walking up the middle of the road with little concern for their safety. Whatever was going on was important enough to merit the roads being closed to traffic.

At that moment, the clock on the church along the road began to chime and there was a quick flurry of movement as the roadway cleared and everyone found their space.

The sixth and final peal of the church bell died away and all around her was complete silence. No one spoke, not even a whisper.

Then, quietly but clearly, the sound of singing came floating towards them.

"Silent night, holy night…"

The single voice was as pure and sweet as a nightingale's, penetrating the sky and reaching up towards the starry heavens above.

Her breath caught in her throat with the beauty of the sound.

The singing was gradually becoming louder and when she leant forward to see more, she was stunned to see the local church choir, dressed in their red smocks with white scarves around their necks, walking along the road carrying olde-worlde lanterns, lit up with candles.

Some of the choristers held their lanterns in their hands, others had them raised up on poles where they swung

91

around, throwing their gentle light across the gathered spectators.

As the music drew closer, she heard more voices begin to sing. The rest of the choir had joined in. Still, no one around her spoke. She'd never known a crowd of people to be so quiet. And then she saw why.

The choir had just walked past her, followed by the elders of the church along with the local vicar and priest. Behind them, the spectators on the pavements had stepped off to join the procession and at this point, they too began to sing.

When the end of the procession had passed and the people standing beside her moved onto the road, Maxwell took her elbow again and guided her into the middle of the throng. Once in place, he started to sing, looking down at her with a smile until she joined in. He then handed her a small lit candle to hold. She was concerned at first that it would go out but relaxed when she saw it was battery-operated.

She walked along in the crowd, through the town, singing the Christmas carols she hadn't sung since her father had passed away. Tears began to slip from her eyes as she recalled his warm, baritone, voice giving its all at the midnight service the night before he died. Oh, how he would have loved this spectacle.

The singers and people in front of her came to a standstill as they arrived in the town square. The choir sang their last notes and the air became still all around. Once again, no one spoke and no one moved.

Suddenly, there was a loud bang and a solitary firework rent the air and its pure white sparkles filled the sky above them. The next thing she knew, lights of every colour were hitting her eyes from all angles and the Salvation Army Band had begun playing "God Rest ye Merry Gentlemen".

The crowd went from total silence to cheering,

hollering and singing along. Everyone was shaking the hands of the people next to them and exchanging hugs. An old-style carousel threw on its light switch, struck up its organ and soon the music was vying with the brass band for attention.

In the space of a few moments, the market square had transformed into a small fun-fair with a coconut shy, a hook-a-duck, a darts stall and even dodgems. There were also some craft stalls selling handmade soaps, candles and cakes.

Polly turned to Maxwell who had remained glued to her side the whole time. She couldn't have wiped the smile from her face if she'd tried.

'What? What was that?'

'Did you like it?'

'Like it? Maxwell, it was beautiful. I've never seen anything like it.'

'It's called "The Procession of the Lights". The town does it every year on the first Sunday of December. As you can see, it marks the beginning of the Christmas festivities.'

'It was stunning.'

'It was. Now, how about we take a stroll around the stalls to see what's on offer before heading over to Dotties's for a hot chocolate and a really decadent piece of stollen?'

'Dottie's opens at night?'

'No, only on this night.'

'Then, what are we waiting for? Lead the way.'

Maxwell took her hand and as he led her through the crowd, the only thing Polly was aware of was the tingling sensation running up and down her arm again.

15

December 6th

'Hi, Polly, did you miss us?'

'Hey, you guys, welcome back. How did it go?'

'Pretty much as expected,' Andy replied with a grin. 'First, Monty had a hissy fit. Then he had a sulk followed by some petty grumbling and finished off with a massive tantrum where he actually stamped his feet! After that, however, it all settled down and everything was fine.'

'I see. Would I be right to assume this is par for the course at these events?'

'You assume correctly. The two words "drama" and "queen" came into their own.'

'I heard that!'

Monty had made his way straight to the kitchen but he was clearly listening in to their conversation.

Andy gave her a sidelong look followed by a cheeky wink. She had to suck her cheeks in to stop herself from laughing.

'Polly, what's this you have here?'

'Oh, Maxwell took me to the light procession last night and there was a stall in the market selling all these wonderful coffees. I picked up a couple of Christmas-flavoured ones and brought in my spare French press so we could try them. Which one do you fancy first – cinnamon and hazelnut, gingerbread, or Christmas pudding?'

'Erm, anything less fancy for the first cup of the day? I'm not saying I'm unwilling to give them all a try but I like my morning coffee to be plain and strong.'

'That's not a problem, Monty, I also got a bag of unflavoured to be on the safe side. Andy?'

'A standard one for me too, please.'

Polly set about making the coffees and took them through to the reception where Andy and Monty were admiring the Christmas tree.

'I must say, Polly, you've decorated the tree and office beautifully. The swags, garlands and lights all look amazing and the tree is glorious. You must have been up and down the ladder no end to reach those top branches.'

'I can't take all the credit. Maxwell helped out and it was he who decorated the top. All my efforts were concentrated on the lower branches. The rest of the office is my handiwork though. He's not getting all of your praise.'

She looked around her and was glad she'd arrived early enough to switch all the lights on before Andy and Monty came in. It really did look quite pretty.

'Maxwell helped with the tree? And accompanied you to the switch-on last night?'

'He didn't so much as accompany me as take me there. I knew nothing about it.'

'Is that so?'

She didn't miss the look that Monty and Andy exchanged.

'Is it a problem? Do you have a company policy about mixing business with pleasure because I didn't know—'

'No, no, nothing like that at all. It's just… well… Maxwell was involved with someone and they only broke up three months ago. I'm merely surprised to hear he's been taking you out.'

'Oh, it's not like that. Not like that at all.'

She quickly explained about her father and her subsequent falling out with all things Christmas and that Maxwell had given himself the challenge of trying to make her love the festive season again.

'He's only being friendly and showing me the different things that the area has to offer at this time of year. It's my first winter in the Peak District – I'm a big city girl out in the countryside for the first time ever. He's just being a very nice tourist guide.'

'Hmmm…'

'You don't think so, Monty?'

'It's just not a very "Maxwell" kind of thing. But look, I'm not going to put a downer on it. And if he succeeds in giving your Christmas spirit a boost, then that's all the better because everyone should love Christmas. Now, we need to bring the stock back in from the van and I need you to help Andy catalogue it, if that's okay?'

'Of course, it is. I'll put these mugs in the kitchen and then you can show me what you need me to do.'

Maxwell tooted his horn and, after giving Bailey a quick pat on the head, Polly ran out to meet him. She'd tried not to dwell too much on Monty's words as she'd set about doing the cataloguing but it had been difficult. Maxwell hadn't made any mention of a recent relationship and she couldn't help but wonder why. He'd been open enough about his ex-wife so why not the ex-girlfriend? Was it because he was over his wife but not the girlfriend? Had he been hurt by the relationship ending and was that why he wouldn't, or couldn't, talk about it? She now wished that Monty hadn't said anything because it was sitting heavy upon her but she couldn't say anything to Maxwell as then he would think she'd been gossiping about him with his brother.

'Hi there, all set for another adventure?'

'Hi yourself and yes, I am. Lead on, MacBeth.'

'What? No question as to where we're going?'

'Nope! I now know you're never going to tell so why waste my breath asking. I am just going to take each day as it comes.'

'Ah, acceptance! This is good. This is progress. This means the spirit is beginning to waken within you.'

'Wrong! This is just me realising that it's easier to get information out of a teenager than it is to prise it out of you!'

Maxwell chuckled as he pulled out of the lane and onto the main road.

'Well, the good news is that tonight's surprise is only a small one. I realise it's a school night, as folks say, and I don't want to encounter the wrath of my brother by sending you into work knackered every day. I also think Bailey will have something to say if I'm stealing you away every night.'

'Yes, I confess that I am feeling a little guilty at leaving him two nights in a row.'

'I'll get him some treats as a means of an apology. And it's not like it'll be happening long-term – there's only twenty-four days of advent so he'll have you all back to himself in a couple of weeks.'

The stabbing sensation in her stomach made Polly gasp aloud.

'You okay there?'

She quickly drew in a breath.

'Yes… yes, I am. I just caught sight of that motorbike and thought he was going to hit us.'

'Hmm, he was going a bit fast for this stretch of road.'

The night sky outside was a rich dark hue with a light sprinkling of stars and she turned her head to stare out while her mind raced. Maxwell had just made it quite clear that this was a short-term thing. He evidently saw this as a friendship and nothing more. Despite everything, she'd found herself hoping that the other side of Christmas would still see them spending time together. The realisation that life would be reverting back to how it used to be had felt like a sharp kick in the guts. Tears began pricking her eyes and it took a lot of swallowing and blinking to push them away. She couldn't let Maxwell see how his words had upset her. He'd made no promises of any sort. Hell, there hadn't even been any kind of advances or insinuations to make her think that there was anything other than friendship on offer here. It was simply so nice to be in the company of someone who was actually thinking about her and was trying to make her happy. That hadn't been the case for a very long time and she'd allowed herself to get carried away with it. She now had a decision to make – cut her losses and pull out of the advent-ures or suck up every joyful moment and deal with the painful loneliness that would be the aftermath later.

'We're here!'

Maxwell pulled into the parking space in the well-lit car park and threw a big grin in her direction. Polly couldn't stop the smile she gave in return and that was when she knew she'd be spending every possible darn moment she could with this man. She'd just make sure she had plenty of tissues, wine and chocolate on hand for the tears that would come later.

<u>16</u>

'Where are we?'

'This is the car park on the other side of town. Haven't you been to this one?'

Polly looked about her, getting her bearings. She could see the church spire rising up above the roofs and knew it was the same one she could see from her upstairs windows when she looked down onto the town.

'No. I don't know this area.'

Over at the far end of the parking area was a medium-sized supermarket. It was one of the big six, unexpectedly tucked away. In front of them, and what appeared to be the back-end of the High Street shops, were cabins, garages and lock-ups, which were all small businesses. There was an antiques shop, a butcher and a cobbler. All were now closed for the night. One of the larger outlets however, a florist, was still open and next to that was a tea-room which had customers seated at its tables.

'Hi, Sue.'

Maxwell waved to the woman standing inside as they walked by.

'Hey, Maxwell, all good?'

'Very good, thank you.'

He held open the door to the tea-room for Polly to walk through. A couple were just rising from the table by the window so she waited for them to pass before taking their place.

'Hmm, so you like tables by the window, do you?'

'I do. I like being able to watch the world go by while taking time out from it.'

'Nice philosophy. I bet you also like the seats above the driver when you're on a bus.'

'Err, who doesn't? Those are the best seats to sit in!'

She peered out of the window, trying to see beyond the car park.

'Where exactly are we? I've worked out we're still in town but can't quite get my bearings.'

'Over there, you have the football club and leisure centre,' Maxwell pointed out the window, 'and behind us, if you walk up the lane, is the main street of the town. You're less than ten minutes away from the office.'

'But the drive here felt longer than that?'

'One-way system!'

'Ah, of course.'

The waitress arrived at their table just then and after clearing away the used crockery from the previous occupants, returned to take their order.

'I'll have a bowl of the winter broth please along with a cheese and ham toastie. Polly?'

She looked at the board on the wall.

'May I ask what's the winter broth?'

'It's delicious. It's meaty and thick with a hint of spice to warm you up.'

Polly smiled at Maxwell's enthusiasm as she gave her order to the waitress but substituted the toastie for a buttered roll.

'I'm guessing this is a regular haunt given your knowledge of the soup?'

'Not as much as it used to be. Its proximity to the football field made it the perfect stop-off after the games to replace the calories burned up on the pitch.'

'You don't play anymore?'

'No. I was the goalie and there comes a point where throwing this much bulk across the ground begins to hurt. I packed it in when Taylor came along because two kids need more time and it's no fun for Daddy to have toddlers clambering over him while nursing bruised ribs.'

'Ouch! No, that wouldn't be fun at all. Do you miss it?'

'Not really. The friends I played with have all moved on with their lives and it's a younger set these days. I'd be very out of place now. I'm happy to be an old fart and sit and watch.'

They were laughing as the waitress returned with their food and there was silence while they ate.

'That was delicious!'

Polly wiped the last few drops of her soup up with the last bite of her roll. It had been everything Maxwell had said.

'Do they do takeaway?' she whispered across to him.

'Yes, why?'

'Because I can see myself coming down for a few of these over the cold months. It was lush.'

'When you do, be sure to ask Monty for his order as he not only likes the soup but he also has a soft spot for their four cheese paninis.'

'Thank you for the tip. It wouldn't do to upset the boss.'

'I don't think you need to worry there. He seems very taken with you.'

'Oh?'

'That's a good thing. Monty doesn't usually take to new folks too quickly – he was burnt more than a few times in

101

his younger days. If he's taken you under his wing, you have a friend for life. Unless you hurt him, of course.'

'I could never do that. He's lovely. Why would anyone want to?'

'He had some hard times growing up. You can't miss that he's gay – it's been clear from a young age – but school kids and teenagers are a cruel breed. These days, the exterior is tougher than it used to be but the inside is soft and can still be wounded. Now, to change the subject, we need to get a wriggle on.'

Two minutes after settling the bill, Polly found herself being guided into the florist's next door to the tearoom and over to a work bench, of which there were six. Maxwell stood behind the one next to her. In a short time, the other four benches were occupied and the lock-up door was pulled closed.

'Good evening, ladies and gentleman, welcome to my Christmas wreath-making class.'

17

December 7th

'Oh, Polly, what a gorgeous wreath. That really does add the finishing touch to the office decorations.'

Polly was hanging one of the wreaths from the previous night on the wooden front door as Monty arrived.

'Don't thank me, the credit for this goes to Maxwell. He made it.'

They both stepped back onto the pavement to admire the stunning creation in front of them.

'Straight?'

'I'm not but the wreath certainly is!'

'Oh, you!'

Polly gave Monty a gentle nudge, recalling the conversation from the previous night. The nudge she received in return was not so gentle and she made a mental note to give as good as she'd just been given in future.

They walked up into the office and towards the kitchen to get the coffee going.

'So, is that where my brother took you last night – wreath-making?'

'Yes, it was.'

'Blimey! He sure knows how to woo a girl… not!'

She felt herself blushing at Monty's comment and turned away to get the mugs out of the cupboard.

'I told you, it's nothing like that. We're just friends. Besides, I rather enjoyed it. It took me a little while to get it together but once I found my rhythm, it was good.'

'Does that mean you also have a glorious wreath somewhere?'

'Yes, mine is now adorning my front door. I confess that I'm rather pleased with it, you know, with it being the first one I've ever made.'

'You do know to spritz it regularly to keep it fresh until January?'

'I do, but how do you know?'

'Our mum. She makes her own, has done for years, and it used to be my daily chore when I lived at home.'

'Right. That'll be why Maxwell donated his to you – as he doesn't need one.'

'Yeah, Mum will have made one for his and Helen's chalets. For the benefit of the kids.'

'I see. So, Helen lives at the holiday park too?'

'She does. Has Maxwell not explained this to you?'

'Like I said earlier, not that kind of relationship.'

'Oh! Well, when he and Helen split, there was the usual conundrum of custody and stuff. Because they're such good friends, they wanted to find a way of keeping the disruption to a minimum. It was Mum who came up with the idea of them both having chalets on the holiday park. Not right next door, obviously, that would be too creepy but on opposite sides of the park so they can come and go without feeling the other is watching. The main house, my family home, is in between so it's the perfect spot for dropping off and picking up the children. It works really well and everyone seems to be happy.'

'But what about when either of them meets someone else? Does that not make it strange?'

'I can't really comment, to be honest. While Maxwell is single now, Helen has been dating a rather nice man but I got the feeling, from the way she was speaking when we met last week, that it could be coming to an end.'

'Oh, that's a pity.'

'It is. She's a lovely woman and I think the problem is that she's looking for the same kind of friendship she has with Maxwell but with added extras. Unfortunately, that friendship is unique and not the kind that makes a marriage. As she already knows.'

'Do you think she and Maxwell would ever get back together?'

Polly focused her attention on pouring out the coffee to ensure her face didn't give her away, regardless of Monty's answer.

'I know the kids would love it and my mother would be over the moon but I can't see it ever happening. Maxwell rarely changes his mind once it's made up on something and he knows that being with Helen wouldn't make either of them happy.'

'Sugar?'

'Well, that's a bit forward, I prefer to be called Monty.'

She let out a groan while giving Monty her best eye-roll.

'It's going to be one of those days, isn't it?'

'Honey, it's always "one of those days" around here.'

He picked up his mug and walked out of the kitchen.

'Oy,' she called after him. 'That's a bit forward, I prefer to be called Polly!'

The loud chuckle that skipped its way back to her made her smile and she was still smiling as she walked towards her own desk.

'So, what delight have you got up your sleeve for my wonderful new staff member this evening, dear brother?'

'I can't tell you. I like to keep these things a surprise right up to the last minute.'

'Seriously?'

Monty turned towards Polly.

'Are you telling me that Maxwell has been dragging you here, there and everywhere and you've known nothing about it until the last minute?'

'Pretty much.'

'And you're okay with that?'

Polly shrugged, trying not to let Monty's indignation on her behalf amuse her too much.

'I was told from the start that that was how it was going to be. I pushed against it for the first few days but realised I was wasting my time, so now I just go with the flow.' She looked at Maxwell and then back to Monty. 'He hasn't let me down thus far so I have no complaints.'

'I see.' Monty looked back at his twin. 'Can you give me any clues for this evening?'

Maxwell pondered for a moment before saying, 'Bird clothing.'

She watched Monty's face as he worked out this cryptic clue which meant absolutely nothing to her and knew he'd found the answer when a big smile lit up his eyes.

'Got it! Oh yes, nice one. In fact, how would you feel about a couple of gate-crashers? Andy and I would love that too.'

'Well, I don't mind but it's up to Polly. Pol – how would you feel about us having company on our date tonight?'

'Oh, err... urm... I don't mind. If... if... it doesn't cause any bother or upset your plans at all...'

'Great! The more the merrier then. Oh, the star on the Christmas tree has slipped. Let me fix that...'

Polly stepped behind her desk, making a show of clearing it up for the night but her mind was darting back and forth like a ping-pong ball! Maxwell had referred to their night out as a date! It was the first time he'd called any of their outings a date. Did he mean it as in "a date" – a courting ritual kind of date – or had he simply used the term because it was easier? Had he even realised he'd said it at all?

'I think the papers are straight now.'

'Huh?'

Maxwell's voice broke into her musing.

'The papers you're bumping on the desk – you've been doing that for about two minutes.'

'Oh!' She looked down at the pile of invoices in her hand that she'd been absentmindedly tapping against the desk.

'Sorry. Just thinking of something I need to remember to do tomorrow.'

'Why not leave yourself a sticky note on your screen? That's what I do.'

'Good idea.'

She quickly scribbled a bit of nonsense on a sticky and smiled at Maxwell as she stuck it on the PC monitor.

'Right, my lovelies, are we ready to go? Andy, just a reminder that you've to say nothing about this evening, okay? Don't be ruining Polly's surprise now!'

'I won't,' he sighed and Polly suspected this wasn't the first reminder he'd had from Monty in the last few moments.

They locked up the office and when the men turned towards the town centre, Polly followed them, listening as they brought Maxwell up to speed on the trip to London. It only took a few minutes for them to reach their destination – The Four Feathers pub in the market square. Maxwell's cryptic clue now made sense.

It was an old pub and Polly had passed it many times, admiring the historic building when she did, but she'd never been inside. They were soon all settled in a booth and she took the opportunity to have a good look around.

The ceilings were low and beamed which meant Maxwell had to duck his head when he returned from the bar with menus in his hand. The ease with which he did it though, suggested to Polly that he was a regular visitor.

The beams were dark wood but the areas between them were painted a pale cream which made the pub look clean and bright. The bar was the same dark wood as were the floorboards beneath her feet. At the opposite end to where they were seated, a large open fire was burning behind a cast-iron guard. The room was decorated in gaily-coloured Christmas decorations, fairy lights and tinsel. She could just see the tips of the branches belonging to the Christmas tree which was hiding around the corner. Christmas music was playing in the background, occasionally being drowned out by the chatter of the other customers around them. The atmosphere was friendly and Polly found herself liking the place. Enough to make a note to bring Ritchie and Scott here the next time they visited.

'Thank you.'

She smiled at the waitress who'd brought over their drinks and took a sip of the beautifully chilled chardonnay.

'Right, part one is eating and then part two is the surprise.'

Maxwell grinned at her and when she looked at Monty and Andy, they were doing the same.

'Seriously, stop looking at me like that. It's like being out with the Three Stooges!'

Amidst chuckling and banter, they decided on their meals and Maxwell retraced his steps to the bar to place the orders.

He hadn't been back in his seat for a minute when Monty commented, 'Polly, it's great to be sitting with a woman who doesn't order a pathetic salad which she'll spend the time picking at and barely eat a lettuce leaf from.'

'Oh, I love my food too much for that. That's the reason I walk to and from work – to burn off the calories I like to consume. I can't be doing with all this body conscious stuff that the media keeps pushing at women. We come in all shapes and sizes and should be allowed to enjoy how we are without being made to feel guilty.'

'I couldn't agree more,' Monty smiled.

'Besides, as I know from experience, beauty on the outside doesn't guarantee beauty on the inside.'

'What do you mean?'

'Well, my best friend in London runs a restaurant in Chelsea and he asked me to lend a hand one week as half of his staff were off with the flu. This was about two and a half years ago. That Laurel Devine, you know, the now much-touted supermodel, came in and she was a bloody nightmare! Three times she sent her meal back saying it was too cold, too burnt or too salty. The fact is there was nothing wrong with the food – she was merely making a scene to get attention and be noticed. Her star was just beginning to rise and she wanted to ensure everyone knew who she was. Naturally, she appeared on several twitter feeds and the like because folks don't go anywhere without their cameras these days and that's what she'd been banking on. I was the one serving her and let me tell you, my hand fair itched to give her a good slap across her pathetic pouty mouth!'

She stopped talking when she saw that Monty and

Andy's shoulders were shaking, tears were streaming down their faces and they'd both stuffed a balled-up hand to their mouths to try and hold back their laughter.

'Err, guys, it wasn't that funny.'

'No, it's not...' Monty spluttered, 'but it is when Maxwell used to date the woman you so want to smack down!'

At this, the laughter overtook him and both he and Andy were almost holding each other up. She noticed other customers looking their way and when she cast a side-long look at Maxwell sitting beside her, she saw his face was bright red in embarrassment although a smile was hovering on his lips.

'Oh, I'm so sorry, I didn't know...'

Her voice tailed off. What could she say? She hadn't known otherwise she'd have kept her thoughts to herself. She wasn't going to retract them though – every word was true and Laurel Devine was a jumped-up little madam. It just went to prove again that even the most sensible of men would fall at the feet of a pretty face with a pouty mouth!

'It's okay, don't worry about it. It's over now so no harm done.'

Thankfully, before any further embarrassment could occur, the first dishes of their meal arrived at the table and the subject was forgotten about.

'It was Matthew Crawley, I'm telling you!'

Polly hissed over the table to Andy who was writing down the answers of the pub's Christmas Quiz – her latest advent surprise and one she was enjoying immensely although Polly hadn't decided if it was the quizzing or the relaxing element of sitting down in the warm indoors that was doing it for her. Either way, she was having a lot of fun.

'Are you sure?'

'Maxwell Watkins, don't question a woman whose biggest passion is period dramas. You have got no idea the backlash that episode generated!'

The next question had Monty bouncing in his seat.

'Green! Santa's suit used to be green.'

'Trust you to know that, Monty.'

'Well, brother of mine, it is kind of my area of expertise.'

This generated more laughter and the happy banter continued right up until they won the little trophy and the other customers gave them a round of applause.

As Maxwell shared the bottle of wine that had come with the trophy, Polly commented, 'It's really nice how the entry fees are given to charity. That's a lovely gesture.'

'They save up all year. Ten percent of the quiz takings is put aside every week and then the full amount taken for the Christmas quiz is added to it.'

'I like that, the community looking out for others less fortunate.'

'It's a great little town, Polly, which you'll find out the longer you're here.'

'To Christmas and community!'

Andy lifted his wine glass and as they all repeated his toast and chinked their glasses, Polly realised that she was actually feeling some of the Christmas excitement in her belly that hadn't been there since she was fifteen years old.

18

December 8th

'Oh, my goodness, do I have an office manager or an abominable snowman in my office?'

'Ha-bloody-ha! Think you're funny, do you?'

'Hilarious, actually. What are you wearing?'

'My coat.'

'I can see that, lovely, but what do you have on underneath?'

Polly let out a sigh. She would have shrugged her shoulders but as there was barely any space to breathe, any additional movement was impossible.

'Maxwell sent me a text this morning telling me to be sure to wrap up warmly for tonight as the weather forecast stated it would be growing considerably colder throughout the day. So, I put on my thermal vest and extra thick jumper. That all fitted fine under your lovely red coat but my grandmother's coat came back today from the dry cleaner's and it's a neater fit so now I can hardly move.'

'Then wear the red coat! What's the problem?'

'I've got my coat back now, Andy, it would be rude to keep wearing the one you guys lent to me.'

'Don't be daft! One more day isn't going to make a difference. Go on, put the red one back on. Besides, it's Christmas and it looks fabulously festive on you. You are a walking vision of Christmas when you wear it.'

'If you're sure…'

'Of course I'm sure. Go on, go get it.'

As she undid the buttons on her cream coat, Polly sighed with relief as the tension against her chest eased.

'Oh, that feels so much better.'

She was just walking back through to the reception when she heard Maxwell's voice calling her.

'Hey, I'm here and I'm ready.'

'Great. Now, you do have gloves and a hat, don't you?'

'Yes, just about to put them on. No need to fuss, I'm not one of your kids.'

'I know, sorry. Just don't want you to be cold.'

She said her goodbyes and walked down the stairs behind Maxwell and out onto the pavement.

'This way.'

He began to stride along the high street and, after running to catch up for the third time, Polly had to ask him to slow down.

'Sorry, I'm so looking forward to this one and am in a hurry to begin.'

They'd come to a standstill outside the last shop on the street where the road led out to the church and the outlying villages. Here, Maxwell tugged the rucksack off his back and pulled out two clipboards with a piece of paper attached to each.

'Right, which board do you want? This one or this one?'

He lifted his hands with each question. Polly pointed to

his left hand.

'That one.'

He passed the board over, bent down to his rucksack again and, when he straightened up, he handed her a thick chunky marker pen.

'That's called a dobber.'

'A what?'

'A dobber. They're used in bingo, which is what we're playing tonight. Welcome to Window Bingo.'

She looked at him as if he was talking in a different language.

'Window Bingo?'

'Yes. Look at your card on the clipboard. You've got boxes with different items inside. As we walk along looking in the shop windows, if you see something there that's on your card, you "dob" it with your dobber. Once all the squares are "dobbed" you call out "House" and you're the winner. Just like normal bingo but with a twist.'

'Unbelievable!' She shook her head. Whatever was he going to come up with next?

'Ready to begin?'

'I suppose the sooner we begin, the sooner we'll be done and I get home to a nice warm fireplace.'

'That's the positive kind of attitude I like!'

His words were accompanied with a light punch on the arm before he pulled the rucksack back on.

'Is there a prize?'

'Let's see who wins the game first.'

'Fair enough!'

They scoured the first few windows in silence and Polly was delighted that she was the first one to "dob" her card. Thank you, green tinsel, she thought.

After a bit, however, the silence was too much. She was used to them chattering and it felt strange for that not to be the case now.

'I'm sorry again for causing you embarrassment last night, you know, with my comments on Laurel.'

'It's okay.'

She wasn't sure but she thought she heard a small catch in his voice and wondered if it wasn't okay at all.

'Do you want to talk about it?'

'Not particularly.'

'How about I tell you mine if you tell me yours?'

He didn't reply immediately and she was beginning to think the subject was closed when suddenly he said, 'Okay, we can do that.'

'Fine. You first. Mine might take a little longer.'

'Honestly, there's not much to tell, Polly. We met just under two years ago. It was Monty's first show and collection where he'd expanded his clothing range to include smaller sizes for men not as big and beefy as myself. However, instead of having blokes modelling the gear on the catwalk with me, he thought lady supermodels would mix it up a bit. Laurel was one of those models. Her looks complemented mine and so we were paired together for the walks. Naturally, the close proximity of the rapid changes and so on, cut through quite a few of the social barriers which are normally removed gradually when you go on dates and we ended up becoming a couple within a few days. It was heady and whirl-windy and I was in a total lust-fog for months. Laurel has this perfect technique of giving just enough of herself to keep you hooked but never enough to make you feel safe in your position. More than once I asked her if we were exclusive but rarely received a satisfactory answer.'

'Was that important to you? Being exclusive? After Helen, you didn't fancy the idea of being able to play the field a little?'

'No, not my style. I've always been a one-gal kind of bloke. Plus, Helen and I had been together for such a long time, I felt rather lost without her by my side. It wasn't Helen that I missed, just the feeling of someone being around. Unfortunately, Laurel was the wrong person to pin my solitary hopes upon. She was frustrated with my reluctance to move to London permanently and I was becoming disillusioned with her for always demanding that I should. I tried to explain about the kids and wanting to be close to them but it went right by her – she gave them no consideration whatsoever and that was her undoing. Slowly, my infatuation began to wane and I could see the spoilt, demanding woman underneath the glamour. I tried to be patient and understanding but for her, it was all of me or none of me. She didn't want to share me although I was expected to share her. Unfortunately, being faithful is not one of Laurel's strong points and, in the end, I had to say my goodbyes as I couldn't deliver what she was after. She wanted the eye-candy on her arm to accompany her to all the "right places" where she could be seen, photographed and show up all over social media the day after. From our conversation the other day, you know my views on that. No way did I want my kids seeing Daddy plastered all over the internet while being a party animal. I began to create a distance between us, gradually so as not to hurt her – these supermodels have egos more fragile than porcelain – until I was in a position to suggest we call it a day as we hardly saw each other anymore.'

'How did that go down?'

'Not very well. She wasn't used to people saying no and she certainly wasn't used to blokes breaking it off with her. She did the dumping – her words, not mine – and how dare I think I was so special that I got to leave her. She then told me that "I" was dumped and flounced out of the room. I haven't seen her since.'

'And that was how long ago?'

'Just over three months.'

'Pretty recent then?'

'Recent enough.'

'Recent enough to still hurt?'

There was a small pause before Maxwell replied. 'No, but recent enough for me to still feel like a failure that I couldn't make another relationship work.'

Her first instinct was to refute his comment but Polly knew from her own experience that those kinds of platitudes were pointless.

'You're wrong to feel that way but I understand that you do. You need to focus on the fact that both parties have to be invested for the relationship to be a success. In Laurel's case, that was never going to happen. There's only one person in her universe and that's herself. You can't hope to win in that kind of scenario. You did the best thing you could – took yourself out of it because you knew it wasn't healthy for you. That takes more inner strength than you realise.'

'Speaking from experience?'

She felt his gaze upon her and she made a point of staring in the shop window and consulting her bingo card.

'Yeah, in a way.'

'I've told you mine, now it's your turn. That was the deal.'

She let out a sigh. Where on earth did she start with trying to explain the disaster that had been her marriage?

<u>19</u>

Polly stared through the window of the haberdashery shop they were currently standing in front of while her mind raced, trying to think of what to say. She must have hesitated longer than she realised for Maxwell's voice suddenly broke into her thinking.

'Look, if it's too painful to talk about, it's not a problem. You don't have to share anything with me. It's not a big deal.'

While he spoke, his hand was gently rubbing her back, just between her shoulder blades, and it was this gesture, more than his kind words, which decided her.

'I do want to tell you, I'm just… trying to work out where to start.'

'I find the beginning is usually the best place.'

'That will make it a longer story.'

'Fine. I'm in no rush. It takes as long as it takes.'

She turned away and walked to the next lit-up window with its beautifully decorated display.

'After my dad died, things kind of turned to shit. For obvious reasons. Mum went to pieces and was really struggling to keep it together. I plunged into a deep well of grief and refused to go to school. We were both mourning our loss but couldn't find comfort in each other. We both withdrew into ourselves and did our grieving alone.'

Tears at the memories blurred her vision and she blinked a few times to clear them. Her eyes scanned around the window display and she was about to turn away when she spotted the little purple fairy hiding behind the grandfather clock. She looked down at her clipboard and saw this was on her card. She used the time it took to remove the lid from her dobber and mark her card to bring herself back under control. This was a time in her life that she didn't speak of and it was still cutting her deeper than she'd realised.

'By the time I returned to school, I'd fallen behind my classmates and ended up having to repeat the year. This led to bullying from my new classmates which I responded to by becoming a bit of a rebel. The only subject I never caused any trouble in was Home Economics. I loved baking, as you know, so I was always on time for the class, never played truant on the days I had Home Ecc and never missed a homework assignment. All my other subjects, however… they could go stuff themselves! Anyway, to try and make this story a little shorter, Mrs Wilson was the only teacher I had time for. We got on well and she looked out for me. Unsurprisingly, I left school with only one qualification – Home Ecc. I didn't want to go to college so Mrs Wilson had a word with a close friend and I ended up with a job as a trainee receptionist at one of the big financial houses in the City, in London. I didn't want to let Mrs Wilson down after her making this effort for me, so even though it was something I had zero interest in, I applied myself, paid attention and learnt the job. It was on my eighteenth birthday that they told me I had excelled in the role and gave me a proper full-time job. I was thrilled.

I was being paid a decent wage and felt like an adult. A few months later, my mum announced her intention to buy a place in Spain with her sister and before I knew it, I was spending Christmas on my own. Okay, the previous two hadn't exactly been a blast but at least Mum had been there so we could be miserable together. That one, however, I was alone, lonely and, therefore, vulnerable. Enter Trevor! More handsome than you could shake a stick at, more charm than oil in Dubai, and perfectly placed to turn the head of any young girl, myself included. He asked me out, I said yes and so it began – him taking me over until I wasn't me anymore. I don't believe it was done with any malice, I was simply young and malleable; he was seven years older and thought he knew it all. So, he led and I followed. He was a trader and I thought he was a god. He had money, the nice apartment, the flash car and the champagne lifestyle. I mean, you find an eighteen-year-old girl who wouldn't have her head turned by all that.'

'I think I'd struggle…' Maxwell murmured.

Polly smiled at him, glad he understood.

'Anyway, we became a couple and lived the high life. His career success seemed to know no bounds. He was the company's golden boy and his client portfolio grew larger by the day. He was flying high and took me along for the ride. When I was twenty-eight, we got married because it seemed the right time to do it. Nothing changed, however, and it was all very much "as you were" but this time with a piece of paper behind us.'

'I'm taking a punt here and guessing the thrill of the partying waned somewhere along the line?'

She glanced up to find his dark eyes watching her and a soft expression on his face.

'You guessed correctly. It was just after my thirtieth birthday. We'd thrown a massive party to mark the occasion and the day after, I had the most awful hangover.

That's when I realised I was spending too many days nursing bad heads and queasy stomachs. I decided that was the end of it. It was time to grow up and be more responsible. It's also when I figured it was time to talk about becoming parents. We'd done the wild partying – we needed to move on. And that's when the problems started. Trevor didn't want kids. Trevor didn't want that level of responsibility. In short, Trevor didn't want to grow up. He liked his life exactly as it was and didn't want it to change. I tried to let it go but that's when we began to grow apart. He continued to party while I would go home after work and have a microwave meal for one.'

'Hmm, sounds lonely.'

'It was, it was very lonely. One night we had a massive row and I said I was leaving. Trevor begged me to stay. He only managed it by promising he would re-think the children thing and to give him some time to come round to the idea. Another twelve months went by; another twelve months where nothing really changed at all, and I again said I'd had enough. If we weren't going to have children, then I wanted out. Trevor was drunk and that's when I found out he'd had a vasectomy not long after I'd first brought the subject up. He didn't want to risk me coming off my contraception and "trapping him" – his delightful turn of phrase, by the way – so he'd faked a business trip in order to go and have the snip!'

'He didn't tell you or discuss it?'

'Nope! That's the happy bit about this male-dominated world we live in. Men can get a vasectomy without their wife's permission but most doctors won't sterilise a woman without her husband being involved, even though it's not a legal requirement. Double standards or what?'

'I would say so. What happened?'

'Well, as you can imagine that really was the start of the end. Except, where I thought it couldn't get any worse, it did!'

'How could it get any worse than that?'

'Easily! You see, when my dad died, he left behind a more than decent insurance policy. It was substantial enough for Mum to put half of it in a trust fund for me and use the other half for herself. I came into my fund at twenty-five, which was also when Trevor found an old, disused warehouse on the edge of Islington – a nice trendy place for any stock trader to live – which was the perfect doing-up project. We bought it, using a rather hefty chunk of my trust fund, and proceeded to "do it up" using pretty much what was left of my trust fund.'

'You bought it outright?'

'Not quite, but the mortgage was extremely low in comparison to what it would have been without the deposit. The mortgage which, I should add, we both paid. By this time, I'd moved up into the role of office manager but despite my monthly pay-packet being a mere fraction of what he was earning, I still paid exactly half of all the household bills. Anyway, after I found out about the vasectomy, I decided I wanted a divorce. I knew it would benefit me more if I took my time and didn't rush into it. So, I played the long game, pretended I was okay but in the background, I was finding out where I stood and the best solicitors for the job. That is, until the day I got a call from the bank asking me to go in. The manager wanted a meeting and *that's* when I found out the evil, twisted little scrote-worm was trying to re-mortgage the house without my knowledge!'

'WHAT? No way!'

'Yes! Every which way! The bastard had forged my signature on the documents and it was only the eagle eye of the clerk, who was collating the file to put it forward for approval, who noticed that the "Y" in Polly was written differently from the original mortgage forms. The manager had called me in to verify it was my signature and that's when all hell broke loose! I found out very soon afterwards that Trevor, in an attempt to keep up with the younger lads on the trading floor, had developed himself a nice little cocaine habit, using money syphoned off his clients' accounts and needed the capital out of the house to pay back what he'd stolen.'

'Bloody hell!'

'I know! You read about these things in books and the like; you never expect them to happen to you.'

'I can't believe it! What happened next?'

'Obviously the mortgage application was halted. The police were called in and things got rather messy for Trevor. In the meantime, I'd been in touch with a solicitor and the ball was already slowly rolling. This development meant my solicitor had the ammunition she needed to go in strong on my demands. Trevor tried to fight it but we got lucky with the judge the day we went to court. She ruled that when the house was sold, I should get the full return of what I had put into it from my trust fund plus ten percent as interest. Any remaining profit was to be divided fifty-fifty once all other fees had been met.'

'Good on her! At least you were treated fairly. What happened to Trevor?'

'His share of the sale was just about enough to cover the bulk of what he'd stolen. He was lucky that property prices in London had risen so well and our house had more than trebled in value since we'd bought it. He tried to fight against the division of the money but to no avail.'

'Was he charged with fraud and theft?'

'No. His company didn't want a fuss – if word had got out it could have tarnished their reputation so he was let go quietly as long as he repaid what he'd stolen. I, or the bank, could have done him for attempted fraud but it wasn't worth the hassle.'

'And then you decided to move up here.'

'I…oh…house!'

'Yes, the house…'

'No!'

Polly grinned at him as she held up her completed bingo card.

'HOUSE! I win! What's my prize?'

<u>20</u>

December 9th

When Polly woke up the following morning, she was surprised by how light and happy she felt. She'd expected to have a sleepless night, tossing and turning, as the regurgitated memories spun around her head. Instead, she'd slept deeply and was now fully refreshed. She glanced at the clock and seeing it was still early, got up and headed down to the kitchen. After switching on the coffee machine and the oven in that order, she went onto the internet to find some more unusual Christmas treats she could turn her hand to. All those she'd tried to date, and had been successful, were now safely filed away for later reference. If Maxwell succeeded in resurrecting her love of Christmas, and he was doing a good job of it thus far, then she may look at booking a stall at some of the Christmas markets next year.

She was scrolling through her search results when one in particular caught her eye – Scollen.

Huh?

She looked closer, reading the recipe and saw it was a scone and stollen mix. She fancied the sound of that and when a quick check of her ingredients came up trumps, she set about making a batch and they were baking away nicely in the oven when she went back upstairs to take her shower and get dressed for work.

Once the scones had cooled slightly on a wire-tray, she put a smaller tray inside a cake tin, placed four of the scones on it and put the tin inside a carrier bag, leaving the lid off so the scones could continue to cool. She took a jar of Bonne Maman strawberry preserve from the cupboard and made a mental note to pick up some cream from the little deli in the market square as she walked past.

Unexpectedly catching herself humming as she locked the front door, Polly paused, smiled and then carried on. She hadn't felt this good since before her dad had died – she reckoned she'd earned the right to be humming about it. It was just as well that Maxwell couldn't hear the song she was now singing aloud for he'd definitely be claiming a victory even if she was all but murdering the poor Shakin' Stevens Christmas offering.

When she arrived at the office, it was to find Monty messing about with a small CD player behind her desk.

'What are you doing?' she asked, while hanging her coat up.

'It's time to indulge in some nice, cheesy, Christmas tunes. Things begin to wind down over the next few weeks so we can relax somewhat and get ourselves geared up for Christmas. Which reminds me, if you need any timeout to go Christmas shopping, just say. You may as well do it during the week when it's quiet than battle the crowds on the weekend.'

'Oh, I couldn't possibly do that…'

'You can and you will. Don't feel you're taking advantage because I can assure you that, come January, things become extremely hectic and you could easily find yourself peeing in a bottle under your desk because the phones won't stay silent long enough for you to have a loo break!'

'He's not exaggerating, Polly.'

Andy came down the wooden steps with a pile of CDs in his hand. A glance at the top one showed her a bright red cover with a jolly looking Santa on it and she gave an inward groan. Her festive singing this morning may turn out to be quite short-lived if she was going to have to listen to Christmas songs and carols for seven hours a day for the next two weeks. She might very well be taking up the shopping offer more than once!

'So, what wonderful event did my brother share with you last night? Did you have fun?'

'Yes, I did. More than I thought I would've done if I'd been told in advance what the activity was.'

'What was it then?'

She filled Monty and Andy in on the window bingo but left out the soul-sharing that had also taken place. They didn't need to know about that.

'And what was your prize?'

'Erm… all Maxwell would say was that he'd be buying the burgers tonight. Does that mean anything to you?'

'Nope, can't say it does.'

Monty shook his head while sneaking a little grin at Andy.

'I saw that. You do know! Tell me!'

'If I did know, I wouldn't say anything and if I didn't know, I still wouldn't say anything!'

'That doesn't make any sense.'

Monty grinned and turned to follow Andy up the steps

to the workshop.

'Eh, Monty, can I just ask one question?'

'Is it about your next advent?'

'No.'

'Okay, ask away.'

'Maxwell… does anyone ever just call him Max?'

She noticed a slight darkening of Monty's face but it went as quickly as it had come.

'No, Polly, they don't. He doesn't like it and he doesn't suit it. Max is too small a name for someone the size of my brother. All that stature requires a good solid name and "Maxwell" does that job just fine. Calling him "Max" diminishes who he is. Well, in my opinion anyway.'

Polly thought about this for a few seconds before replying.

'You know, you're right. I didn't think of it that way. And yes, he is certainly a "Maxwell" – there's no doubt about that.'

As she stood looking at the contents of her wardrobe, Polly checked the text she'd received from Maxwell just as she was leaving the office.

**"I'll pick you up at 6.30pm.
Wrap up very warmly."**

That was it. Nothing more and as usual, no clue at all about what was coming. It was the "wrap up very warmly" part that was causing her a problem. Her closet was full of "London" clothes. As in, clothes not in the least bit suitable for traipsing around the Peak District in the middle of winter but perfectly suitable for a drink or two in a West End wine bar!

'Damn and blast!' she muttered aloud, causing Bailey to lift his sleepy head off the bed to look at her.

'Sorry, sweetie, did I waken you?' She gave his head a gentle pat and scratched under his chin. A few seconds later, his head dropped down onto his paws and she turned back to face down her poor selection of "very warm" attire. One old thermal vest really wasn't cutting it.

Eventually, she settled on a layering process and bundled herself up in a t-shirt, shirt and jumper, thin leggings under her jeans and two pairs of socks on her feet. She also made a mental note to go online when she returned later and sort out some decent thermal underwear and socks. Something told her that there were likely to be a few more requests like this before Maxwell was satisfied her Christmas soul had been saved.

She rapidly dressed herself and was just pulling on her coat when the sound of tyres on gravel alerted her to Maxwell's arrival. Polly grabbed her hat, scarf, gloves and cake tin and ran out to meet him.

It was as she was clambering into the cab of the truck that it dawned on her that she'd probably appeared a touch too eager. Another mental note to self, she thought, try to look less like an over-happy puppy the next time. Maybe cool it a bit!

'Hey, how are you doing? Had a good day?'

'Hi, Maxwell, apart from feeling like Mr Blobby in my twenty million layers of clothing, I'm great and had a great day too. What about yourself?'

'All is groovy over in this corner, thank you. Ready for tonight?'

'Are you going to tell me where we're headed?'

'Of course I'm not!'

'Then I'm as ready as I'll ever be.'

'You've not got long to wait. We'll be there soon.'

'Okay. By the way, I did some baking this morning and

there's a few scones in the tin for you to take home.'

'Oh, wow! Thank you.'

'You're welcome. So, where are we going?' she asked a second time, hoping he might be distracted enough to answer.

'Ah, so the cakes are a bribe? Good try.'

'They weren't but now you mention it… would bribery be an option?'

'No.'

'Oh well, no harm in asking.'

Maxwell hadn't been joking when he'd said soon. Ten minutes later they were pulling into the same car park they'd been in on Monday except this time, all the little shops, outlets and cafés were dark and closed.

It was only when they turned to walk in the opposite direction from Monday night that Polly saw the football field on the other side of the river was all lit up and there was a steady stream of people walking over the bridge towards it. A stream of people that they were soon joining.

'A football match? You're taking me to a football match?'

'You don't like football?'

'It's not usually at the top of my "To-Do" list, I have to be honest.'

'I think you'll like this one.'

'You reckon?'

'Trust me.'

He guided her towards the small stand behind one of the goals and once seated, she looked around to see who else was there. The ground was rapidly filling up and it seemed as though the whole town had turned out for the event.

'I didn't realise the local team had such a good following. I thought everyone was into Premiership clubs these days.'

'This particular event does quite well.'

Before she could question his unusual reply, there was a cheer from the crowd and she looked round to see the players running onto the pitch.

'You have GOT to be kidding? Seriously?'

She couldn't prevent the grin on her face as she turned back to look at Maxwell.

'Yup, seriously!'

Polly returned her gaze to the pitch and laughed along with the rest of the crowd as the sight of fifteen Santas and fifteen elves began to warm up in front of them. This was when she noticed how many children were there as they all ran to the edge of the billboards, trying to catch the sweets being thrown by the club mascot who had also entered into the spirit of things by wearing antlers on its head and a boa made of tinsel around its neck. When the players left the pitch to prepare for the start of the game, all around her, people began to put on Santa hats or pointed elf ears. Maxwell gave her a nudge and she looked down to see him holding out a Santa hat for her to don.

'I'm guessing we're rooting for the Santas then?'

'The Santas are our local team this year, the elves are from the neighbouring town. It alternates each year. The host team are always the boys in red.'

'Is it taken as seriously as a normal derby?'

'You'll see.'

And, see she did. Her sides were aching from laughing by the time the half-time whistle blew.

'Oh, my goodness, I've never seen anything like it!'

'Having fun?'

'Oh, yes, very much so.'

'Now, I believe I owe you a burger – how would you like it?'

Polly was sitting, blowing into her gloves to warm her hands, when Monty and Andy appeared.

'So, you did know where we were going tonight?'

'Sure we did. This game is a big deal and no one misses it. What did you think of the first half?'

'Loved it! I'm not sure what had me laughing more – the substitute elves trying to change the scoreboard, the sight of half-a-dozen Santas chasing them around the pitch, or the way both sides stopped and did Gangnam Style whenever a goal was scored. That is a sight which has to be seen to be believed.'

That had only been a selection of the fun and frolics on the pitch and within ten minutes of the kick-off, Polly had sussed that the only part of this game being taken seriously was how much fun and laughter the two teams could inject into the event. Circus clowns could learn a thing or two from these guys.

'That's why it does so well. And, like the quiz the other night, all the proceeds go to charity. It really brings the town together and helps towards raising the spirit of Christmas. And, talking of which, how's yours doing?'

Polly gave Andy a little grin. 'Rather well, as it happens, but don't let Maxwell know. I'm curious to see what else he has up his sleeve.'

'Your secret is safe with us. Our lips are sealed, aren't they, Monty?'

'Absolutely. I want to see just how creative my brother can be.'

'And, talking of your brother, I do believe he is returning, bearing my prize from last night.'

She quickly guzzled down the very tasty cheeseburger and was just finishing it off when the teams returned to the pitch. As she wiped her mouth with the paper napkin, she turned to Maxwell and said, 'I'm glad I finished that in time. The only thing I want to be choking on this evening is laughter.'

'Then I think,' he replied, watching the Santas empty a

load of red sacks full of footballs onto the pitch and the mock-shock of the elves as they ran about trying to round them up, 'on that one, you're going to be in luck.'

21

December 10th

'Flaming Nora! What a day. I thought you guys said it was a slow, easy wind-down into Christmas?'

Polly flipped the switchboard over to night mode and flung herself back in her chair.

'Today was the last hurrah. The day when everyone runs around clearing the stuff off their desks that's been sitting there for the last three months. As of Monday, everything becomes January's problem. I can guarantee that next week you'll be picking the handset up every so often to check if the lines are still working.'

Andy smiled at her as he placed a glass of Prosecco in front of her.

'Here, have some of this. You've earned it.'

'You know,' Polly said, taking a hefty swig of the lovely, chilled delight, 'if I'd been aware of how freely the alcohol flowed in the fashion business, I'd have looked at getting into it a lot sooner.'

'They didn't have staff drinks in those fancy London trading offices?'

'Only for the traders. The ones who brought in the money. Us serfs, the ones who kept everything ticking over so the rest could do their jobs, were pretty much ignored. We weren't considered important.'

'Well, you are considered very important here. We're only a little team but everyone matters.'

'What matters?'

Andy turned to Monty.

'I was just telling Polly that her contribution here is every bit as important as everyone else's. No one is special around here, not even you.'

'Sad but true. I might come up with the designs but without Andy's flair for cutting and knowing what fabric would work best for the styles, or the seamstresses who help put it together, or the fabulous lady who answers the phones and keeps the admin at bay, none of it would work.'

'Well, I'm more than happy to be a part of your team. Thank you.'

'No, thank *you* for coming on board. It may only have been a few days but we've already noticed the difference.'

Her cheeks began to warm under the unexpected praise so Polly decided this was a good moment to say her goodbyes. Maxwell was picking her up at seven and she wanted to grab a shower first.

'Have a good time tonight.'

She looked at Monty with suspicion.

'Do you know what tonight's event is?'

'Not exactly but I have an idea.'

'Wanna share?'

'Hell, no! Maxwell would kill me.'

'He's your twin brother.'

'And you've seen the size of him. No way. You'll just need to wait.'

'I won't bring any cake in on Monday. I know how much you've been enjoying my baking.'

'Good! I'm putting on weight. No temptation suits me just fine.'

Realising she wasn't going to get Monty to crack, she pulled on her coat, said goodnight and rushed home.

Once she'd given Bailey some fuss and food, and after a nice hot shower, Polly opened the packages she'd received that day at the office. When she'd been told last night that she needed to wrap up warm again for this evening, it had been a mad dash to the internet and an urgent order of thermal socks and underwear had gone through. Thank goodness for instant deliveries – the goods had been on her desk by three o'clock this afternoon.

When said items were adorning her body, she looked in the mirror and appraised her appearance. Okay, as far as sex appeal went, these were never going to win any awards but she could already feel a sweat coming on so they were certainly doing the job they were intended for. Besides, she was never going to be getting sexy with Maxwell; Laurel Devine may be a grade-A bitch but she was a beautiful bitch and Polly was all too aware that she could never compete. Her shoulder-length dark-blonde hair, ordinary blue eyes, more-round-than-oval face, and dress size that mostly hovered around the size fourteen mark, were all distinctly average. Something Ms Laurel Devine was not, which suggested that average was evidently not the kind of woman Maxwell was attracted to. They were just friends and she should get used to that.

A sigh left her body as she finished getting dressed and her mood was subdued by the time Maxwell turned into her driveway.

'Evening. All set for another adventure?'

'Yeah, sure.'

He looked at her as she busied herself with fastening

her seatbelt.

'Are you okay? You sound a bit down.'

'I'm fine. Just a bit tired – it was busy in the office today and I'm not used to having a social life anymore, never mind one that hasn't stopped for ten days.'

'I'm sorry. If you'd rather give tonight a miss…'

'No, no, we're good. I'm sorry for being a grump. You're making all this effort to help me and I'm being a bitch. Please, forgive me.'

'Hey, don't sweat it. There's nothing to forgive. I get it – there has been a lot going on for you. I really don't mind if you want some time out.'

'Let's get going.' She gave him a smile. 'The fact I've been told to wrap up again tells me we'll be outdoors and the fresh air will bring me round.'

'You've guessed correctly.'

He returned her smile, swung the truck round and soon they were on the main road although only for a couple of minutes. A quick right turn had them heading along a track shrouded with tall trees and bushes. The vast canopy of branches overhead created a tunnel effect and the headlights gave it a slightly eerie sensation. This only lasted for a moment till they came to a clearing and Maxwell parked up.

'We're here.'

'Seriously? Are you going to keep using that one on me?' she laughed, as she jumped down from the cab and felt her feet sink into the soft forest floor.

'Now, this is when you really need to have faith in me. I know where I'm going but you won't be able to see a thing once I switch this torch off. Okay?'

'I'm getting a feeling of déjà vu here but sure, I trust you.'

'Fine. Now close your eyes.'

Polly did as he asked and, taking her by the elbow,

Maxwell walked her away from the cab.

'Right, wait here. I need to leave you for a few seconds but I'll be right back.'

She felt him move away and as she stood there, alone in the dark with the smell and sounds of the woods around her, she felt a small shift inside her. It wasn't much but it was enough to let in a sense of peace. Opening up about Trevor earlier in the week had taken a weight off. All this time, she'd carried a sense of shame over her ex-husband's duplicity but talking to Maxwell and seeing his abhorrence at the way she'd been treated, had made her feel less like a fool. She'd trusted someone and they'd let her down. That didn't make her a bad person, it made them the villain for abusing that trust. This sudden revelation had created a sense of lightness inside her that felt quite strange. It had begun as a sort of giddy sensation but here, in this moment of it just being her and nature, it became a feeling of surety. She didn't know quite what she felt so sure about but it was there and it was nice.

'Okay, you can open your eyes,' Maxwell whispered quietly and when she did as he asked, it was as if her eyes were still closed. It was pitch black and she couldn't see anything. She could sense Maxwell by her side but she couldn't see him.

'What—'

'Hush. Just wait.'

Polly stood still, inhaling the fresh, frost-tinged air and was starting to wonder how long they would be standing there when she suddenly found herself standing in a fairy-light filled arbour.

'What the—'

She spun around, taking in the lights around her that had just begun to twinkle.

'Oh, my goodness. This is… oh, wow!'

Over her head and all the way to the ground, the tiny

white lights sparkled and glistened. It was simply stunning.

'Come, this way.'

Maxwell held out his hand and she took it without thinking, still overwhelmed by the lit-up tree tunnel.

He led her through it to the furthest end and, as they stepped out, white strobe lights began to move back and forth, lighting up the trees above, and lanterns placed at ground level showed her the path to follow. As they walked, more strobe lights came on, different colours each time which completely changed the effect of the trees. They went from being haunting in the white, to eerie in red, spooky in green and simply magical in blue and purple.

Still holding her hand, Maxwell led her around a corner and an array of overhead string lights commanded her attention. All shapes and sizes danced gently in the evening breeze above her head and she gazed at them in awe until her attention was captured by the sight of a white doe hiding in the trees. It disappeared quickly but reappeared a few seconds later. It was another clever light illusion and it took her breath away.

They carried on walking through the woods and she was treated to the sight of fireworks in light form, Santas walking through the trees, elves peeking out from bushes, reindeer with flashing red noses scratching around for lichen, until finally, the grand finale, a sparkling golden sleigh flying above the trees being pulled by eight glorious deer.

They walked back through another twinkling tunnel which led to a clearing with a wooden gazebo that was also lit up with softly flashing fairy lights and contained two chairs and a small table set for dinner.

'Would madam like to take a seat?'

Maxwell walked up the two wooden steps and pulled back one of the chairs for her to sit on. A small hurricane lamp on the table contained a lit candle that reflected off the shining cutlery.

'Maxwell, what was all that back there? It was stunning.'

'Every year, we put on a light show through the woods on our land. The grand opening is tomorrow night but I thought you'd enjoy having a special showing of your own. This is the dress rehearsal.'

'It's amazing. You don't do this on your own, do you?'

'Gosh, no. We bring in an expert lighting firm who set it all up and maintain it. In the next clearing along there's a catering van which my parents take charge of. All of this is their baby. My only input is to work with the electricians to ensure they don't damage any of the trees or bushes. Ah, and here comes dinner.'

Polly glanced round and saw a tall, slender woman walking towards them pulling a box behind her. As she drew closer, Polly saw that it was a thermal box on wheels.

'Hi, Maxwell, timed that to perfection, I think.'

'You sure did. Polly, this is my mum, Marian. Mum, this is Polly.'

'Hello, Polly, lovely to meet you.'

'And you, Marian. Both of your boys have told me a lot about you.'

'I hope it was all good.'

'It definitely was.'

'I hope you don't mind being our food taster tonight. We're getting the van ready for tomorrow and I wanted to try out some new items on our menu.'

'Well, Maxwell has already told me what a wonderful cook you are so I would be delighted to taste whatever you have to offer.'

'Super. Well, just let me set up this little table.'

She walked over to the side of the gazebo and brought back a little fold-up table that Polly hadn't noticed and once upright with a red Christmas tablecloth laid over it, began to take items from the thermal box.

'This is chicken tikka on a bed of rice in a pitta bread.'

Marian placed a cardboard, takeaway tray on the table.

'This is a peppered lamb with rice burrito.' More cardboard boxes were brought out. 'That there is beef stew and these cups contain tomato and pepper soup. I've also brought some standard burgers and chips in case none of this is to your liking.'

'That's an interesting choice, Marian, and it all looks delicious.'

'It's a case of trying to expand the selection without too much extra work. These are all dishes which can intermingle.'

'I can't wait to try them out.'

'I want truthful feedback now.'

'Marian, I promise that's what you'll get. I like to bake and you need honest feedback to know what works and what doesn't so I understand.'

'I know you bake – Maxwell shared those scone things you made yesterday. They were delicious. Such a novel idea.'

'Thank you although I can't take the credit – I found the recipe online.'

'They were lush. Anyway, I can't stand here chatting while the food gets cold so you crack on and I'll see you later. Oh, I nearly forgot…' she pulled round the satchel which had been across her back, 'your wine. It's non-alcoholic as we don't have a licence and Maxwell will be driving you home but it's rather nice. Now, enjoy.'

Marian pushed the thermal box to the side with instructions to bring it back with the empty cartons inside when they were done and then slipped back off into the darkness, leaving them alone. They were just dividing up the food when the fairy-lights in the tree tunnel behind them went off. The glow from the candle and the lights on the gazebo wrapped around them, encasing them in a little twinkling and fluttering cocoon. The scent of the woods mingled with the aroma from the food and created something so special that Polly knew she would remember it for the rest of her life.

'Thank you for tonight. Thank you for all that you've done over the last ten days. I know I thank you each time but I really want you to know how much I've enjoyed it all. You've gone to so much effort and I'm impressed by the variety of your *advent*-ures.'

'Polly, I've enjoyed our advent-ures too and it has been so much fun working out different things to share with you. The best bit for me, however, has been seeing you change each day. When we first met, you were carrying a sadness around with you and now that I know you better, I can see where it came from. But now, you're beginning to sparkle. Your eyes shine these days – even when you're tired and feeling grumpy – and for me, that makes all this worthwhile. Now, would you like some chicken tikka first or the peppered lamb burrito?'

As Maxwell divvied up the treats, Polly thought over his words.

She sparkled now?

Did she?

Ritchie had used the same expression last Sunday although she hadn't noticed it herself but later that night, as she stood brushing her teeth, she leant forward to take a closer look in the mirror and found they were both right. There was definitely a light in her eyes that she'd never seen before.

<u>22</u>

December 11th

Polly lay on her side, with Bailey snuggled against her back, and looked out the bedroom window. It was still dark outside but there was a hint of light over in the far distance behind the hills. The heating had only just clicked on and she had no intention of leaving her warm cosy bed for at least another forty minutes. A frost had started to settle when Maxwell had dropped her back home last night and judging by how cold it had been when she'd got up for the loo earlier, it hadn't warmed up any since then.

She wondered what Maxwell had planned for today. All he'd said before he'd left was that it was an indoor day and she could spend it at his place or hers. She chose her place as he'd done so much for her that it would be nice to be in a position to try and give something back. As such, it was her intention to bake some savoury bites and sweet-treats before he arrived at midday so they'd have something to nibble on through the day.

At eleven-thirty, she walked around the house, switching on all the fairy lights and decorations. They'd barely been on through the week – well, she'd been out most nights, it was hardly worth the effort when she wasn't getting in until late – and seeing them all twinkling and glowing brought back the memory of the previous night. Everything about it had been utterly magical. There had been something so amazing about being the only two people in the forest, witnessing all those incredible lights. She knew the atmosphere would have been quite different had there been other people around. But with just the two of them… it had been more special than she had words to describe.

He also held your hand. What about that?

The little voice in her head brought that back to her. How could she have forgotten? How could she have forgotten the feeling of warmth that had slipped through her gloves? The gentleness of his touch while holding her firmly? The tingles that had run up her arm and across her chest when he'd absentmindedly rubbed his thumb over hers while pointing out the hidden gems in the night?

She felt those same tingles traverse her body again as she remembered how nice it had been to just hold someone's hand. To feel connected to another human being. It had been too long since she'd been held in a manner which made her feel that she mattered to someone. Polly hadn't realised how much she'd missed that until now and she was suddenly pierced with a longing to have it again.

Just then, the doorbell rang and the sudden shrill sound in the silence of the house, made her jump.

'Alexa, play soft classical music.'

When the gentle notes of Clair de Lune filled the air from her electronic device, she went to open the door.

'Good day, good day, how are you today?' Maxwell all

but sang as he stepped over the threshold.

'I'm very well, thank you. I don't think I need to ask how you're doing – you seem full of bonhomie and joy!'

'And why wouldn't I be? I'm getting to spend a whole lazy day with my favourite Christmas companion, just chilling and relaxing.'

'Are we now? So, what is the plan for just chilling and relaxing?'

'It's Christmas Movie Day!'

He held up the carrier bag in his hand and she could see the shape of several DVD boxes contained inside.

'Christmas Movie Day?'

'Yup! We simply curl up on the sofa and watch back-to-back movies. Somewhere around five-ish, we'll order in a ridiculously large pizza and guzzle it while we gorge on more cinematic, Christmas wonderfulness.'

Polly gulped and felt her insides curl up in horror. She hadn't watched a Christmas film since her dad had died. It had been one of their things. When her mum went off to do the Christmas shopping, Polly had stayed home with her father and they'd have a mini movie-fest. They'd start with "Scrooge" with Alastair Sim, followed by "A Miracle on 34th Street" with Richard Attenborough and then finish the day crying to "It's a Wonderful Life" with the lovely James Stewart. That had been her favourite. There was no way she was ready to watch it with someone else. She simply couldn't.

She opened her mouth but before she could speak, Maxwell took the films from the bag and began to go through them.

'So, we have "Fred Claus" – very funny, "The Polar Express" – very Christmassy, "Elf" which has me in stitches every time, "The Holiday" and "Love Actually" – both girly rom-coms but pretty good nonetheless, "How the Grinch Stole Christmas" – the Jim Carrey one which is simply brilliant and, finally, the Disney animated version of "A Christmas Carol" – also with Jim Carrey but it's very good.'

He held them up in delight, a smile beaming over his face.

'No "It's a Wonderful Life" or "Miracle on 34th Street"?' she asked, faintly.

Maxwell put the pile on the coffee table and walked over to her. He placed his hands gently on her shoulders and looked down at her.

'No, I didn't bring either of those. They're old classics which I felt might hold memories for you. I purposely made a point of choosing later films that I'm guessing you've never seen and so there'll be no sad feelings to get in the way of you enjoying them.'

'Thank you,' she whispered. 'That was extremely thoughtful of you.'

'Hey, Snowflake, this whole *advent*-ure is to make you a happy Christmas fairy, not a sad one. Do not underestimate the thought that goes into these events. Now, at the risk of being rude, do I smell freshly baked mince pies?'

Polly couldn't stop the laughter that burst from her – a combination of relief and the look of comical longing on Maxwell's face.

'Yes, you do. Why don't you get everything set up in here, while I bring through the yummies?'

'That sounds like the perfect plan to me.'

Polly stretched her legs out as far as she could and let out a yawn.

'Boring you, am I?'

'Not at all. It's just so warm and cosy – I feel totally relaxed. It's a compliment really; that I feel this chilled in your company. It's nice.'

'Shall I stoke up the wood-burner?'

'Sure, if you don't mind. While you do that, I'll go and get plates and napkins for the pizza.'

She wandered into the kitchen, revelling in just how relaxed she felt. It had been a lovely, lazy, afternoon. She'd moved the big footstool that came with her large corner sofa and the two of them had simply vegged out with their feet up, watching movies. They'd watched the Disney version of "A Christmas Carol" first. She'd wanted to get that one out of the way so that, if she did feel a bit out of sorts, the remaining movies would take her mind off it. As it was, however, it hadn't affected her at all and it had been a pleasing start to the day. They were now four movies down with three to go and it was their intermission time while they waited for pizza, garlic bread and chicken wings to arrive.

She scooped some food into Bailey's bowl and poured out a little spot of cat milk for him. It was his daily treat and he loved it.

'Alright there, little man?'

She ran her fingers over his back as he walked past to his bowl. She straightened up, picked up the plates and napkins and returned to the lounge.

'I have to say, that really is one impressive television. Even the kids commented on it as we drove home last week. There were a couple of not-so-subtle hints that I should get one.'

Polly looked over at her 65", all-singing-and-all-dancing television and felt a flicker of pride.

'It was my biggest indulgence when I moved in. I adore watching films and in the absence of a proper cinema room – which I would *really* love to have, by the way – this was the next best thing. Also, anything smaller would be lost in this room.'

'Are movies your only favourite thing? Apart from the baking, of course.'

'I'm a big reader. That's why I have a corner sofa unit – I adore curling up in that corner, with Bailey on my lap, a coffee in one hand and a good book in the other.'

'Is that why you have that unit against the back of the sofa?'

'Well worked out, Sherlock,' she grinned. 'Yes, it's easier to put my mug up there. And, with it being an open-plan lounge, it creates a natural corridor from the hallway to the kitchen.'

'Yes, I can see how that works. I have to say, Graham did a wonderful job with this place.'

'Who?'

'Dorothy's son. He came up with the redesign for the interior. We used to hang out when we were young so I can remember how this all used to look. I can assure you it was nothing like this back then. It looks amazing now.'

She smiled. 'It works for me. I love it.'

'Even with all the fairy-lights and Christmas decorations that my children forced upon you?'

'Yes,' she laughed, 'even with the Christmas stuff all over the place.'

'Polly?'

'Hmm…'

'May I ask a personal question?'

'Sure. What is it?'

'Going back to what you were telling me about being married and stuff, how did Christmas work with your husband? You know, with you being so opposed to it.'

'We just didn't bother with it.'

'Seriously?'

'Yeah. He was a city trader, we both worked in the

finance quarter and the unspoken motto there is "Work hard, party harder!" and that's exactly what we did. The festive season just gave us an excuse to drink and be merry even more than we'd usually be. Not that we really needed an excuse, if I'm being honest. By the time Christmas Day arrived, we'd be a pair of walking corpses and we'd spend the whole day in bed sleeping. Then, on Boxing Day, Trevor would go off to watch football in some corporate box somewhere and I'd either binge on movies or start checking out the travel agents to find some extravagant holiday for the following year.'

'Didn't Trevor have family to see?'

'His folks were all down in Cornwall. He had two sisters and eventually, nieces and nephews. We'd go down a few times in the spring and summer but Trevor hated travelling in the winter. He sent money to his sisters for them to buy gifts for the kids and his parents.'

'I see. Did you never want to go to visit them?'

'Gosh, no! That would have been my worst nightmare. It was bad enough having to take part in the office Secret Santa.'

'I see.'

'What made you ask that?'

'I was just wondering how you've been able to avoid Christmas so thoroughly for all these years, given that it's such a big event in the calendar.'

'Trevor thought it was all over-hyped nonsense and I wasn't of a mind to disagree. That made it easier to downplay it.'

'Right. I—'

Whatever Maxwell had been about to say next was interrupted by the doorbell and the arrival of their pizza.

Once they'd laid it all out on the coffee table, he held up the remaining films for her to make her next selection. 'That one,' she said, grinning as she pointed. 'Since we've just been talking about Trevor, I think "How the Grinch Stole Christmas" will be perfect!'

23

December 12th

'Now, you're quite sure I won't be needing my thermal underwear, thick socks or hiking boots today?'

Maxwell turned to look at Polly as she climbed into the cab of his truck.

'Thermal underwear? Oh, sexy! Tell me more…'

'Behave!'

She gave him a soft slap on the arm.

He made a point of looking her up and down before replying, 'You're looking absolutely fine for today. You have no need to worry.'

A little grin of delight spread across her face as she bent down to place her handbag in the footwell. It was only a tiny compliment but she'd take it. "Absolutely fine" worked for her. It was certainly more than that rat Trevor ever used to give her. "You'll do" had been his stock answer whenever she'd asked him how she looked. He'd never willingly said anything nice about her appearance.

This had only occurred to her last night as she'd been going to bed. They'd finished their movie marathon with the rom-com "The Holiday" and so much of how Kate Winslet was treated by the supposed man of her dreams rang a bell for herself. Rufus Sewell's character was Trevor all over. He was so good looking and charismatic, that people were blinded – herself included – as to what an absolute arsehole he really was. Everything had always been about him and she'd been so desperate to belong to someone, she'd never fully realised how badly he'd treated her the whole time they were together. If anyone had asked her how their relationship was prior to her wanting babies, she'd have said it was good and that had been the turning point but after watching that film last night, she'd come to see he'd been bloody awful right from the beginning. He'd clocked how naïve she was and had really done a number on her.

So, to other people, "absolutely fine" may not be much but for her, it was a lot and she was having it!

'Here we go!'

'What? Already?'

'Yup. Come on.'

The clock on the church steeple above her head chimed one o'clock as she opened the cab door. They were round the back of the church on the opposite side of town. A number of cars were parked up next to them.

'Where are we?'

'Well, that's the church…'

'I can see that!'

'And this is the church hall.'

Maxwell opened the door and she walked through into a room that was larger than it looked from the outside and buzzing with chatter. She could just about make out the sound of Christmas music underneath the voices.

'Polly! Maxwell! So lovely of you to come along.'

'Hi, Marian, nice to see you again.'

Polly found herself wrapped up in a warm hug and a little pang of longing rushed through her as she wished her own mum was as tactile. Once upon a time she had been but after *that* Christmas, she'd closed in on herself and rarely ever showed any affection to anyone. It was almost as though she was too scared of being hurt again. Polly could understand that but it made her sad all the same.

'It's all hands on deck today. Maxwell, did you bring the boxes and hampers?'

'Yes, Mum, they're out in the truck. I'll leave Polly with you while I go and bring them in.'

Polly looked around the room and took in the tables that were almost buckling under the goods on top of them. One was groaning under the weight of food tins, another was loaded up with cakes, another had biscuits and several more had children's toys stacked up.

'Marian, what is all this?'

'Oh, has Maxwell not told you why you're here?'

'Err, nope!'

'We're putting together Christmas hampers for the elderly and vulnerable people in the town. We have a nomination box that is opened on the 1st October and people pop in the names of folks they feel should have a hamper delivered to them for Christmas.'

'And no one takes advantage?'

She immediately thought of how that would have gone down in London. The honesty aspect would have been in short supply.

'Ah, we discreetly check them all out before we put the recipients on the list. Thankfully, most contributors treat it with respect and those nominated usually are deserving.'

'I wish I'd known – I'd have brought some things to donate.'

'Ah, but by being here, you're donating the one thing we never have enough of – time. You're donating your time. We get lots of food and toys donated but very few people will give their time to help put everything together.'

'Well, in that case, where do you want me? What can I do to help?'

Marian led her to a table where a woman was sitting with a pile of papers in front of her.

'Helen, this is Polly, Maxwell's friend. It's her first time helping so can I leave her with you while I go and help Maxwell bring the hampers in?'

'Of course. Nice to meet you, Polly.'

Polly gave a small start. Was this ex-wife Helen? Mother of Maxwell's children Helen? Her colouring was close to Alanna's with her Nordic looks of blonder-than-blonde hair, piercing blue eyes (shift over Daniel Craig!) and cheekbones you could chip potatoes with. The way the woman was giving her the once-over made her all the more certain that her assumption was the correct one.

She sat down next to Helen and for the next few minutes, listened carefully as it was explained that each piece of paper on the table was a list designated to a specific recipient. This allowed for any allergies to be factored in where possible. Each list had a number of items that were to be gathered together from the various tables and put inside a hamper. Once the hamper was completed – it would be finished off with a couple of Christmas crackers and some little tree ornaments – it would be closed up and the string tag attached to the list with the recipient's name and address on, was tied to the handle. It would then be taken away and stored, waiting to be delivered.

'The local supermarkets let us borrow some of their baskets to do this, so off you go. Grab a basket and start picking.'

Helen passed her a list and she looked at the names across the top – Mary and Frank Charlton. Polly didn't know them and she wondered how they would feel at receiving a hamper. Would they be upset at being considered "needy" or would they be grateful that someone had thought about them and cared enough to put their names forward?

She walked along the tables, gathering up tins of ham and fruit etc before picking the items required from the festive fayre table. There were a few items on the list that she hadn't expected to see, such as long-life milk, tins of soup, and part-baked bread.

'Hey, I see it didn't take Helen and Mum long to put you to work.'

She smiled up at Maxwell as she pushed the heavy basket onto one arm so she could reach across for a bottle of alcohol-free wine.

'It sure didn't. Although some of the hamper contents are a surprise. Long-life milk?'

'Some of the older recipients and those with disabilities, rely on carers coming to help but Christmas can disrupt their usual schedule so we like to put in some non-Christmas items for them to store in the cupboard in case of emergencies.'

'Ah, what a good idea. How incredibly thoughtful.'

He walked with her over to the table where the hampers were being lined up, waiting to be filled and replaced.

'I hope this is okay for an advent-ure. I always help each year and couldn't get out of it.'

'It's a good advent-ure. I'm very happy to be here. Isn't the Christmas message about looking after and caring for others? Or, to quote from that movie last night, "Love is all around". It's nice to think that a few hours here for us will add up to many happy hours for other people.'

He gazed down at her for a few seconds and she felt herself beginning to blush.

'What?' she asked.

He brushed a finger gently over the tip of her nose.

'I knew you were special, Polly Snowflake, from the first day we met.'

'MAXWELL!'

Marian's yell cut through the noise of the room and Maxwell rolled his eyes before smiling at her and walking away to see what his mum wanted.

Special?

He thought she was special?

Polly felt her pulse speed up with happiness as she began to pack the hamper. Was it possible that Maxwell was feeling a little more than friendship towards her?

She looked over to where he was standing beside his mum and just as she turned her head, he glanced up and caught her eye. The smile he gave her had her toes curling in her boots and definitely suggested that he had more than just friendship on his mind.

With a hint of a blush on her cheeks again, and a soft smile on her lips, she returned her attention to her task. A few seconds later, however, she began to feel uncomfortable and when she raised her gaze from her list, she found herself staring right into Helen's narrowed blue eyes.

24

December 13th

'My, my, if I were straight, that would be a sight for sore eyes, let me tell you!'

Polly quickly removed her head from the kitchen floor cupboard she was buried in and kneeled back.

'Monty, I think that is what they call a "sexually inappropriate comment" these days.'

'And, if I were straight, I'd never have made it but since I'm as gay as a Maypole, I reckon I can get away with it!'

His eyes gleamed with mischief and Polly couldn't stop herself from laughing.

'You are quite incorrigible, you know that, don't you?'

'Yup! And why shouldn't I be, it's so much fun. Besides, I've had enough shitty things said to me over the years, why should I have to hold back?'

'Maxwell told me you had it tough at school.'

'Not just at school, almost every day since. He looked out for me when we were teenagers but there comes a time when he can no longer fight my battles for me.'

'I understand.'

'Do you? Do you really? Many straight people say they do but most of the time, they really don't.'

'I do. My best friend is gay and I've heard things said to him that no human being should ever say to another. I ended up dragging his ass to martial arts classes so we could both defend ourselves in nasty situations. And there were plenty of them, I can tell you.'

'Oh, martial arts? Which one?'

'Krav Maga.'

'Hey, that's the really mean one, isn't it?'

'If you're saying that's the kick-ass one, then yes, you're right. We got to P5 level. It all becomes more serious after that and we figured we had what we needed when faced with narrow-minded thugs who thought they could have a go at the poofter and his fag-hag!'

'Oh, my goodness, I haven't heard that expression for years!'

'And may we never hear it used in such a derogatory fashion again.'

'I agree with you there. So, your bestie – is he still in London?'

'Yeah. He owns a restaurant which he's very hands-on with, so he's not in a position to leave. Not that he'd ever want to – cut him open and he'd have "London" all the way through him like a stick of Blackpool rock! His husband, Scott, also runs his own PR company down there so it's safe to say they're not going anywhere.'

'Coffee?' Monty held up the kettle.

'Yes, please.' She gave the shelf on the cupboard a final wipe and stood up, shaking her legs which had become cramped from kneeling.

'Do you get to see him often? Do you miss him?'

'No, I don't and yes, I do. Although we do FaceTime

every Sunday morning, much to Ritchie's disgust as he likes his bed on a Sunday but it's the only time that works for us both.'

'What's the name of his restaurant? I might try it out the next time we're down there.'

'It's "Granny Greta's" in Chelsea.'

Monty, who was in the process of pouring the hot water into the French press, banged the kettle down on the worktop and looked at her in astonishment.

Here we go, she thought.

'Did you just say "Granny Greta's"?'

'I did!'

'The "Granny Greta's" that's been all the rage for the last year and which has a five-month waiting list.'

'That sounds about right.'

'So, your friend, Ritchie—'

'— yes, is Ritchie Donaldson.'

'Bloody hell! You do like to hang out with the rich and famous, don't you. A famous restaurateur *and* a famous clothes designer!'

'May I just point out here that the famous clothes designer picked me up. Quite literally!'

'Okay, fair point.'

She grinned as he turned to resume making the coffee.

'How do you know him?'

'He was working in a little sandwich bar near my office in the City. After a couple of weeks, he began to remember my order and would have it ready for me by the time I reached the counter.'

'Why, what made your order so special?'

'It was grated cheese mixed in a bowl with a large dollop of Branston pickle.'

'That sounds gross!'

'It's really not. Most people prefer grated cheese in their sarnies but it's too messy with bits falling out

159

everywhere. But, if you actually mix it in the pickle, the pickle acts like glue and holds it all together. Less mess in the long run.'

'Hmm, I see your point but it's still gross!'

'Anyway, I bumped into him one night in a pub after work, and I thanked him for always making my sandwich, we got talking and haven't stopped since. I'd become rather reclusive after my dad died – none of my school friends understood what I was going through and they slowly faded away. He'd come out to his family and it hadn't been well received so we were two vulnerable people who found strength in each other. I'd do anything for him and I know he'll always be there for me.'

'Does that mean you're the "best friend" he often refers to in his interviews?'

'I guess so. He's not allowed to name me as I don't want that kind of attention.'

'So, what is it about him that makes his restaurant so popular? He's not a chef, is he?'

'Blimey, no! He can barely boil an egg although his sandwiches aren't too bad! Ritchie is simply one of those people who ooze charm and charisma. He is genuinely interested in those around him and it comes through. He appreciates that going out for a nice meal is a special event for people and he wants to make sure they go home having had a good time. His menus are plain, simple food – almost like school meals or what we call comfort food – just well-cooked and tasty. People go to his restaurant the first time to see what all the hype is about. They go back because of the food and the happy, relaxing ambience.'

'Sounds like I really do need to visit, then.'

'Let me know when you want to go, I should be able to get you past that five-month waiting list.'

She gave him a wink and finished her coffee.

'Right, you, get out of my kitchen. I want this place to

sparkle before I go home!'

She took his cup and shooed him out of the room. As the hot water and bubbles filled the sink, Polly thought about what she'd just shared with Monty. She hadn't talked about herself this much in a very long time but between Maxwell and Monty, she was really opening up. It wasn't that she kept herself to herself, it was simply that apart from Ritchie who already knew her inside-out, there had been no one to show any kind of interest in her.

Just then the kitchen door opened and Monty's head popped round it.

'I forgot to ask – did you ever use the Krav Maga on anyone?'

'No, but if you don't leave me alone to get this place cleaned, I just might…'

The door quickly closed and she could hear him chuckling as he walked along the corridor.

She smiled.

Monty would never be able to replace Ritchie as her best friend, but he'd certainly be a good second.

25

'Good evening, how are you today? Recovered from yesterday?'

Maxwell leant forward and placed a soft kiss on Polly's cheek. Startled by this unexpected action, she lowered her head and focused her attention on clearing the already-tidy reception desk and switching the phone, that hadn't rung all day, over to night mode.

'I'm... err... great, thank you. It wasn't that taxing yesterday. It was merely shopping on a smaller scale. And as I'm not averse to a bit of shopping, it was kind of fun. Plus, it was also nice to meet other people from the town. I got talking to a lady who runs a baking group and she asked me to call her in the New Year.'

'Was that Cecily?'

'Yes, it was.'

'Ah, she's a demon when it comes to baking. She's almost on a one-woman crusade to get the town baking. She believes it's something that everyone can do. So, as you can imagine, she and my mum have some interesting discussions,' he said with a laugh.

'She seemed nice enough.'

'Oh, she is. She's just very passionate about her hobby. I reckon you'll both get on well.'

'Good. Now, is there any point in me asking where we're off to tonight?'

'You know there isn't but it's only a five-minute walk from here. I promised you some early nights and this is one of them.'

'Alright then. Well, I'm ready to go if you are.'

She locked the office up and followed Maxwell along the pavement. He took a hold of her hand while sharing the news of his day. She only heard a fraction of what he was saying because her eyes were fixed on the sight of their interlocked fingers. Once again, it felt nice – more than nice, in fact – but it was how natural he'd made the action seem that had her entranced. Trevor had never been one for public displays of affection although, come to think of it, his displays of affection behind closed doors had been sorely lacking too and so this was all new territory for her.

She was still trying to work out if this was a friendly sign of affection or if there was more to it, when Maxwell advised they'd arrived at their destination and she looked up to see him holding open a door next to a sign that read, "Arts & Crafts Centre". What on earth was he putting her through tonight?

They followed a couple in front of them into a large room with several tables set up. Not unlike, she thought, the night they'd done the Christmas wreaths. There was an area for coats to be hung and after they'd removed and hung up theirs, they walked over to the tables and found two, side-by-side, with their names on. The tables were laid out in a circle with two more tables in the middle. One of these held a number of unpainted wooden nutcrackers. When she looked at the items lying on her own table, the penny dropped.

'Are we painting nutcrackers this evening?'

Maxwell gave her a wide grin.

'We most certainly are. Have you ever done that before?'

'No.'

'Cool! Something else new for you. Another new advent-ure.'

'I have to say, Maxwell, you're excelling in finding me new and different things to try. I'm impressed.'

'Twenty-four days of doing things you've done before wasn't going to sell Christmas to you, was it? I had to find some "firsts" to put in the mix.'

She didn't get to reply because at that point, a man and a woman walked to the two centre tables and began to introduce the class.

'Good evening, and welcome to painting your own nutcrackers. This is Anna and I'm Brian. Everyone is fond of these lovely festive figures and what better way to celebrate the season than by having your own bespoke model. Now, there are a number of different designs on the table for you to choose from. These can be as basic as you wish if you're not confident of your skill levels or you can embellish as you desire. Now, for the sake of time, you will note the base coats have been done and we have stencilled on a selection of facial features for your convenience. Anna and I are here to guide you if you have any questions or need a hand. The paints on your desk are acrylic and as long as you don't put them on too thickly, they will dry in approximately thirty minutes – the time it will take for us all to enjoy a cuppa and a mince pie at the end of the session. Now, please, come and choose your nutcracker.'

A few minutes later, Polly returned to her table with a rather regal looking nutcracker in her hand. He had a large moustache stencilled on his face and she hoped she could do him justice.

'Oh, like that is it? You prefer your men to have face-fuzz, do you?'

'Er, no, I really don't but as I won't be snogging this one, I figured it was okay.'

She looked at his nutcracker and saw he'd chosen a drummer design.

'Hmm, I'm wondering what it says about me that my nutcracker is holding a large halberd…'

'A woman not to be messed with, I reckon!'

Her earlier conversation with Monty came to mind as she replied, 'You'd better believe it, mister.'

She pulled on the plastic apron and gloves provided, opened her paint pots and got to work.

'Wow! Check you out! He looks amazing.'

Maxwell was admiring her gleaming nutcracker and Polly had to confess to herself that she was rather proud of him.

'Thank you,' she replied.

Maxwell leant in for a closer look.

'Your lines are so neat and precise. This is really good. I didn't know you were an artist.'

'I'm not but I've spent many hours perfecting a steady hand for icing and cake decoration. I merely extended that skill to what was essentially just colouring in.'

She looked over to his table to see an equally impressive nutcracker sitting there.

'Hey, you're not so shoddy with the artwork yourself. He's as professionally painted as any I've ever seen in the shops.'

'I do like to paint and draw so I came here with a bit of an advantage.'

'I suppose I should have expected that.'

'Really? Why?'

'Your twin brother is creative and has an artistic eye. It stands to reason that there was a good chance you would too.'

'Yeah, that figures.'

They'd just finished clearing up their worktables when Anna called out that the refreshments were ready for those who'd finished. As they walked over to the small café area, Polly sneaked a peek at the other nutcrackers on display and was thrilled to see how good they were. When she glanced back over her shoulder and saw them all standing to attention, she couldn't help but think how distinguished and regal they all looked.

'So, what brought each of you here tonight?'

Anna looked at the painters around the table and Polly listened as they each shared why they'd attended the class. When it came to Maxwell, he simply looked at her and said, 'It's nice to do things that are different and outside your comfort zone. Painting nutcrackers is something we've never done before but now we can say we have. It's always good to try new things.'

He smiled as the rest of the class agreed with him and Polly let out a little sigh of relief that he hadn't felt the need to share the real reason for their attendance. His diplomacy had just made her like him a little more. Which was not good as she already liked him "more" than she felt comfortable with.

<u>26</u>

December 14th

'Oh no we're not!'

'Oh yes we are!'

'Oh no we're not!

'Oh yes we are!'

Polly stood outside the Derby theatre and looked at the large colourful posters advertising their yearly Christmas pantomime. Aladdin could be seen everywhere she turned and the cast of celebrities was impressive. The comedian playing Widow Twankey was one she enjoyed seeing on the television but that didn't mean she was all set to sit through two hours of nonsense for him.

'Why are you so against this?'

'Because they're silly and childish. The last time I was at a pantomime, I was thirteen-years-old and believe me, by that time, the novelty had most certainly passed!'

'Ah, that's because you were at that age where you think you're a grown-up and don't like things that remind you you're still a child.'

'Trust me, it wasn't!'

'Oh, I think you'll find it was. You're going to have so much fun tonight.'

'Maxwell, up till now I've gone along quite merrily with all that you've done but I just don't want to do this. It's too much.'

'Why?'

Polly sighed. She had to tell him the truth. 'Because, it reminds me of how vile I was to my dad the last time we were supposed to go to one, that's why.'

Tears sprung into her eyes and she had to blink hard to stop them rolling down her face.

'Okay, come over here.'

He led her to the seated area just outside the doors.

'I'll be right back.'

He returned five minutes later with two coffees in his hands.

'Here, drink this.'

Polly did as she was told and took a large slug of the warm beverage. Her eyes widened two seconds later and she began coughing.

'What on eath?'

'Oh, didn't I say, I got you an Irish coffee. Figured it might help.'

'You could have warned me first.'

She took a second more cautious sip and, this time, the fiery aftertaste wasn't such a surprise.

'Okay, speak to me. Tell me what happened the last time a pantomime – and I'm not referring to your marriage here – played a part in your life.'

She couldn't hold back the grin at Maxwell's pithy remark and somehow that, along with the coffee, took a little bit of the edge off her anxiety.

She put the coffee cup on the table and placed her hands

in her lap, staring at her fingers as they fidgeted between tight fists and interlocking. It took a moment before she was able to raise her head and look Maxwell in the eye.

'I was fourteen. Dad had bought tickets for the pantomime as he did every year. Even though I'd made it perfectly clear the previous year that I didn't want to go again, he still went ahead and got them. When he told me we were going, I threw the mother of all tantrums. I was a teenage girl – we've got those things down to a fine art! I'd made arrangements to go round to my friend's house and there was no way I was doing something as lame as going to a pantomime with my parents.'

'What happened?'

'My parents went without me. I was grounded for a week and they asked our next-door neighbour to babysit.'

'I see.'

'No, you don't. I was in bed when they came home that night but I wasn't asleep. I heard them talking and my dad was saying how he hadn't enjoyed a minute of it because I wasn't there with them. The disappointment in his voice broke me. I never wanted to hurt my dad. I promised myself that the next year, I would go with them and do so without any fuss, even if I didn't want to. After all, what was a couple of hours? Except...'

She stopped and took another drink of her coffee. A bigger gulp because she needed the courage from the alcohol to say out loud what was coming next.

'Except... the following year he didn't buy tickets. The pantomime wasn't mentioned and we didn't go. I really wanted to make up for how I'd behaved the previous year, so I used my savings to buy us tickets to go after Christmas and gave them to him as a Christmas present. He was so thrilled. So happy. And he held me ever-so tightly when he whispered thank you in my ear. But the tickets were never used. Dad died and I lost out on the chance to make one more memory with him. If I hadn't behaved like a stupid brat the year before, we'd have stuck to the tradition of going before Christmas. And that's why I can't go in there.'

'What was the pantomime you bought the tickets for?'

She gave a sharp laugh as she replied, 'Bloody Aladdin!'

Polly sat quietly in her seat, staring at the stage in front of her. Part of her was wondering how on earth Maxwell had managed to talk her into doing this while the other part was glad that he had. He sat quietly beside her, holding her hand and squeezing it gently every so often to let her know he was fully aware of how difficult this was.

She looked around the auditorium and listened to the voices of the audience as they filtered in. Some people were whispering quietly in the way folks seem to do when they go to the theatre, others were talking in their normal voices, not caring how the sound carried around the room. But it was the animated tones of the children that she was trying to focus on, remembering the days when she had been young enough to find all this exciting and thrilling. It was this that Maxwell had put to her as he'd explained all the good reasons for her to walk through the doors and take her seat. It had only taken one suggestion, however, to make her stand up and move inside and that had been when he'd asked how many memories of these visits had she lost because she was so focused on the ones that hadn't been made. Surely it was better for her to recall the seven or eight good nights she'd shared, sitting in the dark beside her dad, than to keep regretting the two nights she'd missed. It was a logical comment she couldn't argue with and so here she was, trying to keep a lid on the emotions that wanted to explode out of her while she prepared to relive the moments that would inevitably come throughout the night.

'Why are you here with me, tonight, and not your children? Shouldn't you be making your own memories with them?' she whispered.

'They're going to a panto at the weekend with their grandparents. Helen's taking them up to Carlisle on Saturday when she goes to visit her folks.'

'Oh, right. They don't come down here for Christmas?'

'Her brother is up there with them so they take it in turns to visit. Last year they came down to us so this year they'll stay up there with her brother and his family.'

'Right.'

'The kids love it though as it feels like they get two Christmases. They're allowed to open their gifts when they're up there so they can thank their grandparents properly.'

'Well, no kid is going to argue with that!'

'For sure. Oh, here we go…'

The house lights dimmed and the stage curtain began to rise as Polly took a deep breath in readiness for whatever the next couple of hours was going to bring.

27

December 15th

'Oh, bugger!'

Polly let out a groan as she looked at her bloodshot eyes in the mirror. She'd managed to hold it together last night at the pantomime and had even ended up enjoying herself. She'd gone all-in on the audience participation, shouting loudly "He's behind you" on several occasions. She'd sung along to the silly songs, clapped her hands as hard as she could to make the most noise for their side of the audience and had, quite frankly, behaved exactly like the child she'd been too ashamed to be when she was fourteen. She'd still been upbeat on the drive home and when Maxwell had given her a gentle kiss on the cheek when saying goodnight, she'd returned the favour and had felt great about doing so as she'd closed the front door behind her.

It was once she was in bed, lying in the darkness, that the tears had fallen. A tsunami of memory fragments that she'd hidden away – and which Maxwell had so cleverly realised – had come flooding back to her and she'd found herself recalling vague moments of happiness that her guilt had forced out of her mind. Whenever she thought of her dad, it was hard to do so without seeing him as he'd been in those final moments. It had always been a struggle to get past that but the release of these old memories, even if they were hazy right now, would, over time, help her to find a happy place in her heart and head where she could be with him and enjoy the good things they'd shared.

All of that realisation, however, did not help her immediate problem of having eyes so red and puffy, she could barely see.

'Oh, Bailey, look at me! All I need is a slap of lipstick around my mouth and I could double-up as a circus clown! What am I going to do? I can't go into the office like this.'

She peered in the mirror at the cat sitting on the loo behind her but he didn't seem inclined to give her an answer so, letting out a sigh, she picked up her phone and decided Auntie Internet was going to have to come up with some suggestions instead, which was why, when the doorbell rang an hour later, she answered it while peeling two cold, sludgy, teabags off her face.

'Maxwell! What are you doing here?'

'I came to check you were alright this morning. Even though you seemed okay when I brought you home, I was worried that the emotion may have hit you after I left and you were alone. Looking at your eyes now, I think I may have been correct.'

'Oh crap! Are they still all nasty? I'd hoped the cold tea bags would work.'

'They're bloodshot and you can tell you've been crying but not as bad as I suspect they were earlier.'

Polly opened the door for the downstairs loo and had a look in the mirror, letting out a sigh of relief that the puffiness was gone. Yes, they were still bloodshot as Maxwell had said but she could pick up some eye drops from the chemist on her way to the office.

'Thank you for coming to check on me, I really appreciate it. It was thoughtful of you.'

He walked over to her and placed his hands gently on her shoulders.

'Polly, I knew from the beginning there was a likelihood it could all go pear-shaped with this whole "advent-ure" thing but I was prepared to take the risk. You looked so scared that first day, when you were sharing with me what happened to your father.'

'I did?'

This was news to her. It had never crossed her mind that she was "scared" of Christmas. She'd closed herself off from it because she couldn't face the memories but being scared of the season… and yet, now that Maxwell had said this, she could see the sense in it.

'Yes. When I first said that decorating the tree was something you would be doing, fear was the initial emotion to cross your face. It soon turned to horror at the idea but I saw it and that was why I felt I had to push you to open up to me, it didn't seem right for you to be scared of Christmas.'

'I… I… I suppose my mind just linked the trauma of my father's death to the festive season and it went from there. With the subsequent Christmases being so awful and the way my mother closed down, I guess I did develop a fear of it, I simply wasn't aware of it.'

She sat down on the edge of the sofa as a multitude of thoughts tumbled around her head. A few minutes passed and then she looked up at the clock, realised she really needed to get ready for work otherwise she'd be late but couldn't bring herself to move.

Polly didn't know how long she'd been sitting, while her head worked on sorting itself out, but it was the mug of coffee being pushed into her hand that brought her back to the present.

'Come on, drink this up.'

She raised the cup to her lips and then stopped, taking a moment to sniff it suspiciously.

Maxwell laughed above her head.

'It's okay, this one is au natural! No added extras. Not at this time in the morning.'

'You do know it'll be a long time before I trust you with my coffee again…'

'If you say so.'

'I do! Now, if you'll excuse me, I need to get ready for work.'

'No, you don't. I've had a word with Monty and he's given you the day off.'

'What? You can't be doing that – pulling favours with my boss just because he's your twin brother. That's not on. You don't get to interfere with my job.'

She stood up and glared at him, the recollection of Trevor's controlling ways foremost in her mind.

'Hey, calm down! I didn't actually "interfere" as such. Mum has asked me to do something for her today and suggested that you might enjoy doing it with me as it's a task that's better with two people. I asked Monty if he could spare you, told him what Mum said, and he was happy to oblige. So, if you want to blame anyone, take it up with my mother.'

'Hmm, somehow, I don't think I'd win that one. Fair enough. So, what are we doing?'

'You'll find out soon enough but you have time to stick more tea bags over your eyes first – we don't want to scare any young children we meet along the way.'

'Oh you—'

She flapped her hand at him, pretending to hit his arm before making her way to the kitchen where she retrieved the second batch of tea bags she'd put in the fridge to chill.

A confused look found its way onto Polly's face once more as they pulled into the car park by the church hall again.

'What are we doing back here? Do we need to put together more hampers?'

'No, my pretty, but we do need to deliver them.'

'Oh! Right!'

She hadn't seen that one coming and she wasn't sure how she felt about it either. It was one thing putting the hampers together but she'd never anticipated meeting the recipients. What if they turned out to be offended at being considered needy and told them to bog off?

'Is it not a bit early to be delivering Christmas hampers? I mean, there's still ten days to go.'

'We'd normally take them out in the week running up to Christmas but the weather reports are saying that big snow storms could be heading our way next week, so we want to get the deliveries done before that happens. A few of the recipients live in outlying areas which would be difficult to get to if the snow does come.'

'That explains why you've got the hardtop on the truck today. I did wonder.'

'I didn't think it would go down too well if the hampers arrived looking rather windswept, especially after all the effort we've put into them.'

She gave him a grin, closed the cab door behind her and began walking towards the doors of the hall.

'Right then,' she said, 'the sooner we have them loaded, the sooner we get them delivered.'

An hour and a half later, they were on the main road out of the town. The sun was shining and it was a glorious day. Nippy, but glorious. Polly fished her sunglasses out of her bag, put them on and stared out of the window at the magnificent views around her. It was on days like this that she loved the area she now called home although that might be about to change if Maxwell was right about the incoming snow storms. London had had its fair share of snow dumps in the past but she suspected it would be a completely different ball game out here in the open countryside.

In the quiet of the cab, her thoughts wandered back to the night before. Snippets of memories kept popping up but they were gone before she could grasp them and hold them.

'Hey, everything okay over there?'

Maxwell's hand landed on hers and gave it a soft squeeze – just as he'd done most of the night before.

'Err, yes, why?'

'The loud sigh you just emitted kind of suggested otherwise.'

'Oh! I see!'

'Look… I'm really sorry about last night. I shouldn't have forced you to go into the theatre. It seemed like a good idea at the time but now that I've thought about it more, it was wrong to make you do that. I'm no therapist; how the heck am I supposed to know what's good for you and what isn't?'

She didn't reply immediately, taking the time to mull his words over in her head. Had his actions been helpful or not? Her lack of response must have got to him for he took his hand away and she immediately felt bereft by its absence.

'You were right… last night. Making me face up to the monster I'd created in my head was… good. It was good.'

She turned her head so he could see she was being

sincere.

'I don't know what a qualified counsellor would say but it has helped. You see, I think…,' she paused, trying to work out the best words to use that would adequately explain how she was feeling. 'Whenever I think of my dad, I seem to have very few memories. All I ever see is him lying sprawled out in his chair, my mum screaming, blue lights flashing through the lounge window and paramedics swarming around the room. When I manage to push that memory to the side, I'm hit with the guilt of the nights I missed going out with him and the sorrow he felt as a result. Last night, while lying in bed, for the first time in twenty years, I had different memories. I actually remembered the other times we went to the pantomime together. Not every detail, obviously, but little bits. Like the first time he told me to shout out "He's behind you!" along with the other children. I can actually recall the feel of his breath on my ear when he whispered to me to do it. I can't begin to tell you how special that moment is to me now. I'm also getting other snapshots of memories – very briefly. They come and then quickly go again but I'm hoping they'll come back and stay a bit longer so I can see them more clearly.'

'It sounds like something in your head has begun to unlock itself.'

'Yes! That's it! Whichever corner I've pushed all those good times into and sealed off, is beginning to unlock and let its secrets out. I suppose letting out small snippets at a time is a protection device.'

'From the little bit of armchair psychology I have, I do know that in the event of a trauma, the brain takes whatever action it sees fit to protect us. I would hazard a guess that the shock of your father's death made your brain hide all those good memories because something told it you wouldn't be able to cope. Since then, whenever you've given your memory bank a poke, it's thrown that terrifying event at you which has sent you running, too scared to push past it to find all the good stuff hidden behind it.'

Polly gazed out at the hills in the distance as she listened to Maxwell's more-than-reasonable summation.

'All I would say is, don't force the memories to come back to you. Be satisfied with what you've recalled for now and give yourself time to enjoy them. More will follow when it's the right time for them to appear.'

'Okay, Doctor Watkins, I'll heed your wise words and just take them as they come.'

He turned and gave her a quick smile. A smile that melted her heart all the way to the core. She was glad she had her sunglasses on because then he couldn't see the signs in her eyes that would give away how she had fallen for this man and, from the way she felt when he was around, she'd say she'd fallen pretty damn hard.

28

'See that cottage over there,' Maxwell pointed to a small house on a hill in the distance, 'that's where we're headed next.'

'Okay, that's pretty remote. Who lives there?'

'Mary and Frank Charlton.'

'Oh, their hamper was the first one I did. How nice that I get to meet them.'

'They're a lovely couple and also one of the handful of recipients who automatically receive a hamper every year. They're excluded from being nominated.'

'Oh! Why?'

'They're both in their eighties and Frank is now blind.'

'And they live all the way out here? Why don't they move closer to the town?'

'Wait till you meet them.'

After following a twisting road that also had its fair share of ups and downs, they pulled into a small yard by the side of the cottage which, now that she saw it close up, Polly realised was larger than she'd given it credit for. A few chickens roamed around the yard area and a couple came clucking towards her when she stepped down from the cab.

She closed the back door of the truck behind Maxwell once he had the Charltons' hamper in his arms and he directed her towards the back door.

'Give it a firm knock, twice, and then go on in.'

'Just go in?'

'Yes, trust me.'

She gave him a quick look to see if he was messing with her but all he did was smile warmly.

'Are you sure there's not a large dog on the other side waiting to take my arm off as I walk in?'

'I can promise you there's not.'

'Fine.'

They walked up a little cobble path towards a pretty pale blue door with glass inserts. She could see matching pale blue gingham curtains on the other side. As instructed, she gave two firm knocks and then turned the finely polished doorknob.

They'd only just made it over the threshold into a large, warm, kitchen when a little, rotund woman came bustling in.

'Maxwell Watkins! My, how good it is to see you. Come in now, lad, out of the cold. And who's this pretty, young thing you've brought with you? Got yourself a new girlfriend? About time too. I keep telling you you're too special to be single. The love of a good woman is what you need. Aren't you going to introduce us? Honestly, Maxwell! Hello, dear, I'm Mary. And you are?'

'Polly. I'm Polly.'

'Welcome, Polly. Nice that we managed to do all that on our own.'

'Well, Mary, if you'd given me a chance to get a word in, I would have made the introductions. As usual, you were just too impatient!'

'Oh, away with you, you impertinent fella. That's no way to speak to your elders.'

She turned away towards the kitchen sink and catching Polly's eye, she gave her a quick wink. When Polly looked over her shoulder at Maxwell, he had a big grin on his face. She could only assume this banter was part of the way they interacted so she just kept quiet and let them get on with it.

'I'll leave this hamper here on the table for you, Mary. Now, how are you for firewood?'

'Oh, we're fine, we're fine.'

'Well, I'm just going to go out and check. The weather's due to get nasty next week and snow is forecast so I'll chop up some extra for you.'

'Maxwell, we have enough.'

'Mary, I'll be the judge of that. I'd rather you had too much wood cut than not enough. I'll also make sure all the baskets in the house are full. Please do me a favour and keep topping up as you go along so I don't need to worry about you going outside and falling when the bad weather gets here.'

'Okay, I will.'

'Promise?'

'I promise!'

'Fine, I won't be long. Now, play nice with Polly until I get back.'

There was silence in the kitchen for a few seconds after he left and Mary broke it with a sigh. 'That boy, he worries too much about us. We're not his responsibility but he will fuss so.'

'I think it's nice that he's looking out for you.'

'He feels guilty even though I've told him all these years that he has no need to.'

'Guilty?'

Mary placed the old iron kettle she'd just filled onto the range, grabbed a well-used oven-mitt from the hook and put it on to open the door. She threw in a couple of small logs from the basket and gave them a quick prod with the poker before closing the door again. Only once she'd done this, did Mary turn her attention back to Polly.

'Many years back, when they were still in school, Maxwell dated our daughter, Susan. They were only young, early teens if I remember rightly, but Susan was madly head-over-heels for the lad. I could see early on that Maxwell didn't have the same feelings for her and sure enough, after about six months or so, he broke it off. Susan never really got past it and wasn't quite the same afterwards. Finally, when she left school, she went to do charity work over in Africa and has lived there ever since. She pops home every now and again but her life is there now and she loves it. Maxwell, however, feels that it's his fault we're now alone so he looks out for us and makes sure we're alright.'

'You don't have any other children?'

'No, Susan was our only one. Here, you couldn't pass that tray over could you, the one sitting on the dresser at your back.'

Polly turned to pick up the wooden tray and couldn't resist casting her eye over the beautifully carved Welsh dresser.

'Wow, Mary, I love your dresser. It's beautiful.'

'Thank you. Frank's great-grandfather made it. Carved it all himself, so he did.'

'He was a very talented man.'

'They had to find means when farming became less profitable.'

'You're farmers?'

'Oh, not anymore lass. Them days are long gone. We sold most of it off when Frank's eyes began to go. Young'uns today don't want to do farming and we had no one to pass it on to so it made sense to let the Caldwells buy it up. They'd been after the land for years so we were able to make them pay a good penny for it. We've got the yard for my chickens and a couple of daft goats and that's enough.'

'Will you be okay to tend to them if the bad weather comes next week?'

'Thanks to young Maxwell, all will be fine.'

'Maxwell?'

'Come with me.'

Mary took her through a door that led into a long, narrow hallway. She could see another door at the far end and when Mary opened it, it took them out into a large, lean-to style shed. On one side there was a pen filled with hay, straw and a water-trough with a tap attached. On the other side there was a similar setup but this pen also contained a couple of chicken coops.

'Maxwell built this for me a few years back. When we know the bad weather is on its way, I bring the birds and beasts in here and keep them locked in tight until it passes. So, there's no need for either of you to worry about me.'

Polly stepped aside as the old lady turned to make her way back to the kitchen and with a last glance at the shed, she followed her. As each day passed, she was learning more about Maxwell and the kind of man he was. The interesting thing was that she was learning about him from other people. He told her very little of himself but those around him couldn't speak highly enough of him. That in itself said a lot but it also made keeping her feelings for him at bay even harder.

'So, how long have you two been together? Any chance of church bells on the horizon?'

Polly felt the heat rush to her cheeks and she quickly

dispelled Mary's notion of her and Maxwell being a couple.

'Oh, Mary, you've got it wrong. Maxwell and I are just friends. We're not together in that way.'

'Really? You could have fooled me.'

Polly looked over at Maxwell sitting in the chair by the fire and gave him a look, imploring him to back up her statement. He, on the other hand, just shrugged, took a bite of the cake Mary had insisted they shared, and leant forward to pick up his mug of tea.

'We only met two weeks ago, Mary, I can assure you, we are just friends.'

'Oh, lass, it only takes two minutes to fall in love. I knew as soon as I cast my eye on Frank there that we'd be together for the rest of our lives. And I was right, wasn't I, Frank?'

'Hmph! Didn't give me any choice, woman! You'd made your mind up and I knew it was useless to argue with you.'

The slim-built man sitting in the chair opposite Maxwell spoke his words through a smile and Polly was under no illusion that he loved his wife very much and most likely hadn't put up much of a fight all those years ago.

'You just knew a good thing when you saw one,' Mary replied.

'I'm not going to disagree with you there, dear. Now, is there any tea left in the pot?'

Mary leant forward and gave the teapot a shake.

'No, it could do with refreshing.'

'I'll do it.'

Frank stood up and much to Polly's amazement, put his hand on the teapot, lifted it up and walked out the room unassisted and unaided.

'He was born in this house, love, and he'll die in it,'

Mary said with a gentle smile. 'He knows every inch of the place and never bumps into anything. The furniture is just the way it was when he was a kid. We update it but never move it.'

Maxwell smiled over at her just then and she recalled what he'd said to her in the truck. They didn't move because they didn't need to. Frank was better off here in the place he knew like the back of his hand and Mary seemed more than capable of looking after them both. For all that though, Polly was glad Maxwell had taken them under his wing and looked out for them.

Thirty minutes later they were saying their goodbyes, Mary seeing them off with hugs, kisses and the firm instruction that she wanted to be top of the guest list when they tied the knot seeing as how she was "calling it first".

'I've seen how you both look at each other, it's on the cards, you mark my words!'

Polly decided it was simply easier to agree with her than get into another discussion on the topic.

As they drove out of the yard, waving furiously, Polly spoke through the gritted teeth of her smile.

'Thanks for your input back there. Why didn't you step in and tell Mary that we're simply friends?'

'Because she's an older lady who believes in love. She's had a long and happy marriage and she wants the same for others. Let her have her dreams, what harm can it do?'

'Fine. Whatever makes her happy.'

'That's the spirit. Besides, is being married to me such a horrible thought?'

Polly looked at him in shock before deciding this was the perfect moment for a little revenge.

'Maxwell, I was married to Trevor for almost six years. Anything would be an improvement on that – even you!'

<u>29</u>

December 16th

'Here, poppet, you look like you could do with one of these today. Everything alright?'

Polly looked up as Andy placed one of Dottie's magnificent hot chocolates in front of her. He'd even added whipped cream *and* mini-marshmallows. Boy, she must have been looking down in the mouth for the double treat.

'Oh, thank you, Andy, that's very kind of you. I'm fine, honestly.'

'You've been subdued today, lovely, and that's not like you. I know we don't talk as much as you do with Monty – the downside of me being stuck in the upstairs office most of the time – but I'd like to think we're friends too.'

'Of course, we're friends, Andy.'

'That also means you might find it easier to talk to me than to Monty over matters of the heart. Especially if those heart-felt matters are connected to his twin-brother.'

'Oh no, please don't tell me it's that obvious…'

'It's not obvious but it doesn't take a genius to work it out. So, am I right in thinking you've taken the headlong dive into loving the other Watkins brother?'

'I… I think I have. I really don't know. I feel all over the place, if I'm being honest. Sometimes I think, "Yup, I love him" and then other times I'm completely at a loss to describe what I feel. I'm also worried that I'm latching onto him because he's the first person to show me this level of kindness in such a long time.'

'Why on earth would you think that?'

'He's a kind and thoughtful man, Andy. Not only have I seen it for myself but other people tell me too. I met Mary Charlton yesterday and she couldn't have sung his praises any louder if she'd tried. Mind you, she also told us we were getting married and she wants an invite to the wedding!'

'She did WHAT?'

Polly was glad that Andy managed to swallow the mouthful of chocolate he'd just taken before he exclaimed so loudly.

'You heard me.'

'What did Maxwell say to that?'

'Nothing! He said nothing! He just went along with it.'

'Seriously?'

'Yes, seriously.'

'Hmm, now that's interesting.'

'Is it? In what way?'

'In the way that, if you don't have feelings for someone and another person tells you marriage is on the cards, you'd be pretty quick to put them straight on their thinking. The fact that our boy *didn't* reject the suggestion tells me he wouldn't be averse to the idea at some time in the future.'

'Nooooo! Are you saying… noooo… he can't…'

'Can't what? Like you? Be in love with you? Why not?

If you're in love with him – or seriously "in like" – then why can't he feel the same for you?'

'Because I'm… well… I'm just me. A bit boring, not very exciting and rather ordinary. I've met Helen, she's beautiful. I've seen Laurel Devine, she's also beautiful. Anyone who's been with women like that is not going to be attracted to me.'

'Oh, Polly, I don't know who did a number on you, honey, but they did it good! Who on earth ever told you that you were ordinary? Huh? Did they walk with a white stick? You are beautiful in your own special way.'

'Thanks, Andy. That's the polite way of saying I'll never be on the front page of Vogue.'

'With the right makeover, you probably could. Let me tell you, half the women who grace the front cover of Vogue and all those other kinds of magazines wouldn't be there if it wasn't for the magic of good makeup artists and spectacular lighting. The kind of beauty you have would never work on a magazine cover because what makes you special is the beauty that radiates *from* you. And you can't photograph that.'

'I'm sorry? You've lost me.'

'Polly, you are pretty on the outside, you really are. You have lovely blonde hair, gorgeous blue eyes, rosy cheeks and lips that even I wouldn't have a problem kissing. You are the quintessential English Rose. What makes you extra special though is that you also have an inner beauty and it radiates from you. Your smile not only lights up the space around you but you smile often and every person around you feels like you're smiling just for them. You're kind and you're quick to do things for others. Remember how you got the job here – because you answered the telephone. Only a small act but a thoughtful one. In the short time you've been here, we've seen all the kind things you do for us and for other people. I saw you helping a young mother with her pram the other day in the street. I overheard you telling Karen she no longer had a job here – you could have been cruel but you weren't. You did it kindly and also advised her where she may find alternative employment.'

Polly burst out laughing at that.

'Oh, Andy, I'm not that kind. I sent her to see the troll I'd walked out on earlier that day!'

'You didn't?'

'Yeah, I did! But thank you for all the other nice things you've said.'

'There's no point in me saying them if you're not going to believe them. Give you and Maxwell a chance. Don't overthink it. In the words of those Oasis boys, you gotta roll with it. And let me tell you, you might think you're the lucky one if Maxwell falls in love with you but I can assure you that he's also damn lucky that you're in love with him. Love's a two-way street, don't ever forget it. Now, if you'll excuse me, I have to go and finish putting together the end of year receipts to pass on to our accountant as January is the lovely tax point of the year and I'd rather not have that hanging over my head through Christmas.'

On impulse, Polly stood up and gave Andy a hug along with a kiss on the cheek which he returned before walking off up the steps. After he'd disappeared, she walked over to look out of the window to the street below. As the shoppers and pedestrians walked by, she pondered over what he'd said and as dusk began to fall, she made a few decisions.

Yes, it was time to stop being so down on herself.

Yes, she had fallen in love with Maxwell.

No, he wasn't Trevor who had caused so much damage.

No, she wasn't going to overthink it.

And so yes, she had to let go and let whatever was going to happen, happen.

It was time to finally just *roll with it*.

<u>30</u>

'Why are we going to a garden centre? Is there something you need for work?'

'Maybe…'

They'd just driven into the car park of the large garden centre on the outskirts of town. The bushes dotted along the borders had twinkling fairy-lights weaved through them and a large inflatable snowman bobbed about outside the main door. Tinny-sounding Christmas carols could be heard through the outdoor loudspeakers.

'Oh my!'

They walked through the doors and Polly stopped in amazement for it felt like she'd stepped into some kind of winter wonderland. Straight ahead was a corridor of fairy lights, not unlike the one she'd walked through in Maxwells' forest, and beyond it she could see display upon display of Christmas decorations. Maxwell took her hand, just as he'd done that night, and she walked through the lights beside him. On the other side, there was a house display where each room was all done up with a different colour and effect for Christmas. The dining room was

191

predominantly green while the lounge was all shades of red. The conservatory was a dream in white while a cast-iron igloo to the side sparkled in blue.

Vast floor-standing vases were filled with strings of beads that glistened in the glow of the fairy-lights mingling between them. Gorgeous hurricane lamps sat here, there and everywhere, showing off a plethora of tree baubles that came in every colour. Battery-operated candles shone all around and snow globes in every shape and size twinkled and sparkled.

Feeling like her head was on a swivel, Polly turned every which way to take it all in. It was Christmas overload and she found herself revelling in it.

She ground to a halt, however, when she came to a length of shelving filled with stuffed toys and animals.

'Why are these here? I wouldn't have expected a garden centre to have toys.'

'Ah, these aren't just any stuffed toys. These are special.'

'They are?'

She leant forward to have a closer look. Maxwell put out his hand and took the paw of a teddy bear between his fingers. Suddenly, the bear started to sway from side to side, his mouth moved up and down and he began to recite, "The Night Before Christmas".

'Oh my! Oh my! That's fantastic. How clever.'

'You've never seen these animated toys before?'

'No, never. Oh, gosh! Do they all do that?'

Before Maxwell could reply, she was off along the aisle, squeezing the paws and feet of the various elves, mice, teddies, dogs, cats and reindeer – bringing them all to life and the cacophony of their songs and voices filled the air.

Polly squealed in delight. She'd never seen anything like it in all her days. At that moment, her inner child had taken over and she let herself enjoy every little childish second.

'Having fun?'

She hesitated before looking up at Maxwell and was relieved to see him grinning down at her. She'd been briefly afraid that he'd be annoyed with her antics but then she remembered what she'd told herself that afternoon. He was not Trevor and she shouldn't judge him as though he was.

'This is all so wonderful. Why didn't they have these when I was a kid? It's not fair!'

She stuck her lip out in a childish pout and Maxwell burst out laughing.

'Now you look just like Alanna when she doesn't get something she wants.'

Polly laughed along with him as she walked past all the toys again, switching them on and off, one at a time, until she came to the one she liked best. It was a little white Scottie dog, wearing a Santa hat and singing "Merry Christmas, Everybody". Its little hat moved around in time to the music and it bopped from side to side as it sang. She could feel the smile spreading over her face as she watched it.

'I'm having this one,' she declared, bending down to pick up a boxed one from the floor below.

'You're buying a Christmas item willingly and without coercion?'

'I sure am! Deal with it!'

'And my work here is done!'

'So, is that it? I can go home now?'

Maxwell grinned at her.

'You think I brought you here just to look at dancing teddy bears? Oh no, I've got something even better for you. Come on.'

He took her hand once again and weaved his way past

193

the displays, through the doors that took them out the back of the shop and along a path until they came to the vision that is every child's dream – Santa's grotto.

It truly was everything a child could wish for. A log cabin stood in the middle of a snow-covered garden surrounded by a white picket fence. Sparkling icicles hung from the roof, a frost-covered lamppost resided by the gate, a snowman was standing to attention in the garden and elves chirped festive greetings beside the shining red front door. A small wisp of smoke wended its way out of the chimney and spun around the shining star sitting at the top of the huge Christmas tree positioned slightly off to the side.

'Wow! This is gorgeous. I love it.'

'When was the last time you sat on Santa's knee?'

'Blimey, when I was about six or seven, I expect. Although I don't think that's allowed these days.'

'No, it's not, which is probably a good thing as it might be rather awkward now you're older.'

'What do you mean?'

'Why, that you're going to speak to Santa.'

'Ha ha! Nice one, Maxwell. I think I'm just a bit too old for that now.'

'We're never too old, which is why, for one night every year, this place has a Santa's grotto for adults. No children, just grown-ups so they can remember the magic of being a child.'

'Honestly? You're teasing me…'

'No, I'm not. Look at the people in front of you.'

Polly looked along the little queue and sure enough, there wasn't a child to be seen, it was all adults.

'I'm really getting to speak to Santa Claus?'

'You really are.'

Unable to stop herself, Polly threw her arms around Maxwell and placed a big fat kiss on his lips. She then hugged him tight and when she let go, he left his arm across her shoulders and they stood like that until it was her turn to go in.

'That is just *so* not fair! How come you got the mixer?'

They were sitting in the café of the garden centre, enjoying a couple of toasties and admiring the presents they'd received from Santa.

'Clearly Santa thought I'd enjoy it more.'

'I'm sure you would really rather have the ice-cream van.'

Polly looked at the small boxes of Lego toys sitting on the table in front of them. Maxwell's hand crept over towards the cement mixer she'd received and she gave it a sharp slap.

'Paws off my mixer, dude. It's mine.'

Maxwell laughed.

'I never put you down for being so possessive.'

'You don't know how much I loved Lego when I was a kid.'

'Then, in that case, please allow me to regift my ice-cream van to you.'

He pushed it over the table towards her.

'Don't be daft, that's your present from Santa. You can't give it away.'

'Yes, I can, because if I take it home, I'll have two children arguing over who gets to build it. You'll be doing me a favour.'

'Would you have said the same if you'd received the cement mixer?'

'Yes, I would and for the same reason.'

'Then tell you what, they can hide out at my house and you can come over sometime and we'll make them up together.'

'Cool! It's a deal. Now, eat up your toastie – I promised you an early night in with Bailey this evening.'
Polly took a bite of her toastie and as the cheese and ham filling thrilled her taste buds, she wondered if Maxwell's words were a clue that their time together wouldn't come to an end on Christmas Eve after all.

31

December 17ᵗʰ

Polly was looking out the office window, waiting for Maxwell to arrive. He'd said he would pick her up at four so she'd come into the office early that morning to make up the time. Having already had the day off on Wednesday, she didn't want Monty or Andy to think she was a slacker.

She wondered how it would be between them this evening after Maxwell had kissed her goodnight when he'd taken her home the night before. It hadn't been a full-on snog but it most definitely had been a kiss between people who were more than friends. She'd felt quite giddy when she'd floated into the house a few minutes later and poor Bailey had nearly had the life squeezed out of him when she'd picked him up in delight.

Now, however, it was the awkward date that comes after the next step has been taken. Did Maxwell regret the kiss? Was he happy they'd kissed? Would he kiss her again?

From her own perspective, the answers were no, she didn't regret the kiss. Yes, she was happy he'd kissed her. And, hell yes, she would kiss him again. She just really hoped he was singing from the same Christmas carol songbook as she was.

The sight of the pick-up truck coming along the road spurred her into action. Polly grabbed her things, yelled out a goodnight to Andy who was still in his office, buried under numbers and receipts, and was shoving her arms into her coat as she flew out the door onto the pavement.

'Good evening, young Snowflake, are you ready for another advent-ure full of fun and delight?'

'I most certainly am.'

'Excellent. Now, let's just have one of these and we can be on our way.'

He leant over, placed his hand gently on her cheek and turned her face towards him whereupon he placed his lips on hers and kissed her hello.

Polly returned the gentle pressure while every nerve ending in her body sang with joy. When he pulled away a few seconds later, she had to refrain from moaning with disappointment and her lips felt like their best friend had run off and left them behind.

She opened her eyes in time to see his sweet smile before he turned away to watch the traffic while waiting for an opening to pull out into.

'How was your day? Did you do anything exciting or important?'

'Now, that depends on what you call exciting or important. If you think walking around the National Arboretum, checking their trees are in good health, then yes, it was exciting and important.'

'I'd say ensuring their trees are healthy was fairly important. It would be rather pants to be walking around the memorials, remembering the souls who gave up their lives in combat, only to have a dirty big oak tree suddenly keel over and flatten you. I reckon it would put a bit of a dampener on the day.'

'I rather agree.'

He bestowed his schoolboy grin upon her and she tried not to squirm in her seat as her body turned molten.

'What about you? Any handsome supermodels walk through the office today?'

'If they did, I totally missed them due to being buried in the filing room trying to do some archiving. Honestly, I really don't know what that Karen one was doing in her time there but it sure wasn't work!'

'She wasn't one for putting her back into things, I'll say that. A shirker rather than a worker.'

'Hmm, well, she's giving me plenty to do while it's all quiet.'

'I'm sure Monty and Andy appreciate it.'

'Tough if they don't! I do what needs to be done.'

Maxwell burst out laughing at her bolshy response.

'There's no messing with you, is there?'

'Not when I have an office to run and keep ship-shape.'

'So, do you have any clue on where we're heading this evening?'

'Well, I haven't found a crystal ball while sorting out the office so that would be a no.'

'Oh, you are a feisty one tonight!'

She returned his grin. 'It's been known to happen.'

'I hope you like tonight's outing. It's something I enjoy but it's not for everyone.'

'Oh, I'm intrigued now. Feel like giving up a hint or two?'

'Don't be daft, of course not!'

'Fine. So, apart from tonight's surprise, what else do you enjoy doing when not healing Christmas Grinches? You mentioned you like to draw – is that the only thing?'

'I love reading.'

'Oh, you never said when I mentioned it was one of my preferred pastimes, last week.'

'I think the subject kind of moved on before I had a chance to. My job is a fairly active one so it's nice, like you said, to just snuggle down in a quiet spot and lose yourself somewhere far flung and interesting.'

For the rest of the journey, they discussed what genres they liked and what authors they mutually enjoyed. It was only when they rounded a bend and Polly saw the stately home on the opposite hill all brightly lit up, that the conversation ground to a halt.

'Gosh! That is stunning. Is that where we're going?'

'It sure is. Polly, meet Chatsworth House.'

'Fantastic! I've wanted to visit here for a while but haven't gotten around to it yet. I saw a programme on the television about it and it sparked my interest. Are we going inside?'

'We absolutely are. And you're sure you don't mind this?'

'Why on earth would I mind? I'm thrilled.'

'Stately homes and the like aren't everyone's cup of tea. Some people find them boring.'

'I love history. I could never be bored in places like this.'

'Well, that's great to hear because we have a ton of them across the Midlands and I'd be more than happy to show them to you.'

'I like the sound of that.'

Maxwell parked the truck and she indulged herself in a tiny, inward, "squeee" of delight as she got out the cab. It certainly was looking like Maxwell planned to stick around when all her advent-ures were done.

'Well, what do you think? Like it?'

'Maxwell, I'm simply speechless! This place is amazing.'

Polly stood in the huge room inside the stately home and admired the vast fireplace which was so big, she could have stood upright inside it with room to spare. On either side were two gigantic Christmas trees, decorated with large red and silver baubles. To her right, was a third tree, half as tall again with matching décor. Above it, two small iron balconies leaned out into the room and she wondered what the point of them was as they were too small for an orchestra or band to sit in. In fact, they were only just big enough for one person to stand in.

She followed Maxwell through the ornately decorated rooms and corridors that had become even more stunning in their Christmas attire. Besides the multitude of Christmas trees in every colour scheme she could think of, there appeared to be a theme of children's stories for she'd spotted the Mad Hatter and Alice in Wonderland, Toad and Badger from The Wind in the Willows and she was now admiring a glorious Winnie the Pooh and Piglet as they attempted to put up some decorations. She was also sure she'd just heard someone exclaim that Paddington was in the next room.

'I have to say that I love coming here at Christmas. It has a magical atmosphere which I've never felt anywhere else.'

'Maybe the walls have absorbed the atmosphere of every Christmas celebrated over the last four or five hundred years and it oozes out to envelope the visitors as they walk round.'

'Or,' Maxwell grinned at her, 'it's all the ghosts. I'm sure there's been a few deaths around here across the centuries!'

'Oh, Maxwell! Behave! I'm trying to join in with your

romantic Christmas notions and you come out with that!'

They giggled like children as they made their way through the last few rooms before, inevitably, coming out into the gift shop.

Polly gravitated towards the books and soon found herself immersed in a Victorian book about cakes and baking. The photographs were rich and colourful and there were some quite complicated confections that piqued her interest.

Maxwell caught up with her as she waited in the queue to make her purchase.

'Whacha got there?' he asked, peering over her shoulder.

'Yet more recipe books that I really don't need but can't resist.'

'You have a few cookbooks then?'

'More than I dare to count.'

'Just like my mum. She can't resist recipe books. Adores them. But, despite the shelves full of them, she only ever uses the same two or three.'

'Ah, but it's the knowing they're there that's the buzz.'

'I suppose.'

'Surely there must be something – a tool or the like – that even though you have several of, you still buy more.'

'I guess I do have a thing about antique screwdrivers. I seem to have a box full in my garage but still buy more. I like old ones with wooden handles. They're far more tactile than the modern plastic things.'

'Well, there you go.' She smiled at the cashier as she swiped her credit card and picked up the brown paper carrier bag the books had been placed in. 'For your mum and I, it's cookbooks, for you it's screwdrivers. We all have our little foibles.'

They stepped outside into the cold dark night and Polly pulled her hat and gloves on. They walked around the corner and she let out a mew of disappointment.

'Aw, the market's all closed.'

Sure enough, the last few stall holders of the resident Christmas market were putting up the shutters on their little wooden cabins. The majority were already closed and in darkness.

'I'm sorry. I wasn't able to get away any sooner to bring you earlier.'

'It's okay. At least I got to see the house.'

'There's always next year.'

'Indeed. It'll be something for me to look forward to.'

'Wow! Looking forward to Christmas now? What have I done to you?'

'I really don't know, Maxwell Watkins, but I think I like it.'

With those words, she spun round to face him and, putting a gloved hand on each of his cheeks, pulled him towards her and kissed him soundly.

32

December 18th

'I'm sorry to leave you alone all day again, Bailey. I'm turning into a horrible mummy. I promise, there's only a few more days of this advent-ure thing left and we'll return to normal.'

Polly let out a yawn as she rolled over in her bed to give her cat a big cuddle. He didn't seem to mind her recent absences but she felt guilty about leaving him so often. Thankfully, it was only short-term and some semblance of normality wasn't too far away.

That wasn't to say she hadn't enjoyed her daily surprises and she was still impressed with the number of activities Maxwell had come up with. Although she could have done without the early rise this morning. As per usual, the information given had been sparse and all she had to work with was "I'll pick you up at seven and wear comfortable shoes".

Dead on seven am, there was a toot outside and, giving

Bailey one last hug, she rushed out the door.

'Oh, hello? New car?'

A shining silver Tesla was sitting gracing her gravel.

'Good morning, my lovely little Snowflake, how are you?'

Maxwell bent down to give her a welcoming kiss that lasted a little longer than a usual hello kiss would. When he finally let her come up for air, her head was spinning and she was holding his arms just a little tighter thanks to the wobbly sensation in her knees.

Once inside and belted in, he answered her question.

'No, old car actually that I don't get the chance to drive very often. It's no use for day-to-day business – the suspension would be knackered in a week if I took this to work – so it only comes out for high days and holidays when I'm driving on proper roads and not dirt tracks.'

'Hmmm, so that means we're going somewhere that's on "proper roads" – interesting.'

'I hope it will be. It's a bit of a trek though, so you may as well settle back and relax.'

She did just that and they were soon on the motorway heading south. She really couldn't fathom where they were headed and when they veered off at the Watford junction, she grew even more curious while racking her brains, trying to think of anything unusual in the area. After all, Watford wasn't far from her old London stomping ground but try as she might, nothing came to mind that would fit the criteria Maxwell seemed to have for her events.

He parked in the car park next to the train station, took her hand and led her onto the southbound platform. A few moments later, a train for London Euston arrived which they boarded.

'London! You're taking me to London? Isn't that like taking coals to Newcastle? I don't think there's much in London to surprise me.'

He simply smiled and replied, 'We'll see.'

It was only a short journey into the capital and soon they were standing on Euston Road with Maxwell looking at the map on his phone, trying to get his bearings. While he did this, Polly stood quietly by his side and wallowed in the sights and sounds around her. The hustle and bustle of her home town was as familiar to her as the back of her hand and a wave of home-sickness welled up in her chest. She was surprised to find herself blinking back tears and they were nothing to do with the thick exhaust fumes in the air.

'Okay, this way.'

Maxwell took her hand but had only taken a few steps when he glanced at her and stopped.

'Hey, are you okay? Here…'

He pulled a tissue from his pocket and handed it over. She quickly dabbed her eyes while giving him a watery smile.

'Thank you. I'm sorry.'

'Don't apologise. I'm the one who should be sorry. I never gave any thought as to how it would feel for you to be here.'

'I'm alright. It's just… it's the first time I've been back since I left and I've only just realised how much I've missed it. When I made the decision to leave, I couldn't get away fast enough and once out of here, I didn't look back. It's… well… London has a vibe that is all its own and you either love it or you hate it. I thought I hated it but now know that I love it and always will. It's a part of me that won't ever go away.'

'Do you think you'll come back here to live again in the future?'

'No, I don't believe I would but we never know what tomorrow will bring. Let's say that it's not in my immediate plans nor any I can see in the future.'

'That works for me. So, now that I've managed to upset

you, let's see if I can make it up to you with a few surprises. I think I know a few places that you may not have visited while you were here.'

'That's quite a challenge you've set yourself, Mr Watkins, I hope you know that.'

'I'm quietly confident. And the first one is this way… let's go.'

He led her across the road, along and down several side streets until finally, just as she was convinced that he was lost, he stopped in front of a row of tall, terraced houses.

'Does this look familiar to you? Recognise it at all?'

Polly looked around her before shrugging.

'I can't say it does.'

'Excellent. Then here's to surprise number one.'

They walked along the street until they came to a bright red door with a simple Christmas wreath on it. The sign next to it read, "Charles Dickens Museum".

'We're going in here?'

'Yes, we are. After all, he's "The Man who Invented Christmas" so it seems appropriate to visit his museum.'

'Charles Dickens invented Christmas? Are you sure about that?'

'It's generally considered that his story, A Christmas Carol, led the way for how we now celebrate the festive season.'

'Well, in that case, I would say this is a good place to start. Come on.'

She grabbed his hand and marched through the door.

'And that seat… how uncomfortable must that have been? Sure, he'd have had some good swivelling moments on it but to sit for hours upon hours as he wrote his stories? Let's just say he's gone up in my estimation if only for his perseverance!'

'I'm sure it wasn't that bad.'

'Maxwell, are you kidding? Have you seen how long his books are?'

'Did anything else impress you or was seeing where he did his writing the pinnacle of the visit?'

'Oh, the house itself was lovely and I do have a soft spot for Victorian décor. Plus, seeing it all decorated for Christmas was nice. Thank you. Thank you for thinking of it – it's a place that has never crossed my mind to visit.'

'You're welcome. Now, onto our next destination. This way.'

He kissed her nose, took her hand and a few minutes later, they were making their way down into the Underground.

'How do you manage to have Oyster cards?' she questioned, after he handed one to her before skipping through the ticket barrier.

'Monty. He keeps some at the office because they come in handy when he needs to come down. I asked to borrow a couple for today so we'd be saved the hassle of buying tickets.'

'You do know you can just use your contactless debit card…'

'I do but I prefer the Oyster cards. I'm a bit paranoid about cloning and stuff.'

'Fair enough.'

They walked through the corridors of Russell Square until they came to a halt on the westbound platform.

'Will we be on the tube for long?'

'For as long as it takes to reach where we're going.'

Polly gave a small grunt under her breath. It didn't matter what angle she took, in an attempt to get information, he was always onto her and her sly intentions. She sneaked a look at him from the corner of her eye and found him grinning as he watched her.

'What are you grinning at?'

'You! I love your persistence. I admire the fact you don't give up. Maybe you have some of Mr Dickens' perseverance in you.'

She was about to reply when a tube came onto the platform and the thrill of feeling the hot air being pushed up the tunnel along with the vibration of the train – yet another piece of home she'd forgotten about – made her forget the sharp retort which had been on her lips.

They found two seats together and travelled along in silence. Polly closed her eyes, sat back and lost herself in the swaying sensation that came with riding on the tube.

'Okay, next one's ours.'

'Oh, sorry, what was that?'

'We're off at the next stop.'

'Oh, right. Hyde Park Corner?'

'That's the one. Are you alright? Did I lose you again?'

She followed Maxwell to the doors as the train began to slow down.

'A little,' she replied. 'I've only been away nine months or so but it feels longer. I think I kind of pushed everything London-related out of my head and threw all my energy at settling into my new home in the Peak District. I suppose I felt putting all of London out of my mind would make it easier.'

'And did it?'

'Yeah, it did. It's just being back now—'

'Is it upsetting you? We can leave any time. You only have to say.'

'No, it's definitely not upsetting me. It's… it's home, you know? I just wasn't prepared for it, that's all, but it's not a problem, okay?' She rushed to reassure him on this point. 'It's hitting me in the soft spots. I'm fine though, honest. It's good to be back.'

They'd been so busy talking that she hadn't been

paying attention to the route they were walking and it was only when she heard the squeals and the Christmas music that she looked up to find them almost in front of the gates which led into the huge "Winter Wonderland" that took up residence in Hyde Park at this time of year.

'No way! You're taking me to the "Winter Wonderland"? Fantastic!'

'Fantastic? Am I really hearing this from the woman who only two weeks ago told me she avoided all things Christmas like the plague?'

'You know you are! I've already told you – I'm a convert. Now come on, let's get in there.'

This time it was she who was rushing ahead, dragging Maxwell behind her and ignoring the sound of his laughter in her ears.

33

'I'll bet you're glad now that I advised you not to have any glühwein until later.'

Polly glanced up at Maxwell as he worked on staying upright on the ice rink. She, on the other hand, was skating with growing confidence and was currently skating backwards as she spoke.

'How on earth are you so good? I'm only just keeping my balance here.'

'Ah, misspent teenage years. Too many nights over at the Ally Pally and not enough studying or doing homework.'

'Ally Pally?'

'Alexandra Palace to you. I grew up in Muswell Hill – the Pally was no distance away. I spent a lot of time there – either on the ice during the winter or sneaking in under-age drinking during the summer.'

'And that's why you're so good now at this ice skating malarky?'

'Hey, this was your idea!'

'I didn't know I'd be hitting the ice with Jayne Torvill!'

'Hardly! I go forwards and backwards. That's it. And to be honest, I'm amazed I've not already hit the deck because it's been a *loooooooong* time since I was on blades.'

'You're enjoying it though. You haven't stopped smiling since we came out here.'

She swivelled round and took his hand.

'I used to love it when I was a kid. It's all coming back to me now. I used to just go round and round for hours. I hated it when they would clear the ice so they could clean and refreeze it. I was always amongst the first back on.'

'Did you go with your friends?'

'No, not really.' She thought for a moment and then continued. 'I kind of got in with what would be called the "wrong sort". They were the kids who didn't care what crap you had going on at home because they had their own crap to deal with so they didn't ask too many questions. They just wanted to find fun in whatever form they could because it helped them to forget. And that worked for me.'

'I can see why that would be.'

'But it did mean that I learnt how to do this, however…'

She let go of his hand, pushed hard on her right foot and flew off across the ice, weaving amongst the other skaters. She wasn't going fast but the feel of the wind against her face felt so good that she let out a laugh full of joy. She sped past Maxwell who was beginning to pick up the pace and called out to him.

'Come on, slow-coach, you can do better than that.'

After she'd completed three circuits, Polly slowed down and held out her hand. Maxwell took it and pulled her closer to him.

'You looked so free just then. You were like a snowflake dancing across the ice.'

'It felt good. I feel good. Every day it feels like more weight is being lifted off me. I didn't realise how much it was crushing me. Thank you for everything you've done.'

Maxwell veered off towards the crash barrier, pulled her into his arms and held her tightly before dropping a kiss on her lips.

'Polly, you don't need to keep thanking me. I get all the thanks I need when I see you laughing and smiling and relaxing within yourself. Seeing the light of happiness in your eyes is the biggest "thank you" you can give me. Now, how about we get back onto terra firma and grab a cup of something warm along with a bite to eat?'

Her stomach let out a rumble and she giggled, glad that the music was loud enough to cover the sound.

'What are we waiting for? Let's go.'

'You go and grab that table over there – I'll get us a couple of hot chocolates.'

'Don't forget the cream and marshmallows.'

'As if I would!'

Polly headed towards the bench table underneath the canvas awning and was pleased to feel a heater just overhead. She placed their cartons of noodles and hotdogs down before undoing her coat and taking off her scarf. She straddled one of the seats and watched Maxwell as he gave the drinks order to the man behind the counter. Her stomach rumbled again so she broke a piece off one of the hotdogs and nibbled on it while she waited. She wasn't sure if she'd be able to eat all of the long sausage and the noodles but the rich smell of the noodle bar had filled the air as they'd walked past and they hadn't been able to resist stopping to buy some.

'Here you go. Although these are almost a meal in themselves.'

Maxwell placed two mammoth sized hot drinks on the table and was just undoing his jacket when a squeal rent the air.

'MAXIE! OH, MY GAWD, MAXIE! IT'S YOU. IT'S REALLY YOU!'

The next thing Polly knew, Maxwell had disappeared behind a curtain of long, black, wild gypsy hair.

When he was finally released, Polly's heart plummeted when she saw Laurel Devine emerge from the flowing black mane, her arms wrapped firmly around his waist.

'I wasn't sure if it was you, Maxie, until you turned around. It's wonderful to see you again.'

'Hi, Laurel, how are you?'

'All the better for seeing you now, you delicious beast. What are you doing here?'

He didn't reply straight away, leaning over instead to pull a paper napkin from the dispenser on the table and wipe his lips. When he tossed it onto the table, Polly noticed the thick lipstick smears rubbed on it.

'I'm here with my friend, Polly. We're in London for the day. Polly, this is Laurel, Laurel, meet Polly.'

She felt the laser beam of Laurel's dark, dark, brown, almost black, eyes go through her. She was being sized up but it only took an instant for the other woman to dazzle her with her wide, photogenic smile. Clearly, she'd been written off as someone non-threatening.

'Hi, Polly.'

There was no time to answer before her attention was returned to Maxwell.

'Now then, Maxie, why don't you and I meet for a drink later? We can catch up on old times…'

Polly had picked up her hot chocolate and just about choked on her first mouthful as she watched Laurel's red-tipped finger tap Maxwell on the chin before being drawn down his chest towards the belt on his jeans.

'I'm sorry, Laurel, that won't be possible. Anyway, what are you doing here? I thought this was totally "not your thing"!'

214

He drew quotes in the air to emphasise his words.

'Photoshoot for some publicity thing. I don't know what. I only go where my agent tells me to, you know that.'

'I see. Well, it's been nice seeing you again but my food's getting cold so if you'll excuse me…'

'Oh, Maxie. Look at the rubbish you've got there. You know it's bad for you. You put on weight, grow fat and it makes your hair and skin all skanky.'

Laurel looked straight at Polly as she uttered these charming words. In that moment, Polly was glad she was sitting down because the Krav Maga moves she'd told Monty were long forgotten suddenly found themselves itching to be let loose.

Maxwell didn't reply to Laurel's bitchy comment. He simply sat down, picked up his hotdog and took a mighty bite, completely ignoring the supermodel standing by his shoulder.

After a moment, and with a hoity toss of her hair, she turned and stormed off.

'Has she gone?'

'Yes?'

'And the pitbulls?'

'The what?'

'The two blokes who were standing off to the side – they're her bodyguards. Have they gone too?'

'Oh, I didn't realise they were with her. Yes, they left just behind her.'

He let out a sigh and pushed the half-eaten hotdog away.

'I'm so sorry about that.'

'What have you got to be sorry about? So, you bumped into your ex and she was a bit of a bitch. These things happen.'

'It's the first time we've crossed paths since we split up. It's just kind of thrown me a little.'

'Do you still fancy her?'

'What? No! Absolutely not.'

'Are you sure?'

'Yes. I mean, she has the kind of looks that would turn any man's head but she's lacking in far too many other areas.'

'I think she was keen to remind you of the areas she's not lacking in.'

'That's just Laurel – the eternal flirt.'

'Okay.'

Even though she thought she was going to choke on them, Polly forced several forkfuls of noodles down her throat. She was not going to let Maxwell see how Laurel's sudden appearance had affected her. How she now felt dowdy and uninteresting when compared to the stunning beauty of the model who lived such an exotic life and who'd most likely rather die than do something as boring as baking a cake.

Maxwell pushed back the sleeve of his jumper, made a show of looking at his watch and then stood up, pulling his jacket closed to zip it up.

'Well, come on then, we can't sit here all day. Things to do, things to see.'

She gathered her stuff together and followed him back out into the crowd that was swelling by the minute. Even though he took her hand as he had done before, and pointed out various little cabins of interest in the Christmas market, Polly felt his actions and cheery demeanour were forced. The shine had gone off the day and she no longer wanted to be there.

They were walking up Park Lane towards Oxford Street, the noise of the traffic replacing the music that had previously been assaulting her ears, when Maxwell pulled her to the side, wrapped her in a warm embrace and kissed her deeply.

'Look, don't let her spoil our day,' he whispered. 'We were having a good time and we still can. Forget about her, she's history. We're the here and now, okay?'

'Okay.'

'Good. Now for the next event.'

Polly couldn't help but burst out laughing as he dragged her onto one of the open-topped buses and up the stairs so she could "see the Oxford Street lights close up". They alighted at Piccadilly Circus and walked along Piccadilly itself so they could take in the majestic beauty of Fortnum & Mason before picking up a tube at Green Park which took them back to Euston and then home.

The crunch of the gravel under the car wheels woke her up and Polly opened her eyes to see them pulling up in front of her house.

'Here you go, sleepy-head. Back home all safe and sound.'

Maxwell got out of the car, walked round, opened her door and held out his hand. She took it and he walked her to the front door.

'I'll pick you up tomorrow afternoon at one. Have a long lie in, you'll need to be fresh for what's coming next.'

She didn't get a chance to answer before he lowered his head and kissed her. A kiss that carried more promise than any he'd given her before. He pulled her closer to him and her arms found their way around his neck. She stretched up onto her toes so as to hold more of him to her. A moan escaped and floated away on the wind and she didn't know if it had come from her or from him.

A moment later, the sharp sting of the cold air needled her cheeks as Maxwell slowly pulled away.

'Goodnight, my little snowflake.'

He placed a gentle kiss on her forehead and then got back into the car.

She stood waving goodbye and it was only when she

closed the door behind her, did she realise she was pulling in large gulps of air to try and ease the spinning sensation flowing round her.

Never before in her life had she been kissed like that and she really hoped there were many more where that had come from.

34

December 19ᵗʰ

'I think, my beautiful Bailey boy, that Mr Maxwell is being a little cheeky? Would you happen to agree?'

She turned her phone towards the cat to let him see the message that had just pinged up.

"It's really cold out today; wear the sexy underwear!"

Bailey stuck his nose on the screen, sniffed it, looked at her and then began grooming his undercarriage, letting her know that he had zero interest in either her phone or the words typed upon it.

Polly wrapped her arms around him and gave a gentle squeeze.

'Oh, Bailey, he's soooooooo lovely and you're the only being I have that I can talk to.'

She looked longingly at her laptop but knew she couldn't call Ritchie. This was his busiest time of the year and she knew he would be shattered. It wasn't fair to disturb him on this occasion, no matter how much she wanted to or how much he would love to hear her news.

She picked up her book and tried to concentrate on the dark thriller but it was no use. After five minutes of reading the same paragraph three times, she put the paperback down, got up and went into the kitchen. When she felt this restless, there was only one thing to do.

Bake!

After checking her ingredients, and making a note of what was running low, she decided that a Gingerbread Swiss Roll with Eggnog Cream was perfect. It wouldn't take too long to make and it was pretty festive. If it worked out well, she could add it to the list of potential bakes for the Christmas markets next year.

It wasn't long before she was mixing and whisking while her head was in the clouds, filled with thoughts of Maxwell.

When the man of her daydreams arrived at her door a few hours later, two Swiss Rolls were sitting proudly on the kitchen island.

'Have you been baking again? It smells wonderful in here.'

'I have. Come and taste – you can give me your opinion.'

She cut a slice from one of the rolls and he ate it while she pulled on her boots.

'That,' Maxwell pointed at the cake on the plate with his fork, 'is amazing! It's so light and the fusion of ginger and eggnog is delicious.'

'Good enough to sell?'

'Absolutely!'

'Great! I'll add it to the list.'

She put the cakes into two separate tins and handed one to him.

'For your mum. I'd like her feedback too.'

'What, my opinion not good enough for you?'

'It absolutely is but additional feedback is always welcome.'

'Well, you can pass it to her yourself. She's invited you to dinner this evening.'

'Oh, that's kind of her. Please let her know I accept and I look forward to seeing her later. In that case, can I leave the tin here and pick it up on the way there?'

'Sure. I figured you'd need to feed Bailey before we go.'

'We'll be back about five-ish, then?'

'The time at which you will return home before dinner will not be unreasonable.'

They exchanged a grin as she gave Bailey a kiss and cuddle before following Maxwell out the door. Nineteen days and he still hadn't slipped up when she tried to worm information out of him. Would he make it all the way to the twenty-fourth?

'It'll be better if we leave the truck here and walk. Are you okay to do that?'

'Sure. I've got my thermals on so I can handle the cold.'

'You took my advice then?'

'Naturally. You've lived here all your life so I'm not going to argue with you over the weather. Which reminds me, I saw on the news this morning that the promised snowstorms won't be bothering us after all.'

'No, the wind direction changed and they've moved further north.'

'That's good to hear.'

They chattered about various weather events they'd experienced as they walked and soon arrived at the market square where a small crowd was gathered, standing next to the cenotaph.

'Okay, what's going on this time?'

'You'll see, all in good time.'

Maxwell said hello to a few people he knew nearby and introduced her to them. She was in the middle of chatting with a woman who'd mentioned she wanted to spend a few days in London the following summer, when a loud tin horn went off.

'Roll up, roll up. All those participating in this year's "Calderly Top Christmas Treasure Hunt" please step forward.'

'That'll be us.'

Maxwell placed his hand on her elbow and moved them both forward to the centre of the crowd to stand in front of a man who was talking into a loudspeaker.

'Okay, most of you know how this works but as I'm seeing a few new faces, we'll go over it again. Angie here has an envelope for each team which she is handing out as I speak. You cannot open the envelope until I blow the horn for the game to start. The card inside contains the first clue. At each destination, you will receive a card with the next clue. The winning team will be the first to arrive at the final destination with all ten cards.'

'I really hope you're good at working out cryptic clues because I'm rubbish,' Maxwell murmured in her ear.

'I've never done a treasure hunt before so I don't know if I am or not.'

'Then it's new to both of us.'

'What? This is your first one too?'

'Yeah. I thought you might like a task where both of us are on an equal footing.'

A woman walked over and handed them their envelope. They were team number seven.

'If it makes you feel any better, seven is my lucky

number.'

Maxwell looked at her and grinned.

'Well then, my little snowflake, I'd say that's a good omen to be starting on.'

Just then, the air horn blew and everyone scrambled to open their envelopes. Maxwell pulled out a Christmas card, opened it up and read out the first clue:

> *To get this started, you need to go,*
> *And find a kiss under the mistletoe.*

He looked at her and she looked back at him.

'Well, any suggestions?'

Polly thought for a moment before a large smile spread over her face.

'Yes, I think I do.'

She looked around the other teams and noted that they were still looking confused.

'Come with me.'

She took his hand and wandered slowly away from the crowd, trying not to draw attention to their departure as she didn't want the other teams following them.

She made a point of looking in a few shop windows, easing them towards a small lane that ran down to the main road and she pulled Maxwell into it as they passed the opening.

'Quickly, before they're aware we've got this sussed and come after us.'

They ran to the other end of the lane, along the main road and then back up a second alleyway.

'Are you sure you know where you're going?'

'Yes,' she smiled, 'trust me.'

Five minutes later, she was leading him into the churchyard where the procession had begun on the night of the Christmas lights switch on. She walked over to the opposite side of the church and pointed up at the tree branches above.

'Look.'

Maxwell followed her finger.

'Mistletoe!' he exclaimed.

At that moment, the vicar of the church appeared and he was carrying a pile of envelopes in his hand.

'How did you know to come here?' Maxwell asked her.

'I was curious to see the church after the light parade so came along for a look on one of my lunch breaks. I spotted the mistletoe then. This location made sense because I expect the clues will all be within walking distance.'

'Good afternoon, are you both doing the treasure hunt?' the vicar asked.

'We are,' came the unified reply.

'Then you need to kiss before you can receive the next card.'

Polly giggled as Maxwell replied, 'That will be a small price to pay,' before lowering his head and kissing her soundly on the lips.

She could feel herself blushing at him behaving like this in front of a man of the cloth but when she glanced at the vicar, she caught him laughing.

'I would say the price has been firmly paid. Here is your card. Good luck. Now, you may want to get a wriggle on, I can see a few teams just along the road there. Don't let them catch you up.'

'Thank you, vicar.'

Polly gave him a warm handshake before they walked out the churchyard on the opposite side from the road and away from the other hunters.

Maxwell opened the second card and Polly leaned over to read it.

These bells don't often ring a lot,
Rarely when cold but always when hot!

Polly racked her brains. What on earth could that mean? She was trying to dissect the clue when Maxwell suddenly said, 'Fire station! It's the fire station.'

'Of course, it is!'

He grabbed her hand and they scurried off along the path, laughing as they went.

35

'This one is impossible.'

'No, it's not. Read it out again.'

Maxwell opened the card and read out the clue for the second time.

> *No creature was stirring, the night before,*
> *To find out the rest, you must go to this store.*

'It's clearly a reference to the poem, "The Night Before Christmas" which means we need to find a book store but which one? We've been to them all.'

'We're missing something,' Polly mused.

Something was niggling at the back of her mind and she desperately tried to grasp hold of it. Suddenly, it came to her.

'Oh, hang on a minute…'

'What?'

She smiled.

'I think I've got it!'

'Where are we going?'

'To Fred's Pet Shop.'

'The pet shop?'

'Yes, the pet shop! Come on!'

Two minutes later they were standing in front of Fred's Pet Shop and there in the window, was a large cage with a couple of mice running around and playing on their little toys. Next to the cage was a picture book of the favourite Christmas poem and the words "…Not even a mouse," were written on the glass.

'You, my little snowflake, grow more amazing with every passing minute.'

Maxwell gathered her up in a quick embrace before they stepped inside the shop for their next card.

'How many do we have now?' Polly asked when they came back out.

'This is number nine. Only one more to go.'

'So, hurry up and open it.'

Polly found herself hopping from foot to foot in excitement. This afternoon had been so much fun and it looked like they were still in the lead.

'Oh, this one is pretty easy.'

'Thank goodness! We needed a break after that last one. Where are we going now?'

Maxwell passed her the card which she opened and read aloud.

It's behind you, oh no, it's not.
Can you find the last clue, before you lose the plot?

She looked up.

'That has to be the theatre, surely.'

'That was my thinking, too.'

'Then let's go.'

They all but ran to the small theatre on the corner of the town square but found it in darkness when they got there and no sign of any living soul.

'Maybe we need to go to the stage door? You know, the "it's behind you" part.'

Maxwell led the way down the side of the theatre towards the back but when they got there, it was also in darkness. No signs of life and certainly no cards.

'Hmm, well, now I am confused.'

'I can't see anything that could be considered a clue.'

Polly was looking up, checking out the metal fire escape to see if anyone was hiding up there but there wasn't. They were all alone.

'Come on, let's go back to the front doors. Maybe we got here quicker than the person with the cards.'

They returned to the front of the building and they'd just stepped back into the square when Polly suddenly stopped in her tracks. Maxwell walked into the back of her and she stumbled slightly before finding her balance.

'Oh, that is good! That is SO good.'

She turned to look at Maxwell.

'I'm telling you, the person who came up with these clues deserves a medal!'

'And how do you work that one out?'

She inclined her head towards a small newsagent across the square from the theatre.

'Look at their window.'

'Huh?'

'The sign in their window.'

'Hallmark Christmas cards sold here?'

She rolled her eyes.

'No, the other sign.'

'Get your New Year fireworks now.'

'Yes!'

'I still don't get it.'

'The last line in the riddle – "before you lose the plot". It means the Gunpowder Plot. Guy Fawkes. Fireworks!'

'Well, bugger me! That is genius!'

'I hope so! I may just have made a leap too far in my deductions.'

'Only one way to find out.'

They ran over the square and burst through the door of the tiny shop.

'Are we in the right place?'

The lady behind the counter bestowed a big warm smile on them.

'If you're treasure hunters, then you most certainly are. And you're also the first here.'

She pulled an envelope from under the counter.

'Here you go. You're on the home stretch. Good luck.'

They stepped back outside and Maxwell was about to open the card when Polly grabbed his arm.

'No, stop. We need to go back to the front of the theatre first.'

'Why?'

'To avoid giving the clue away to any rival teams who might arrive before we work it out.'

'Do you know, Polly Snowflake, I would never have put you down as being this cunning before today.'

'Put it down to all the thrillers I read. It's good to know I've learnt something from them.'

'What does the last clue say? How much brain power do we need for that as I think mine is almost used up?'

'Let's have a look and see, shall we?'

Polly opened the envelope, took out the card, opened it and read quietly:

It's nearly over, how do you feel?
Can you get it tied up before the last peal?

'Oh, blimey.'

'Indeed! Does any of that mean anything to you,

Maxwell?'

They strolled further into the square and looked about them, trying to see anything which might lend an idea as to where they had to go.

'We need to get a wriggle on, another team has just gone into the newsagent.'

Polly tried not to sound overly-concerned but she was just finding out that she had a broader competitive streak than she would have previously given herself credit for and was shocked by how much she now wanted to win this event. It would be so unfair to have led the way all this time and then be pipped at the post.

'I… I… I'm done, Polly! My brain has just turned to mush.'

'Come on, Maxwell, it's the last hurdle. We need to look at it closer.'

She opened the card again and they both read it out slowly.

'Hold on,' Polly pointed at the card. 'Look at the word peal – that's how you spell the ringing of bells. It's something to do with bells.'

'Oh, well done. So, it's something bell… or bells.'

'Right. So, "tied up" – could that be rope? String? Ribbon? Oh, what's that expression? Think, Polly, think…'

She scrunched her eyes closed, forcing her mind to make the vague connection floating around in it.

'Tied up with a pretty little bow! That's it. So, that could be a bow and bells?'

She turned towards Maxwell and found herself being smothered in a bear-hug of an embrace.

'Polly, you really are a genius. Come, we need to go this way and be prepared to run because the other team may decide to follow.'

He grabbed her hand and they ran as fast as they could

out of the square. A loud holler behind them confirmed what Maxwell said.

'This way, I know a shortcut.'

She held onto Maxwell's hand as tightly as possible and did her best to make her shorter legs cover the same distance as his much longer ones as they ran along roads and alleyways until finally Maxwell stopped at a tall, black wooden gate and, using his height advantage, put his arm over the top, felt about and unbolted it, pushing her through quickly before locking it again behind them.

A security light went on and she saw they were surrounded by wooden tables and benches. They were in a pub beer garden.

Maxwell took hold of her hand again, opened a door and took her inside the building. She could hear the clattering of dishes along with shouting.

'Are we in a pub?' she asked, as she followed Maxwell, still running, along the narrow corridor.

'Yes, it's The Bow and Bell. You worked it out.'

They burst through the door into the bar area and Maxwell shouted out, 'We're here! We've done it! We're finished!'

A loud cheer went up and they were enjoying the wild applause when the front doors were flung open and the team who'd tried to follow them traipsed in.

'We're here, we've won!' they shouted out. 'We're the first to arrive!'

'Oh, no you're not!' everyone yelled, as the barman presented the winners with two large glasses of mulled wine.

'Where do you want me to put this?'

'Over there on the worktop would be perfect, thank

you.'

Polly went over to the massive wicker hamper and tore off the cellophane wrapping.

'Here, you take these.'

She took out the bottles of wine and passed them to Maxwell.

'Don't be daft, Polly, you keep them. You did most of the brain work, you should have them.'

'Maxwell, it was a team effort. Besides, I am more than happy with the rest of the prize which I very much doubt you'll have a use for.'

She let her hands trail over the glorious red mixing bowl set with a matching rolling pin, measuring spoons and apron. The vast catering size tub of mincemeat and bag of flour had her itching to get to work.

'I'm sure I could find a use for them. Don't you have enough baking utensils already?'

'Wash your mouth out, young man! There's no such thing as enough when it comes to baking stuff!'

Maxwell laughed as he picked up two bottles of wine.

'I'll take these two and leave the others for us to enjoy another time.'

She walked around the island into his embrace and they passed a couple of minutes kissing until Bailey jumped up and meowed in their ears.

They slowly peeled themselves apart and after giving the cat some fuss and food, Polly picked up the tin with the Gingerbread Swiss Roll in it and they went back out to the pick-up truck.

'Is anyone else coming to dinner tonight?'

'There's us, Mum and Dad and a couple of their friends – Tina and her husband, Errol. I think Mum's trying out a new recipe she's found for cooking duck.'

'Oh, I like duck.'

They'd barely pulled into the yard in front of the old

farmhouse when the door opened and Marian practically ran towards them.

Maxwell hurriedly removed his seatbelt and jumped out of the car. Polly followed suit and was closing the truck door as she heard Marian cry, 'Oh, Maxwell, we have got a problem.'

Before anyone could ask what the problem was, a scream pierced the air.

'MAXIE! MAXIE! OH, MY DARLING MAXIE!'

Once again, in front of her eyes, Polly saw Maxwell disappear behind a profusion of long, black, wild gypsy curls and heard the words, 'I've come back to you, my Maxie, and I'm never going to leave you again.'

36

December 20th

'Damn it! What the hell does that woman think she's playing at?'

Monty was striding up and down the reception area while Polly nursed the grande hot chocolate Andy had made a special visit to Dottie's to obtain.

When Monty had walked in and saw her face that morning, he'd pretty much forced her to tell them everything that had occurred over the weekend. All was fine until she got to the bit where Laurel Devine had seen Maxwell in London. That part of the story had elicited a growl from Monty but he had said nothing, allowing her to continue with her tale.

Upon uttering Laurel's name a second time and advising him that the woman was now holed up in a cabin on his parents' holiday site had, however, been a step too far and a string of expletives had sprung forth from his lips.

He spun round and strode back in her direction.

'Please tell me that Maxwell informed the she-devil to sling her hook and bugger off.'

Polly cast her mind back to the night before and the awkward situation she'd found herself in the middle of.

'Not immediately, no. We went indoors and your dad was in the process of setting another place at the table. Laurel and Maxwell went into the lounge, closing the door behind them. Your mum took me through to the kitchen and thrust a large glass of wine in my hand.'

'Wine? After a shock like that, you needed something much stronger. So, what did she say?'

'Apparently, Laurel turned up just after four o'clock, demanding to see Maxwell. Your mum explained he was out at which point Laurel demanded she call him and tell him to come home. Your mum refused.'

'Good on her!'

'What I don't understand, Monty, is why didn't Laurel just call him herself? They dated; she must have his number.'

'Maxwell changed it when they split up as he wanted a clean break. Laurel was phoning at all hours of the day and night, calling him all sorts of names and expressing her disgust that he'd left her.'

'Well, that's another thing that's confusing me – if Maxwell was the one to break up the relationship, why was Laurel saying she had come back to him?'

'Most likely because, in her vain, empty head, she's twisted the situation to make her look better. I'd heard a rumour that she was telling people she'd broken off the relationship. No doubt a face-saving exercise which she now believes to be true.'

'I see.'

'What happened after that?'

'Dinner was ready and your mum called them through to come and eat. I was sitting next to Maxwell for the first course and he apologised for her arrival.'

Polly didn't think it was necessary to give Monty the full rundown on how much Maxwell had apologised, how he'd held her hand under the table and had squeezed it so hard, conveying to her that he needed her to try and understand.

'Did he say that he'd told her to leave?'

'Not in so many words.'

'Surely, he must have told you more throughout the meal?'

'He most likely intended to but I made the mistake of getting up to help your mum carry the dirty dishes to the kitchen and returned to find Laurel sitting in my seat, practically draped over Maxwell. She was like an octopus – as fast as he moved one of her hands from his person, the other one would move in and take its place. I had no choice but to take her place at the opposite end of the table and was perfectly positioned to watch it all.'

'He wouldn't be such a fool to go back to her, would he?'

Polly closed her eyes at Andy's question. It was one she wasn't qualified to answer and the thought of it made her lower intestines feel like they were being ripped from her body.

'I'm really hoping not, Andy, but for all that he's my brother, I just don't know his thoughts on this one. I can only pray that the way he feels for Polly here is strong enough to override any latent desire he may have for the model.'

'Are you sure he feels something for me, Monty?'

Even though she knew Maxwell held her in some regard, right at this moment, Polly needed to hear reassurance from another quarter. She had to be told by an outsider that what she'd been seeing wasn't a figment of her overly-desiring imagination.

'Oh, sweetie,' Monty knelt in front of her and took a hold of her hand while Andy, sitting beside her on the sofa, placed an arm around her shoulders, 'you would have to be blind to miss the way he looks at you. I really don't think you have anything to worry about. He's going to tell the not-so-Devine bitch to take a long walk off a short pier. I just know he is.'

'How can you be so sure?'

'Because he's my twin brother and I'll bloody well kill him if he doesn't! What did he say to you when he dropped you home?'

'He didn't take me home, your mum's friends dropped me off as they were passing right by the top of my road. He just said he would sort it out before I got into their car.'

'Oh, man!' Monty shook his head. 'I sometimes wonder if he ever gets it. What an idiot. Look, you hang on in there. Everything will work itself out, I promise you.'

Polly was signing for the delivery of a package when a text came in from Maxwell saying he'd pick her up straight from the office that evening. A little smile of irony crossed her face that he should contact her at the same time his Christmas present had arrived.

She asked Monty if he'd mind her taking a slightly longer lunch as she needed to do some supermarket shopping. With so much of her spare time being taken up with her "advent-ures" she'd been struggling to find the time to fit in the big shop that needed to be done. And with Christmas now looming large on the horizon, she wanted it over with before the shops became rammed and the shelves were emptied.

Monty was happy for her to take the time and she used the opportunity to put extra food down for Bailey when she took the groceries, and Maxwell's gift, home.

The rest of the afternoon passed quickly as she continued to deep clean the office and she was now pacing up and down, waiting for Maxwell to appear. She didn't know what she was going to say or how she should act.

Andy, bless him, had told her that the fact he was continuing the festive tasks was an indicator that Laurel's presence in their lives would be short-lived.

She jumped when she heard the door slam at the bottom of the stairs and the heavy footsteps on the wooden treads. Her arms were snaking their way into the sleeves of her coat when Maxwell walked through the upper door.

'Hey, how are you? Are you okay?'

Without any hesitation, he walked over and pulled her into his embrace, holding her tightly against him.

'I am so sorry about last night. I still can't believe Laurel turned up like that. We had a long talk this morning and she gets it now. I've managed to make her understand that we're over and she has to leave.'

'Has she gone now? Is she away?'

Maxwell let out a sigh.

'I'm afraid not. She doesn't drive and the driver she'd hired to bring her up wasn't available until the morning to come back and get her. By this time tomorrow though, she'll be gone. I promise.'

'Hey, bro, what's this I hear? Don't you be upsetting my Polly – this woman is a godsend and I don't want to lose her.'

'I've just been telling Polly that Laurel and I had a long chat and she's leaving in the morning.'

'She damn well better.'

'If she doesn't, Monty, I'll send you round to see her. If that doesn't have her running for the hills, nothing will.'

'Very funny. Just… don't let her ruin your life again. This time, you have far more to lose.'

Maxwell pulled Polly close to his side.

'I know, Monty, I know.'

The radio was the only sound inside the cab of the pick-up. Polly simply didn't know what to say and the atmosphere was strained. The bonhomie Maxwell had shared with his brother seemed to have been left behind in the office.

'Is there any point in me asking where we're off to this evening?'

This drew a smile from Maxwell and that one small gesture was enough to make her relax a little.

When they pulled into the vast hospital car park a short time later, she looked at him in surprise.

'Just trust me. This will be the best night of your life.'

She followed him through the automatic doors and along the brightly lit corridors. The smell of the building hit her and she was pondering on exactly what created it as they entered the lift. Disinfectant was the obvious contender but there was something else that she couldn't put a finger on. So engrossed was she in trying to solve the puzzle that it wasn't until Maxwell stopped at a set of double doors and pushed the buzzer, that she looked up to see where they were.

A blue, eye-level, sign soon told her they were outside the Oncology Ward.

'Maxwell, what—'

The doors opened before she could finish her question and they were quickly ushered into a side room by the ward sister.

'Maxwell, how wonderful to see you again. Thank you for doing this. As always, we are deeply grateful for you giving up your time.'

'Suzie, I've told you before – the pleasure is mine. You

don't have to keep thanking me, I'm more than happy to do it.'

'And this is your helper?'

Suzie looked at Polly and Maxwell quickly stepped in to make the introduction.

'This explains the second bag that was dropped off.'

'Indeed, it does.'

'Then I shall leave you both to get ready.'

'Maxwell, what's going on?'

The minute the door had closed behind the nurse, Polly swung round to face the man smiling behind her.

'All will be revealed in the next few minutes. Now, I believe this one is yours.'

He picked up two suit-hanger bags, weighed them in his hands and passed one over to her.

'I'll draw this curtain across to preserve your modesty as you change.'

Polly hung up the bag on a hook behind her, pulled down the zip and just about passed out when she saw the outfit inside.

'Maxwell Watkins! I'm asking you again – what the HELL is going on?'

37

Once she was changed, Polly pulled back the curtain and was greeted by the sight of Maxwell in full Santa Claus regalia. With his height, he looked magnificent although padding had been used to present the jelly belly the jolly old man was famous for.

'You know, I really should hate you for this,' she muttered, as she walked over to the mirror and carefully attached the pointed ears which had accompanied her elvish outfit.

'But you don't…' he whispered, lifting her hair out of her collar and kissing the back of her neck before letting it slip through his fingers.

'How can I? Listen to that.'

She lifted her hand to indicate the sweet sound of children's voices singing "Jingle Bells", floating down the corridor, in anticipation of the great man's arrival.

'You'll be a brilliant elf. You've seen the film – you know what to do.'

'Hang on a minute, did you know about this when we watched that together?'

'The idea came to me as we were watching it. I do this gig for the kids every year and it seemed the perfect way for you to share it with me.'

She was about to reply when there came a gentle tap at the door. Maxwell walked over to find Suzie on the other side.

'They're all ready for you,' she whispered.

'We're on our way.'

Maxwell walked over to the corner, moved the wheeled screen and picked up the big red sack lying behind it.

'Time to roll, Snowflake, are you ready?'

'As I'll ever be.'

They walked out into the corridor and with a loud "Ho! Ho! Ho!" Santa swung his sack onto his back and strode towards the area where the children were waiting. Polly, deciding that this was a "may as well join them" moment, picked up her feet and skipped along behind him. They entered the room to a cacophony of cheers, whistles and clapping.

Suzie led Santa to sit in a chair which had been decorated with balloons and tinsel. A smaller chair covered in paper snowflakes was lined up beside it.

'Now then, children, let's all give Santa, and his elf, Snowflake, a big, loud hello.'

The children yelled their greeting at the top of their voices and Santa waved to them all.

'Good evening, children. How lovely it is to be here with you tonight. Have you all been good this year?'

'YES!' came the resounding reply.

'Well, I know that you are telling the truth because Sister Suzie over there wrote to tell me how wonderful you all are and asked if I could possibly find a little bit of time to visit you before Christmas Day. When I mentioned this to Snowflake, she was most insistent that we visit and she also gathered up some spare presents. Would anyone here like a present?'

A forest of little hands flew up into the air and Polly couldn't help but smile at their enthusiasm. While Maxwell had been speaking in his deep, Santa voice, she'd had a discreet look around the room and her throat had tightened at the sight of children with hair loss, dark circles in skeletal faces and IV drips attached to their arms. Several were lined up in small chairs in front of them and the nurses had moved the beds round for those who were unable to leave them.

'Now then, children, what I'm going to do is call out the name on the present I take from my sack and that person will put their hand up. Snowflake here will bring your gift to you, okay?'

'Yes, Santa.'

'Good, good! Right, before we begin, I loved the sound of your singing as we arrived so how about we have another song? Who knows "Away in a Manger"?'

Hands shot up again and soon the enchanting melody of the children singing was flowing around her. Polly did her best to join in but had to stop a couple of times to clear her throat when it became too emotional for her.

All too soon, the singing came to an end and she plastered the biggest smile she could onto her face and began helping Santa deliver his gifts.

Twenty minutes later, the red sack was empty and the squeals of joy had subsided.

'Snowflake, please could you help me with this?'

Polly turned around to see a little girl, about eight or nine, holding out a bright blue wig.

'Of course, I can, Maisy. Is the blue one your favourite?'

Maisy had received a number of toy wigs in all colours and styles including a beautiful long blonde plait like Elsa's from the film "Frozen". Polly only knew this because of the packaging but she'd made a mental note to look for the film and watch it.

'I like all the colours, Snowflake, but tonight I'm wearing the blue wig because it matches my socks.'

She lifted her feet up, lost her balance and rolled back on her bed. She was giggling as she sat back up.

Polly held up the wig on one hand, teased the tresses out with her fingers and then turned to face Maisy.

'The best way to put on a wig is to lean your head forward like this,' she pushed her chin down towards her chest and leant forward, 'and then you throw your head back like so…' With a flourish, Polly tipped her head back. 'Now, you try it and I'll put your wig on for you.'

Maisy did as she was asked and Polly slipped the vibrant blue hair over the soft, fluffy down on the little girl's head. Her heart contracted painfully in her chest and, for a moment, her smile was lost. It seemed so wrong that these innocent, young children should be dealing with such a despicable disease.

'How does it look?'

'Beautiful, Maisy. You look beautiful.'

'I'm so happy that Santa gave these to me. I asked my mummy but she said blue and pink hair would look silly.'

'Well, let me assure you, that you do not look silly at all. You are stunning. And I know you're really going to rock the pink wig when you wear that one.'

This elicited another giggle before Maisy's face turned serious.

'Snowflake, can I ask you a question?'

'Of course, you can, poppet.'

'Why are you so tall? I thought elves were supposed to be little.'

'Ah, you see… it's kind of like this… I ate too many vegetables when I was a young elf.'

'You did?'

Polly had to work hard on maintaining her serious expression when faced with the giant blue saucers that Maisy's eyes had become.

'I did. Have you seen the film, "Elf"?'

'Yes.'

'Then you know how much elves like sugar and maple syrup.'

'I know they do. That's really bad for your teeth.'

'It is. And I like those things too but I also liked Brussel sprouts and cauliflower and peas. And I ate lots of them and this is what happened. I grew up and up and up.'

'Santa Claus is really tall – did he eat lots of vegetables too?'

'He absolutely did. Mountains of them.'

'Wow! I don't like vegetables very much.'

'Do you like tomato sauce and gravy?'

'Hmmm. Yes. They're yummy.'

'Then put lots on your vegetables and you'll find they taste so much better.'

'I will. I need to grow up tall because I want to drive a train and I won't be able to see out of the window if I'm small.'

'Indeed, you won't and that would never do. You'd be bumping into trees and sheep and cows…'

Maisy burst out laughing and they were still talking nonsense when Maxwell came over a few minutes later to tell her it was time for them to go.

'If we leave the elves alone for too long, Maisy, they get into all sorts of mischief back home at the North Pole,' he said, still using his Santa voice.

'Bye-bye, Snowflake, bye-bye, Santa. Thank you for my wigs.'

'You're very welcome, Maisy. Merry Christmas.'

They weren't far from home when Polly was finally able to speak. Once they'd changed and slipped out of the ward, she'd been unable to hold back the tears. Maxwell hadn't said anything when he passed her the packet of tissues from the pocket of the cab door.

'Do you do that every year?'

'I do. Have done for the last ten years. My father did it before me. We have the build, you see.'

'Does it get any easier?'

'No, it doesn't. I get through it by forcing myself to see the joy on their little faces when I arrive and not the medical equipment around them.'

'I'm guessing the parents put in the presents.'

'No, that comes from the town. A portion of the charity money we raise each year is put aside for this. Suzie gives us a list of the children's names and what they want Santa to bring and we try to fulfil the request. It's not always possible but most of the time, the gifts are actually rather simple.'

'Like Maisy's wigs.'

'Exactly. They weren't expensive but the happiness she'll get from them is priceless. Life has dealt them a blooming crappy hand; the least we can do is try to make it a little less crappy.'

'Thank you.'

She felt his eyes on her in the dark.

'For what?'

'For sharing. It was tough, being there, but I'm glad you included me. It was… special. It's good to be reminded that there's always people worse off than yourself.'

He took her hand and held it gently for a moment before giving it a squeeze and releasing it.

They were driving up the hill that led to the top of her lane when Maxwell suddenly said, 'Uh oh, what the heck?'

She looked up out the windscreen and saw big fat snowflakes hurling themselves against it.

'Er, I thought you said we were going to miss the snow? That the wind had changed direction or something…'

'That's what the weather report said at the weekend.'
'Then I think they got it wrong,' she replied, as they pulled into her driveway and saw the fresh white flakes already laying down their blanket.

38

December 21st

'I'll bet you're glad you don't go outside, Bailey. I'd lose you if you went out there!'

Polly was sitting on her sofa looking out at the patio. Or rather, where the patio would be if there wasn't about a foot and a half of snow piled up against the patio doors. It looked like the wind had been blowing down from the hills because a closer inspection – as in a look out the window – showed her that the snow had drifted up against the doors. There wasn't actually that depth of snow all over the garden.

There was enough though! She'd gone out to check the bird bath after she'd had her shower and breakfast and the snow had been up to her ankles. She hadn't been impressed with Ritchie's farewell present of a pair of fluorescent pink wellie boots earlier in the year but she'd sent up a silent prayer of thanks when she'd slipped into them this morning.

She was watching the news on the television, astonished at the swathe of white which appeared to be covering all of Britain from the Midlands in England right up to the central belt of Scotland, when a text came through on her phone.

"Hi Pol, due to the weather, Andy & I have decided to close the office now until after New Year.
Enjoy your extra days. Luv Monty.
PS – you'll still be paid. A bonus for all the cleaning you've done! Lol lol x"

'Oh!'

She sat down at the breakfast bar, composed a reply and after hitting "send" sat back and wondered what to do with herself. The book she was reading was pretty good – maybe a day curled up on the sofa with Bailey and a coffee would be nice. After all the excursions with Maxwell lately, it would be rather lovely to just kick back and relax.

Pleased with her decision to have an easy day, she was heading up to the bedroom to retrieve her book when she heard her phone ping again. Polly did a U-turn on the stairs and returned to the lounge.

"Hey, Snowflake, I'll be with you in two hours. Dress up warm.
Definitely wear the sexy underwear! M. xxx"

She sat for a moment, trying to decide what to do between now and Maxwell's arrival. If she curled up with her book as intended, there was every chance she'd lose track of time and end up rushing about to get ready. She was into the last third where all the action was ramping up and the temptation of "just one more chapter" would be too great. A glance in the direction of the kitchen reminded her of the big tub of mincemeat she'd won in the treasure hunt and which was still sitting on the worktop. A sudden desire for some Viennese mince pies hit her and the decision was made.

'Sorry, Bailey, I'm afraid our chill-out session has just been delayed. It would seem that even extreme weather conditions will not deter Mr Maxwell Watkins from his endeavours!'

The fluffball purred loudly as his chin received an unexpected scratch then Polly retraced her steps back towards her bedroom to lay out what she planned to wear before baking up a storm in the kitchen.

'Hey, you good to go?'

Maxwell leant down and kissed her before she had a chance to answer. Once he let her back up for air, she nodded before turning to lock the front door.

'Blooming heck! What have you got on your feet?'

'Oi, don't mock the wellies!'

'They're pink! Very bloody pink!'

'Yes, they are, I'll give you that, but they will also keep my feet dry and that matters more to me than being a fashion statement.'

'Well, at least I'll be able to find you if you fall in a ditch!'

'Cheeky sod!'

She walked around him and then stopped in her tracks.

'Er… where's the truck?'

Polly looked around but all she could see were the large footprints in the snow where Maxwell had walked from the gate to her door.

'It's back home. I wasn't driving out in this.'

'So, how did you get here?'

'I walked. Well, most of the way and then I got a lift. It's not so far when you walk through the woods. At most a mile and a half as the crow flies. It's the winding road route that makes it further in the car.'

'Right. I didn't realise you were as close as that.'

Just then the sound of howling ripped through the air.

'What on earth—'

She spun around to look at Maxwell and saw him grinning widely.

'Give me your hand. Boy, have I got a good advent-ure for you today!'

He held her fingers tightly between his as he half-dragged her up the slippery hill. Her wellies may be keeping her feet snug but their grip in the snow was next to useless.

At the top of the hill, they crossed the main road. She was glad to see the snow lacked any tyre tracks as the thought of vehicles trying to go down the steep hill didn't bear thinking about.

On the opposite side of the road, Maxwell sprang over the drystone wall and then held out his hands to help Polly over. As she landed in the snow next to him, the howling turned to barking and when Maxwell stepped to one side, she was treated to the sight of a low-slung sled and eight beautiful Huskies standing waiting a little further into the field.

Utterly speechless, she simply stood looking. She'd finally run out of words having already used up her "wows", "amazings", "brilliants" and "stunnings" – she had nothing left that would do justice to this latest surprise.

'Good advent-ure?'

'Yes. So very, very, yes!'

'Wanna ride on the sled?'

'Oh, yes please! Double yes with extra bells on it.'

He led her over to the dogs and sled and introduced her to Simone, the musher.

'I'm sorry? Did you say "musher"?'

'Yes. Dog driver to anyone not involved in the sport of mushing.'

'I see.'

She was quiet for a moment, thrilled but confused by their presence.

'Okay, guys, I'm sorry but can one of you please explain how… why… whatever… you are doing here? I'm trying to get my head around it.'

'Simone competes in dog sledding around the world and just so happens to live a few miles from here. When I saw the snow this morning, I knew she'd be out running the dogs on the sled and so begged the favour of a ride from her.'

'He's a very persuasive chap and we go back a long way so I didn't have the heart to say no. Then, when he told me he was trying to impress a beautiful lady…'

'Hey! I did not say that!'

Simone laughed and winked at Polly.

'Maybe not in so many words but I got the picture. And you definitely are a beautiful lady.'

The blood rushed from her brain to her cheeks which must have been the reason for her inability to come up with a suitable response so she chose to change the subject.

'Would I be correct in thinking these are all Siberian Huskies?'

'You would.'

'I thought so because they all have blue eyes.'

'What difference does that make?' Maxwell asked.

'Malamutes, which are very similar to Siberian Huskies, have brown eyes. Huskies can have brown or blue eyes but pure-bred Malamutes can only have brown eyes.'

'Well, check you out, Barbara Woodhouse!'

'Am I allowed to pet them?' she asked Simone, ignoring Maxwell's quip.

'Later, once they've been run and burnt off some

energy. Now, if sir and madam would like to hop on board, we'll get going. Apparently, there's more of the white stuff on the way so we need to make the most of this bright sunshine while we can.'

She followed Maxwell over to the sled and memories of her reindeer ride came back to her. This sled couldn't have been more different. She'd had to climb up into the reindeer sleigh, this time her bottom was mere inches away from the snow. Maxwell sat down first and she had to position herself between his legs, leaning against his chest. He crossed his arms over her as Simone wrapped some fur-lined throws around them and tucked them in before taking up her position behind and above them.

'Okay, are you ready?'

'Are you ready?' Maxwell whispered in her ear.

'Yes, I am. I really am.'

'We're good here, Simone, ready when you are.'

'HIKE!'

The dogs, which had been lying and standing when they'd arrived, were all now standing to attention and on Simone's command, began to run. It didn't take long for them to gather speed and they were flying across the field.

Polly let out a small squeal when she saw they were heading towards the open gateway in the wall but they flew through it with plenty of room to spare and onto an open pathway. She wasn't sure if they were on a road or a farm track because it was covered in snow but she assumed it would be the latter as there could be no way the sled would be allowed on the public roads.

She felt Maxwell's arms tighten around her and she relaxed back into him. She was perfectly safe. Simone had total control of her dogs and so she decided she literally would just sit back and enjoy the ride.

39

'Oh, that was so much fun! I loved it.'

Polly was kicking the snow off her wellies by the front door. Maxwell was doing the same.

'I'm thrilled you enjoyed it so much. It wouldn't be for everyone but I like to think I know you well enough by now. When I saw the snow this morning, it was the first thing I thought of, hence the phone call to Simone.'

She closed the front door behind them and let out a little groan of joy.

'Aaaahhh, that feels so good. Underfloor heating is the best. Wellies are great for keeping your feet dry but they do lose out on the warmth part, even with the thermal socks.'

'You need to get yourself a pair of real wellington boots, those out there are just fashion items and no good for this kind of weather.'

'Right! I'll bear that in mind.'

She threw a grin over her shoulder as she walked into the lounge. Bailey was still in the same spot he'd been occupying when she went out and it didn't look like he'd moved at all.

'Can I tempt you to a big hot cup of coffee and some mince pies? I made a batch of Viennese ones earlier.'

'Oh, yes please! I love Viennese mince pies, they're my favourite. It's so hard to find nice ones though. They always have too much biscuit topping and not enough filling so they're really dry to eat.'

'I quite agree. That's why I learnt to make my own with just enough of the biscuit topping to give you the texture and flavour and loads of mincemeat to avoid the feeling of eating sawdust.'

'Yes, that's exactly what they can be like!'

She filled the kettle and flipped it on before taking the coffee jug from the cupboard. Maxwell sat on one of the bar stools against the island.

'Help yourself, Maxwell, they're in those tins in front of you.'

She watched from the corner of her eye as he opened the tin and inhaled the rich spicy scent before picking out a pie and biting into it. The immediate look of pleasure was all she needed to see. The pies were good.

When she placed his coffee in front of him, he was pushing his fingertips onto the counter in order to pick up the crumbs which had dropped. She passed him a side plate and told him to have as many as he wished.

'Don't say that, I'll end up eating the whole tin.'

'Then you'll be doing my waistline a favour. Besides, the filling used in these barely made a dent in that tub we won so I can easily make more.'

He put two on his plate and she did likewise. After placing the lid back on, they walked through to the lounge.

Polly looked out of the window as they sat down.

'I'm still getting the hang of the weather patterns up here but that sky over there above the hills is looking really dark.'

Maxwell looked out to where she was pointing.

'Hmmm, you're right. It looks like we've got another dump on its way.'

'I switched off the news earlier before the weather update – do you know how long they expect this to continue for?'

'The last I saw before leaving this morning is that we should expect more snowfall and a thaw isn't anticipated until next week – possibly Wednesday if we're lucky.'

'Blimey! Oh!'

A thought hit her out of the blue and she couldn't believe she'd forgotten about the uninvited guest over at the holiday site.

'Are you okay?'

Maxwell had a look of concern on his face.

'Laurel. You said last night that her car was coming today to pick her up but…'

Her voice trailed off as they both turned to look once again at the snow outside.

'Shit! I… I totally forgot about that.'

'You forgot? How on earth could you forget?'

'Very easily! Mum had the sense to put her in a cabin well away from mine and I was up and out this morning before she'd have even opened her eyes. In my mind, she'd already gone but as you have just pointed out, she won't be. Unless she's decided to hike back to London which will never happen. Damn it!'

He stood up, picked up his plate and mug and returned them to the kitchen.

'I'm sorry, Snowflake, I need to go. It's growing quite grey out there and while I know the woods well, the snow changes everything and navigating in the dark is less fun. I also suspect that Mum may have been lumbered with Laurel all day so I need to go and rescue her. I'll be in her bad books now for sure.'

'Would Laurel impose upon your mother?'

'Yes, she would. Looking after herself is something she can't do. There'll be no food in the cabin because it wouldn't occur to her that not everyone is prepared to drop everything to run around after her and she should bring her own supplies. And even if the cabin was stocked up, she'd STILL turn up at the farmhouse expecting to be waited upon.'

He ran his fingers through his hair and Polly saw how concerned and agitated he'd become.

'Then you'd better get going. Marian strikes me as a lady who won't hold back on letting her displeasure be known.'

'You've got that one right.'

He walked out to the door and began pulling his boots on while Polly went into the kitchen, topped up one of the tins with mince pies and put it in a bag.

'Here,' she handed it to him at the door, 'a peace offering for your mum. It might just be enough to soften her temper.'

'Thank you, you're an angel. I can't see them making too much of a difference but we can hope.'

He pulled her into an embrace but the kiss she received was swift and fleeting before he opened the door and rushed off. There wasn't even a wave as he marched through the gate.

Polly closed the door and locked it up for the night as she wouldn't be going back out again. She walked slowly into the lounge and sat down on the sofa while her head whirled with all sorts of thoughts and her heart drummed with all kinds of emotions.

Her biggest concern was how abruptly Maxwell's manner had changed when she'd brought up Laurel. They'd gone from being chilled and relaxed to him being flustered and jumpy. Was it really concern for his mother that had caused the change or was there still a hangover from his relationship with Laurel that he wasn't aware of? He said he no longer had feelings for her but was this a form of bravado and deep down, he still did?

A heartfelt sigh slipped from her lips. Polly knew that this was something outside of her control and she just had to hope the time they'd been spending together of late had made enough of an impact on his heart to push out anything he still felt for the other woman.

40

December 22nd

'Now that, Bailey, was a darn good book! What an ending!'

Polly closed the cover on her e-book and snuggled back down under the blankets. Bailey crawled up the bed and came to a stop in the crook of her arms. She burrowed her nose into his dense, soft fur and cuddled him close. After a restless night where her mind refused to switch off, she'd finally drifted into sleep just after three am. To make up for that, she'd treated herself to a long lie in, with breakfast in bed, this morning.

Now that her thoughts were no longer being distracted by the tense action of her thriller, her brain decided it was time for her to think about Maxwell again. He'd made no mention of meeting up today when he'd left last night and as the snow was just as thick this morning as it had been yesterday, she figured he'd finally run out of things they could do. In fairness, he'd done really well to find something new and different for the last twenty-one days, so she couldn't hold it against him if the weather had stymied him at the last few hurdles.

Her phone pinged and she twisted round to get it from the bedside table while trying not to disturb Bailey. The screen showed it was a message from Maxwell.

'Bailey, I swear that man is developing the ability to read my mind! How is it that just as I think about him, a text comes in? I mean, seriously? How does he do it?'

She tapped in her pin number and opened up the message.

"Morning! I hope you're well. I'll be with you at noon. You'll need the hot undies again. LOL XXX"

'Wow, three big kisses now, Bailey. I think the boy might be getting serious. What do you think?'

The cat opened one eye and let out a little mew.

'You think I should quit overthinking it and have a bit more sleep before he arrives?'

Bailey gave a little snuffle as he pulled his tail up over his face.

'Fair enough, oh wise grey one. I will follow your advice.'

And with those words, she set an alarm on her phone, dropped it onto the bedside table and followed Bailey's example, although due to the lack of a big fluffy tail, she pulled the duvet up over her face instead.

'I don't believe you! Is this really what we're doing today?'

'It sure is! So far, you've had a sleigh ride and a sled ride. It seems only right to complete the hat-trick with some proper sledging. We've got one each!'

Maxwell pointed at the two plastic sledges propped up against the wall next to the door.

'And where will we be doing this sledging?'

'The hills over there, out your back.'

'What? The hills I can see in the distant horizon from my lounge window?'

'That's the ones.'

'But they're miles away.'

Polly didn't mind a nice hike when the weather was fair but she knew she'd be done in by the time they got there from traipsing through the snow. Maxwell seemed to forget that not everyone had his long legs.

'They're not that far. It's only a mile and a half.'

'That's a mile and a half in deep snow.'

'Do you have a better suggestion?'

'Yes! Why not use the hill on the lane? It's steep enough and has enough length at the bottom for a decent run-off.'

'There's the small matter of traffic, Snowflake.'

'Look, Yeti—'

'Yeti?'

'Yes, Yeti! If you're going to keep calling me Snowflake, then it's only right that I return the favour. It's not fair for you to go without a pet name!'

Maxwell let out a burst of laughter.

'Fine. If it makes you happy.'

'It makes us even. Now, as I was saying, Yeti, there are only four houses on this lane and not one of them has moved their cars since yesterday morning. Apart from the lack of tyre tracks in the lane, I can see their driveways from my upstairs windows and all the cars are buried under snow. If they are planning on going anywhere, they won't be moving at speed so we'll have plenty of time to get out of their way.'

'Okay. You present a good argument, come on. Get those feet in your wellies.'

Within a few minutes, they were standing at the top of the lane. Polly walked out onto the main road to check for any traffic but it was all clear. She was surprised to see some tyre tracks in the snow although they looked as though they were made by one vehicle. When she pointed them out to Maxwell, he advised her that it was probably one of the snow ploughs and gritters making their way back from the big A-road which skirted around the town.

'Why didn't they grit this road?'

'Most likely they didn't have any left on board after doing the ring road but if the snow was still falling, it would have been buried underneath and wasted.'

'So, when will this road be done?'

'The ring road takes priority and then the main roads are next. If there are no further snowfalls, or heavy ones at least, you could see this done tomorrow or the next day. It will all come down to whatever the weather is bringing next.'

'Then it looks like we'll be completely safe to do our sledging here.'

She looked down the lane and checked for any potential obstacles like bins outside the gates but it was all clear. In fact, it was the perfect sledging course and she couldn't wait to get going. She hadn't been sledging since she was a child—

WHAM!

Polly grabbed the top of the dry-stone wall and used it to steady her from the memory which had slammed into her head.

She was on a sledge, a red plastic one similar to the sledges Maxwell had brought along today, and she was flying down a hill. The wind was rushing past her face and a pair of long legs covered in thick brown cord and tucked into black wellingtons were wrapped around her. An arm was across her chest while the other was holding the rope at the front of the sledge. She was giggling and laughing while shouting "Faster, faster" and she could feel the rumble of her dad's laughter against her back. When they'd reached the flat area and came to a stop, she was straight off the sledge, grabbing the rope from her father's hand and shouting, "More, more, more" while rushing back up the hill as quickly as her pink-clad, seven-year-old legs and red wellie covered feet could go.

They'd made numerous runs that day but she now recalled the best one. As the slope had become busier, they'd had to change their downhill course which took them across an overhang they hadn't seen. The next thing Polly knew was that they were both flying through the air before dropping down with an almighty thump. The sledge and her father disappeared as she went rolling off down the hill and came to a stop in a snow-filled ditch. She now recalled that when her dad had pulled her out, she'd been laughing so hard her sides were sore and her first words were, "Can we do that again?"

'Polly, what's wrong?'

Maxwell's voice cut through her thoughts and she realised she was actually laughing out loud while gripping the wall.

'Nothing's wrong,' she assured him, 'nothing at all. I was just hit by a memory of sledging with my dad when I was little and it made me laugh.' She shared what she'd remembered with him.

'It sounds to me like you were always one for an adventure, even at that young age.'

'It does seem that way, doesn't it? I wonder why I changed?'

'Maybe because the person who made you feel so brave was taken from you. Don't underestimate how deeply such a loss can affect you.'

'Yeah, that could be it. I suppose it's easy to be brave when you know there's someone around to protect you.'

'So, how brave are you feeling now? Are we sharing a sledge or is it one each?'

She looked up at him and grinned.

'You're on your own, mate! I'm going to race your ass to the bottom!'

'Is that so?'

'It is so!'

She took one of the sledges, placed it between her feet, dropped down onto it and with an almighty push off, lifted her legs and pulled them up in front of her.

'WHEEEEEEEEEEEEEEEEEEEEEEEEEEEEEEE EEEEEEEE' she yelled, as she hurtled down the slope.

She'd come to a slow halt just before the hedging at the bottom of the lane and was hauling herself up when Maxwell slid up alongside her.

'Good?'

'Bloody brilliant!'

And with a laugh, she grabbed her sledge and began making her way back up the hill.

41

'Now, you promise you'll come over for drinks after Christmas?'

'I promise. Thank you.'

'No, thank *you*, I can't remember the last time we had such fun.'

The day had grown dark, the street lights had come on and Polly was saying goodnight to her neighbours as they all made their way back indoors.

She and Maxwell had been on their sixth or seventh run down the lane when Emma and Matt had walked out their gate, all wrapped up and pulling sledges behind them.

'We've come to join in, if you don't mind. You look like you're having such a good time.'

'Hey, the more the merrier.'

Maxwell had been quick to greet them and soon the men were bonding over techniques to make the sledges go faster.

Twenty minutes had barely gone by when the family who occupied the house at the furthest end of the lane had come out to join in. The children were mere toddlers but that didn't stop them having a jolly time although their father had spent more time filming them than playing with them. Eventually, Polly had gone over to him and offered to do some filming of him and his wife together with the children. It didn't seem fair that he wouldn't be included in these moments when they were watched back in years to come.

The last person to join them was Mrs Sophie who was Polly's closest neighbour. She was an older lady who had once been a schoolteacher and carried herself with an authoritative air. Everyone called her Mrs Sophie although she was actually Mrs Sophie Reynolds. No one could recall what had happened to Mr Reynolds and no one dared ask.

Not wishing to be left out but unable to join in the fun of the sledging, she'd arrived at her gate, warmly wrapped up and pushing a hostess trolley with two large flasks of hot chocolate and homemade chocolate cookies.

She'd declined the offer of a turn on the sledges initially, citing her old bones as a good reason to give it a miss but the silver-tongued Maxwell had talked her round and she'd had a good old laugh as the men took it in turns to pull her along on the flat and then take her half-way up the hill from which she'd sledged down on her own.

'Oh, girls, what a day I've had. Thank you. Now, if you'll excuse me, I need to go and change my Tena lady!'

With a wink, she turned and pushed her trolley back to the house. Once the door was closed behind her, Emma had turned to Polly and asked, 'Did she just say what I think she did?'

'She most certainly did!'

The women looked at each other for a couple of seconds and then burst out laughing.

'Oh, I'll never look at Mrs Sophie in the same way again after that,' Emma coughed through the giggles that she couldn't seem to stop.

'Ah, good on her! She's still got some life about her,' Polly grinned back.

The fading light had seen Maxwell saying goodbye. As he'd walked over through the woods to her again that day, he had to leave before darkness fell. He'd left the sledges with her so she could continue to play with her new friends. Those had been his exact words and she smiled as she once again kicked the snow off her boots outside her door. She felt she had made new friends today and she was looking forward to getting to know Emma better. Some of the banter they'd exchanged together and with their respective partners, suggested that the woman shared the same sense of humour and would be good company. She would absolutely be taking up the offer of meeting for Christmas drinks next week.

All warmed up from her hot shower and a bowl of pasta, Polly sat down to do something she hadn't done since she was a teenager – wrap Christmas presents!

After she'd ordered Maxwell's gift that day, she'd dithered and pondered on whether she should get gifts for the rest of his family who had somehow become a part of her life. She didn't know if it was the right thing to do and if it would seem too much with having only known Maxwell himself for just a few weeks.

She'd worked on a process of elimination. Monty and Andy were definitely in the running for a gift as they'd been so kind to her. She'd decided to get them one of the new-fangled hot chocolate machines that were now all the rage as they both loved their sweet beverage although Dottie might be less pleased at the drop in her takings. The decision on a gift for the children was taken from her hands when she was looking online for some new, festive, cookie cutters and a child's baking set had popped up in her search. It was just so cute that she'd been unable to resist and so had bought one each for Alanna and Taylor. This then led her onto Marian. Maxwell's mother had been so kind and friendly and when a book of Victorian Cooking had jumped out at her in the Chatsworth gift shop, Marian had been the first person she'd thought of and it had been bought alongside the baking book she'd chosen for herself. For David, Maxwell's dad, she'd had to do a spot of re-gifting. When they'd chatted on Sunday night over dinner, she'd found out that they shared a love for jigsaw puzzles. Polly had ordered one for him the following day but thanks to the weather, it had yet to be delivered. Fortunately, she had a couple of unopened puzzles which she could use as substitutes although she wasn't sure if they would be to his taste, but needs must.

That had left Helen. Although they'd only met the once, the woman had been pleasant enough despite the hard look Polly had caught sight of, and it didn't feel right to be giving gifts to all of her family and not include her. In the end, she'd bought her a small bottle of the perfume she'd been wearing when they'd met – it was one Polly herself wore occasionally and she'd recognised it.

As she spread the wrapping paper out in front of her and placed the little cuts of sticky tape along the side of the coffee table, she suddenly felt the need for some mood music.

'Alexa, play Christmas music, please.'

When the last gift was wrapped and she had a little festive stack of presents in front of her, Polly felt a surge of excitement flow through her. It was a feeling she hadn't felt for many, many, years.

It was her Christmas spirit finally breaking free.

42

December 23rd

'Mum has asked me to tell you that you're invited over for dinner tomorrow night. Well, to give the evening its proper title, "Buffet and Boards Night". A number of family and friends are invited to partake in a buffet and play board games.'

'That sounds like fun.'

'It usually is. Everyone gathers at four o'clock and they play whatever games they want until seven-thirty. Then teams are made up and we hit the Trivial Pursuit. The buffet is set up in the dining room for people to pick at, as and when they wish. It's a nice, relaxed time.'

'Then I accept the invite.'

'Mum will be pleased.'

Maxwell had arrived on her doorstep at eleven that morning with no prior warning. He hadn't looked in the best of moods when she'd opened the door so Polly had just stood back, let him in and said nothing. When Trevor

269

had walked about looking like that, she'd learnt that it was best to stay quiet until it either blew over or he was ready to talk and get it off his chest. She'd employed the same tactic with Maxwell and after coffee, mince pies and Bailey straddling his lap, he'd slowly unwound. She still didn't know the cause of his ire, although she certainly had her suspicions, and she wasn't sure she wanted to ask.

'That bloody woman is doing my head in! She won't leave me alone!' he suddenly spat out.

Ah! Her suspicions had been right. Laurel Devine was at the root of the issue.

'Want to talk about it?'

'Not really but I think I'll explode if I don't.'

'I'm all ears.'

'I shouldn't be burdening you with this.'

'Maxwell,' she moved beside him and wound her fingers through his. 'You've listened time and again to me talking about my dad, my mum, my ex-husband… I think you've earned the right to offload onto me. So, tell me, what's been going on?'

'Oh, she's just being a total pain. I told you the other day about how she can't do anything for herself so she's expecting us all to drop whatever we're doing to entertain her. She's bored because she arrived thinking I was just going to fall back into her arms and is very put out that I haven't. I tried to be courteous and invited her to join us on our recent adventures but she wasn't interested.'

He'd done what?

Polly gasped, utterly shocked by this revelation. He'd invited that she-devil to come with them on their special days?

What?

What did that mean?

Maxwell continued to stare out of the window and missed seeing her concerned expression.

'Did you think she would join us when you asked?'

'Gosh no, what we were doing was far too physical and too much fun for Laurel to be interested. The only pastimes she likes are the ones where all the attention is on herself. I simply asked so I had a comeback when she inevitably threw it back in my face. Which she did this morning.'

Polly slowly let out a breath and prised herself off the "high doh" her Scottish grandmother always used to exclaim about whenever she was strung up over something. He'd extended the invitations safe in the knowledge they'd be declined. Phew, that was a relief.

'What happened this morning?'

'Oh, she only turned up at the door of my cabin wearing nothing more than a thong, a fur coat and a pair of stupid high-heeled boots.'

BOINGGGG!

Polly was right back up on that high doh thing again!

'She did… she did what? Please, tell me you're kidding me.'

'I wish I was, Snowflake! I just about died when I opened the door and saw her there. I was expecting Helen with the kids' presents and instead, I found something else wanting to be unwrapped.'

'What did you do?'

'Well, I had to get her indoors before she caught her death of cold. The stupid woman had walked across half the site in that state. She was blue by the time she got to mine. Fur coat or no fur coat – she wasn't going to stay warm for long with zero clothing on.'

'And then?'

She really hoped she was managing to keep the jealousy out of her voice because inside, Polly was raging fit to burst.

'Then, she opens the coat, drops it to the floor and tries to get all sexy on me!'

271

Thanks, she thought, *that's what I really wanted to hear, Maxwell.*

'Erm, too much information there, Yeti.'

'Oh, of course, sorry. Anyway, to cut to the chase, I forced her into one of my sweatshirts, a pair of jeans, and marched her back to the farmhouse. I had to get her out of my cabin as quickly as possible.'

'Why? Were you tempted to take her up on her offer?'

'What?' This time it was Maxwell's turn to gasp. 'No, absolutely not. It's just… she'd stayed there with me in the past when we were up this way and after we split up, it took a while to stop seeing her around the place. I didn't want to risk being in that position again.'

'Of course. That makes sense.'

Polly felt her heart tumbling down through her body. You would only have such a concern if you still carried feelings for that person. If you were over someone, they could be in your space but not leave an imprint after they'd left. Her worry from earlier in the week came flooding back to her – did Maxwell still harbour feelings for Laurel that he wasn't aware of?

'I'm sorry, I missed what you said there. Can you say it again, please?'

With a great deal of effort, she pushed her concern to one side and listened to Maxwell's tale of woe.

'I said, I left Laurel with Mum who was none too pleased to see her again. She takes picky eating to whole new levels and has been demanding egg-white omelettes and for her food to be cooked in accordance with her keto diet.

'Her what diet?'

Maxwell laughed. 'That's exactly what my mum said. Followed by telling her in no uncertain terms that she'd get what she was given and the only exception she'd accept was if Laurel was vegetarian. Which she definitely is not.

When Laurel retorted spitefully that she'd put on weight if she ate that sort of rubbish, Mum just sniffed and said it wouldn't do her any harm as she'd seen more meat on a butcher's pencil.'

'Marian doesn't spare her words!'

'She certainly doesn't. After that, Mum walked out of the room muttering she was my problem and I need to sort it.'

'But, what can you do? You can't drive her back home, can you?'

'No. Not only are the roads still blocked but the thought of being in the same space as her for that length of time is enough to drive me nuts. I'd probably end up doing her a damage which wouldn't be good for anyone.'

'Is there any more news on when the roads out of town will be cleared?'

'No. The last I heard is there's a shortage of gritters and it's now looking to be after Christmas.'

How was it possible for Polly to feel her heart sink even lower when it was already down in her boots? You didn't need to be a rocket scientist to know that the longer Laurel was around, the greater the chance of Maxwell's feelings for her being resurrected and coming back to the surface. And when all was said and done, no matter what way you turned it, Polly didn't stand a snowflake's chance in hell of holding onto her yeti while the supermodel was in town.

<u>43</u>

'Why do I need to wear this?'

'To know which team you're on.'

Polly pulled the bright orange hi-vis vest closed and squashed the Velcro strips together.

'Do you mind holding this while I put mine on, please?'

Maxwell handed her his rucksack.

'What are we doing that requires me, or us, to be in teams?'

She looked at the crowd around her. They were in the car park adjacent to the football ground and there were stewards walking about with clipboards and bags of different brightly coloured vests.

'Oh, you'll soon find out. I can promise you though, it's going to be fun.'

'Hmm, we'll see.'

It had been quite the surprise when Maxwell, after spilling his woes all over her lounge, had looked at his watch and exclaimed, 'Crap, is that the time? We need to hurry or we'll be late.'

She'd then been told to put on her "sexy" thermals

again – thank goodness she'd now taken to washing them every night – and to get wrapped up, they were going out.

In the space of twenty minutes, she was dressed, booted up and they were rushing out the door and down the lane into the town. They'd scurried through the streets which were busier than she'd expected and several of the shops were open for business. She barely had time to wish she'd known this sooner before they were speed-walking down the alley that led towards the river and the football ground. It was with only a couple of minutes to spare that they'd "registered" onto their team.

A whistle ripped through the air and all the chattering ceased. An air of anticipation began to build and soon a voice came over the tannoy.

'Ladies and gentlemen. Welcome to the twenty-third Calderly Top Chucker. You all know the rules by now but for those of you who don't, they're very simple. There are no rules!'

At this, a loud cheer went up followed by much laughter.

'However, as a reminder, when the whistle blows, each team must return to their designated stand immediately. Any chucking which occurs before the start whistle or after the finish whistle will see that team disqualified. Now, can you all gather together into your group colours, please. Your team marshall will be with you momentarily to take you to your designated stand. Thank you.'

'The Calderly Top Chucker? What on earth is that?'

'You'll find out in about ten minutes. I think you'll like it.'

It wasn't long before their team marshall came over and advised them that they had been allocated the west stand and they should follow her round.

'Well, that's a stroke of luck. The west stand is covered and has the best loos. It'll make waiting in between bouts more comfortable.'

They walked through the turnstiles which had been opened up and made their way out to the seated area around the football pitch. Or rather, the deep, snow-covered pitch which had a two-foot high, piece of plastic orange netting stretched across it. Polly calculated it was roughly where the halfway line would be.

'Have you worked it out yet?'

She stared at the pitch for a few more seconds.

'Nope! Still haven't got a clue.'

Maxwell chuckled as the tannoy crackled into life again.

'Could the blue team adults and the yellow team adults please take their places.'

The two groups wearing the hi-vis vests in those colours walked down onto the pitch, one on each side of the netting.

The tannoy crackled again.

'On your marks, get set, GO!'

A piercing whistle blew and the teams flew into action.

'Oh, my word!' Polly exclaimed. 'It's a snowball fight!'

'It sure is! A good old-fashioned snowball fight.'

She watched as the snow on the pitch was gathered up, rolled into snowballs and thrown in all directions.

'All the teams on this side of the netting are our groups, so we support them. The teams over on that side,' he pointed at the areas furthest from them, 'will be our opponents, so we can boo them.'

Polly glanced around her and heard her fellow orange-clad team members shouting their support to the blue team directly in front of their stand and applauding when the opposition took a good hit.

'Are there winners? Or is it all for fun?'

'There are independent adjudicators who make the

decisions after each round. The rounds last ten minutes. The team which collectively appears to be wearing the least amount of snow is declared the winner of that round. There are three rounds and whichever team colour has the most wins on each side goes up against the top team on the other side for the final. We also have the juniors but their rounds are only seven minutes.'

'Do they give out prizes?'

'The winning group gets a badge. It's nothing fancy – just a round badge with "Winner" on it and the year. It's a thing in the town to try and have as many of these badges as possible.'

'Do you have any?'

'I do.'

'How many?'

'Including my junior badges, I have fifteen.'

'Wow! That's quite a lot.'

'I've been lucky to be on some good teams.'

'Or have they been lucky to have you? I'm guessing your build has been to their benefit.'

He shrugged. 'Maybe.'

Polly turned her attention back to the action on the pitch. So far, it looked to her as though the blue team were winning this bout.

'That bloke there,' she pointed, 'he's not throwing, just making the snowballs. Are team tactics employed here?'

'Oh yes! People will play to their skills so those who know throwing is not a strength will make the snowballs for those who are better at it. The glory is shared at the end of the day so we all work together.'

'Then I think I may be better placed making the snowballs, I don't think I'm the best at throwing.'

'Have a go at both and see how you get on. Now, you need to wear these.'

Maxwell handed her a pair of latex gloves.

She took them and looked at them in confusion.

'Why?'

'They help to make better snowballs. The snow sticks to your fabric gloves and impedes both the quality of your snowballs and your throwing. Put these over the top. I have fifteen badges which makes me a bit of an expert so I know what I'm talking about.'

He helped her to put on the gloves and she returned the favour. A loud whistle came over the tannoy and the first round was finished. The blue team were declared the winners. She then watched in amazement as a bunch of teenagers ran out onto the pitch with large bin bags and began scattering out fresh snow.

'They gather up the snow from the town centre and bring it here. It means there aren't any large piles of snow getting in the way around the town and that each team has a fair supply of snow.'

When the teenagers ran off the pitch, the next announcement came over the air. The orange team were up!

Polly followed Maxwell and her group down the steps of the stand. She did a quick head count and worked out there were about twenty of them. Some of the parents with children had stayed behind.

'Okay, Snowflake, let's see what you've got!'

The whistle blew and all around her white snowy missiles began to fly. She decided to err on the side of caution and worked on building a stack of snowballs for Maxwell and the man standing next to him to use. She did this for a few minutes until she realised that the group seemed to have more ammo providers than ammo throwers. As she debated whether to change her role, she spotted a woman just across the net who was tall with long, black curly hair. Polly knew it wasn't Laurel but the resemblance was just enough to get her dander up and the next thing she knew, she was pelting snowballs with all her might. The frustration of the last five days released itself through her fingers and the poor woman didn't stand a chance. When the whistle blew for the end of their round, she looked like a walking snowman.

'Okay, Snowflake, we need to have a talk about the supposed lack of throwing skills you think you have. You were a demon!'

They walked off the pitch as the victors of that round and Maxwell took a flask of hot chocolate from his rucksack.

'I guess all that hand-mixing when I bake has some benefits,' was all she said, figuring that the real reason behind her ability was something he was better off not knowing.

'That's it, you're officially a Calderly Topper. You have your Chucker badge – you're one of us now!'

Polly glanced down at the little plastic badge sitting proudly on the chest of her jacket and smiled. She'd managed to avoid venting her spleen on any future solitary victims and her shots had been well distributed and well-aimed. She'd definitely earned the right to be on the winning team.

'I'm surprised you didn't bring Taylor and Alanna today. I'm sure they would have loved that.'

'Helen feels they're a bit young yet. She's said they can participate when they're ten and better able to defend themselves.'

'It also gives you a few years to train up their throwing arms.'

'There is also that.'

He threw her a smile as his arm came across her

shoulders and he pulled her to him, holding her tightly against his body until they reached her front door.

'Right, I'd better get home to relieve my mother of Laurel's presence. I'll call you tomorrow.'

He lowered his head and kissed her for several moments before finally releasing her. They were both breathless and he stared into her eyes for a few more seconds before stepping back and releasing her.

'Tomorrow,' he whispered, blowing her a kiss and then turning to stride quickly out of the gate.

44

Christmas Eve

Polly stepped back and admired her handiwork. Thirty-six Viennese mince pies were laid out cooling on the wire trays in front of her. She'd sent Marian a text last night, after getting her number from Monty, asking if she could bring something for the buffet this evening. Marian had replied that she wouldn't say no to more of the delicious mince pies Maxwell had brought round a few nights ago.

She went to the cupboard and pulled out a smaller cooling tray which she placed alongside the others on the worktop. After carefully inspecting each pie, she put the least attractive ones to one side. She'd keep those for herself. The rest would accompany her this evening.

Maxwell had sent a text saying he'd come for her at three o'clock and to ensure Bailey was fed as she'd be home late. To this end, she'd already fed him his main meal but had put an extra one in his timer bowl just to keep him going.

She was now going to enjoy a long soak in a bubble-filled bath before getting dressed. She'd really dithered over what to wear and had pulled out almost everything in her wardrobe. How on earth could she find something that was reasonably dressy but that she'd still be able to walk a couple of miles in. From the corner of her eye, she caught a movement through the window and when she walked over for a proper look, she saw a snow plough moving slowly along the road above the house. She ran down the stairs, pulled on her wellies and upon walking up the lane, was thrilled to see patches of grey tarmac beginning to show underneath the salt and grit which had just been laid. With a bit of luck, Maxwell would be able to pick her up in the truck. She took a photograph and sent it to him to let him know. She waited for a reply but when one didn't come, she merely shrugged, went back indoors and returned to her bedroom to sort out her evening attire with more confidence.

It was a few minutes after three when Maxwell pulled onto her driveway in his pick-up truck. The tins filled with the mince pies were stacked on the hallway table, ready to be passed to him. The bags containing her Christmas presents had been placed underneath and she'd give them to Maxwell when he brought her back home later tonight.

She was just pulling on her coat when he knocked on the door.

'Hey, perfect timing. These are the mince pies for your mum, do you mind putting them in the cab for me while I lock up?'

'Of course, no problem.'

He placed a quick, soft kiss on her cheek as he took the tins from her hands. She locked the door and followed him, giving him a smile as he held the door open for her and gave her a hand up.

'Oh, so gentlemanly. It must be Christmas,' she teased.

'Hmm, it must be,' he murmured but she couldn't help noticing that he seemed distracted.

'Is everything alright?' she asked as he got into the driver's seat.

'Oh, er… yeah, yeah. Christmas Eve, you know. Always worrying you've bought everything you need, done everything that needs to be done and have enough batteries for the kids' toys.'

'I see.'

She actually didn't. Her sixth sense was screaming at her that something was wrong but as Maxwell didn't feel inclined to share it with her, there wasn't much she could do. She knew Laurel Devine's presence was the root of the problem but that was a conversation Polly didn't want to have a second time. Perhaps now the roads were being cleared, her driver would be able to come and collect her. Maybe *that* was the reason Maxwell was out of sorts. Was she leaving and he didn't want her to go? Had she succeeded in getting back under his skin? Only one way to find out…

'So, now that the roads are passable again, is Laurel's driver coming to pick her up today? Or has he already been? Is she gone?'

'No, she's still here. The driving agency had no one spare to come for her. This is one of their busiest days and everyone was booked. We're stuck with her now until after Christmas.'

'After Christmas? Oh no!'

Her heart sank. Just when she'd thought it couldn't get any worse, it had.

'You can imagine how well that has gone down with my parents.'

'Not very?'

'You've got it in one.'

There wasn't much more she could say, or wanted to say, so she just looked out of the window until they pulled up to the farmhouse. Several cars were already parked there which suggested the other guests had arrived.

Between them, they carried the cake tins to the house and Maxwell led her through to the kitchen.

'Polly, you're here. Welcome to our little Christmas party. What can I get you to drink? Oh, Maxwell, dear, just pop those tins over there and take Polly's coat.'

Marian fussed about, poured her the glass of white wine she'd requested and after exclaiming delightfully over the mince pies, took her through to the lounge.

'I'll leave you in David's care, Polly. He'll introduce you to everyone. I need to return to the kitchen.'

'Oh, is there anything I can do to help?'

'No, not at all, dear. You're a guest. I'll be through shortly. I only have a few bits to finish off for the buffet. Once they're out of the oven and plated, I can sit down and join in.'

David came over and walked her around the room, introducing her as he'd been instructed to do and she soon found herself in a team with another couple, Alistair and Kirsty, who asked her if she'd like to join them for a game of snakes and ladders. Soon she was so engrossed in trying to avoid the reptilian pitfalls that it was a while before she realised Maxwell wasn't in the room.

And neither was Laurel.

Icy fingers ran down her spine as her brain instantly came up with a trillion scenarios on why this might be and none of them were good. She heard voices in the hallway and saw Monty and Andy come through the door. They waved to her and smiled before David approached them and took them off, no doubt to assist Marian with something. She turned her attention back to the game and upon throwing a five, found herself sliding down the largest snake on the board and all the way back to the second row of the game.

'Oh, tough luck,' said Alistair, who then went on to throw the four he needed to win.

'Ah, this was fun. I haven't played that since I was a girl,' Kirsty smiled.

'I think I fancy a wee pick at the buffet before starting anything else. Polly, would you like to join us?'

'Thank you, Alistair, but I think I should go and say hello to Monty. He's my boss and it may not go down so well if I don't.'

'Very well. See you in a bit.'

She watched them go and then went to find Monty.

'Hi, Polly, you're just in time to help with cutlery rolling.'

He and Andy were in the kitchen wrapping paper napkins around forks and spoons and placing them in jars to sit on the buffet table.

'Hi, guys, thank you for the extra days off, that was very kind of you.'

'Oh, not a problem. There wasn't much going on so it just made sense to begin the holidays a few days earlier given the weather. What did you do? Anything exciting?'

She filled them in on the activities Maxwell had arranged and expressed how impressed she was that he'd managed to work around the snow.

'Ah, that's Maxwell for you. He's always been quite ingenious that way. When we were kids, he was the one with the imagination and who came up with the best games to play.'

'So, where is he now? I can't imagine your mother letting him off entertainment duties if she's got you both sorting the cutlery.'

Monty and Andy exchanged a look.

'What? Tell me, what's going on?'

With a sigh, Monty shoved his rolls of cutlery into a jar and turned to look at her.

'This afternoon, when Maxwell left to pick you up, the less-than-delightful Ms Devine decided to down half a bottle of Dad's favourite moonshine liqueur all in one. Apparently, she was angry and depressed at the amount of time Maxwell has been spending with you rather than with her. Mum walked into the kitchen just in time to catch her glugging down the dregs of the bottle.'

'Oh, bugger!'

'Yeah! Bugger indeed! That stuff's fifty percent proof and takes no prisoners. One shot of it has my head spinning so half a bottle doesn't bear thinking about. Mum's been at the end of her tether with Laurel for most of the week, what with her constant whining and catering demands. She didn't like her when she and Maxwell were actually dating and she now loathes her for all the trouble she's been causing. You see, Mum really likes you. She thinks you're good for Maxwell and was adamant that he kept his promise to you for your advent-ures, so she's kind of stepped in to keep Laurel occupied while he was with you but that also means she's borne most of the crap. She had no choice but to text Maxwell when he was on his way to get you to let him know what she'd done and warn him what he'd be coming back to.'

'Ah! That explains why he was so preoccupied when we were driving back although he never said anything.'

'He wouldn't. He sees Laurel as his problem and not something you should be involved with.'

'So, where are they now?'

'Out in the garden. We've been told there was a nice vomiting session just after you both arrived and he's out there with her now, hoping the fresh air will help to sober her up.'

At that moment, Marian's voice rang out as she called for Monty to hurry up with the cutlery. He picked up two of the jars and walked out.

'Hang in there, Polly, she won't be around for long.'

Andy gave her arm a gentle squeeze then picked up the remaining jars of cutlery and followed Monty to the dining room.

Seeing she was alone in the kitchen, Polly went over to the back door and slipped out. She found herself in the conservatory, looking out into the garden beyond. The plethora of outdoor Christmas lights, shining snowmen and brightly-lit Santas made it easy for her to see the couple sitting side-by-side on the bench. Maxwell had his arm around Laurel and her head was resting on his shoulder. As she stood there, Polly watched him turn and lay a kiss on Laurel's head.

Alone, in the dark, her heart broke into a thousand pieces.

45

It was half-past ten, the games had been packed away and the guests were now milling about, putting on coats and gathering up their belongings. Marian was handing out plastic boxes filled with leftovers from the buffet. Polly was doing her bit to help by stacking the empty plates in the dishwasher.

What a night it had been. How she'd managed to smile, laugh and act as though all was normal, she would never know. Helen had arrived with Alanna and Taylor a few minutes after she'd come back in from the conservatory and the children had been ecstatic to see her, giving her hugs and asking about Bailey. Their happy chatter about Santa Claus coming that night had helped to keep her distracted and they'd joined together to play tiddlywinks with Monty and Andy. They'd been halfway through the game when Maxwell had walked in with Laurel clinging to his arm. They'd been stuck together like that for the rest of the evening and there had been no opportunity to talk with him. Not that there was much she could say. It was perfectly clear that Laurel had got what she'd come for –

Maxwell was back in her clutches and plain Polly Snowflake hadn't stood a chance.

'Do you want to come in the car with us, Polly?'

'Where are we going?'

Monty smiled at her.

'I'm sorry, I'm not allowed to say.'

'Oh, I—'

'Polly will be coming in the truck with me. This is her last advent-ure, we'll be sharing it together.'

Maxwell looked down at his brother and the expression on his face was one that Monty clearly knew not to argue with.

'Okay. If you think that's a good idea, then fine. We'll see you shortly.'

Andy and Monty walked out of the kitchen, leaving them alone.

'Don't bother with the rest of those plates, Polly, Mum can sort them when she gets back.'

'No, I want to finish. There's only a few left and then the dishwasher can be running while we're out. Where are we going anyway?'

'You'll find out shortly. Now, go and get your things. I'll finish loading the machine.'

Ten minutes later she walked outside to the pick-up truck and was stunned to see Laurel sitting in the front passenger seat. She looked at Maxwell and he gave her a beseeching look, one that asked for her understanding.

Oh, she understood alright! She'd been relegated in every way. Removed from his side and pushed to the back. Or in this case, the back seat.

Without a word, she climbed in and sat in stony silence for the whole of the journey. When the truck parked up, she was out before the engine had been turned off and was surprised to find herself in the car park behind Monty's office and Marian, David, Helen and the children waiting for them.

'Monty and Andy have gone ahead to secure our seats but we need to be quick. They won't be able to hold them for long.'

Marian slipped her arm through Polly's and they all walked down the little alley that brought them out onto the main road of the town where she found herself being gently guided along until they came to the lit-up church where the notice board welcomed them to the Christmas Eve service.

'Oh! We're going in here, are we?'

'We do it every year, Polly. It's a family tradition. It's always a lovely service and such a nice way to go into Christmas Day.'

When they were inside, the children ran ahead to join their friends sitting on the front pews. Andy and Monty were sitting eight rows back from the front and she could see the relief on their faces at their arrival. Judging by how busy the place was, she suspected they'd had their work cut out trying to keep the seats. David stood to the side to allow her to slide in first with Marian following. He then placed himself next to his wife with Helen on his other side leaving Maxwell and Laurel to squeeze in on the end. Polly was as far away from Maxwell as it was possible to be and she wondered if they had contrived this arrangement between them. After all, Maxwell wouldn't want his family to be embarrassed in front of the whole town by having his old flame and recent small fling sitting on either side of him.

Well, fine! If that's how it was going to be, she would brazen this out the best she could. After tonight, she wouldn't have to see him again and he could return to his glamorous lifestyle with his glamorous supermodel girlfriend by his side. It now seemed that all his talk of walking away from that world had been exactly that – just talk!

She felt the tears pricking her eyes and she blinked several times, determined not to let them fall. She only had about an hour or so to go and it would all be over.

She could do this!

'Wasn't that a lovely service?'

'It was very nice, Marian. And the children singing "Little Donkey" was super cute.'

Polly, despite her sorrow, had found the service both touching and soothing. She was surprised to find she felt quite peaceful although she knew this was only temporary. It would pass soon enough.

As they walked up the aisle towards the doors, people were stopping each other to pass on their season's greetings and Polly soon found herself alone, separated from those she'd arrived with. Rather than trying to find them in the crowd, she walked out to the churchyard and stood to one side so as not to be in people's way. It was a clear, fresh night and the stars twinkled overhead. The snow was still piled up around the grounds of the church but the path had been cleared to ensure the safety of those who'd attended this evening.

'Ah, Polly, there you are. Come on, let's go.'

Maxwell appeared in front of her, Laurel, unsurprisingly, still clutching his arm.

'But I haven't yet wished your parents or the children a Merry Christmas. The people in the pew behind us got in there before I had a chance to.'

Maxwell hesitated but didn't get the chance to reply as Laurel decided she'd had enough.

'Oh, Maxie, it's cold out here. Please, can we just go, I've had enough hanging about…'

Polly saw him clench his jaw at the sound of Laurel's

whining tone and for a moment, she felt sorry for him. The moment was fleeting, however, and she quickly hardened her resolve. He'd made his choice, now he had to live with it.

'Okay. Sorry, Polly, we have to leave now.'

'Fair enough. Let's go.'

She set off at a pace, her shoulders back and her head up. No way was she going to let him see how upset she was. In a few minutes, they were back at the truck and as soon as he clicked the lock, she opened the door for the back seat and climbed in. As Laurel got in the front, she turned her head and threw a small smile of victory in Polly's direction. This time, it was she who was clenching her teeth as she turned her head to stare pointedly out of the window.

When they pulled into her driveway, Polly was once again out of the truck before Maxwell had cut the engine. Her key was already in the lock when he caught up with her, carrying the tins she'd packed the mince pies in earlier.

Was it really only a few hours since she'd stood here, all excited and looking forward to a night that had now joined her father's death and Trevor's betrayal as one of the most painful she'd experienced over the years?

'Here you are,' he said, handing the tins over.

He then bent down, placed a perfunctory kiss on her cheek, turned and walked away. Halfway to the truck he stopped to look back at her. She held her breath, waiting… hoping he'd say something which would give her an atom of belief that they still had something.

He drew in a breath and she waited to hear what he was about to say but then his shoulders sagged and all she heard was, 'Merry Christmas, Polly.'

By the time she'd closed the front door, he was driving out of the gate and out of her life.

For a moment or two, she stood stock still on the

doormat, not really knowing what to do with herself. It was the arrival of Bailey, coming to see why she was taking so long to give him his fuss, that prompted her into moving. She placed the tins on the side table, took off her coat, hung it up and kicked off her boots.

It was when she picked the tins back up that she spied the bags of gifts still sitting under the table. Maxwell had gone before she'd had a chance to give them to him.

The sight of the brightly coloured presents was her breaking point and dropping the cake tins on the floor, she let out an almighty wail, ran up the stairs and, throwing herself on her bed, proceeded to cry her broken heart out.

46

Christmas Day

With a groan, Polly sat up and tried to open her eyes but her mascara, combined with her tears, had clogged them shut and she had to use her fingers to gently prise them apart.

'Bailey, remind me the next time my heart is broken, to make sure I'm wearing waterproof mascara.'

The cat nudged her elbow in response although she didn't think it was an affirmation of her comment. More likely a reminder that it was after nine o'clock and he hadn't been fed yet.

She stumbled down the stairs, quite literally plonked some meat out of a tin into his bowl and then returned to her bedroom where she sat on the edge of the bed and tried to think. She could really have done with talking to Ritchie but he'd still be sleeping after the inevitable late-night Christmas Eve party he'd planned for his staff when the restaurant had closed and then they were off to Scott's parents for Christmas dinner. She was going to have to sort this one out on her own.

When it was all boiled down, she had two choices. She could give in and allow herself to wallow in the pain that was swimming through every pore of her body or she could woman-up, accept that the last twenty-four days had been a time of unexpected fun and amazing experiences and move herself forward. If Maxwell wanted to be with a skinny, anorexic, bony bitch of a supermodel, then that was his choice and he'd be the one who'd have to deal with the inevitable fallout when it came. Because if there was one thing Polly was quite sure of – Laurel Devine was the kind of person who was more intent on winning rather than looking after the prize she'd won.

Her heart clenched at the thought of Maxwell feeling what she was feeling now. She wouldn't wish it on anyone, even if they did bring it on themselves. By wishing Maxwell ill, she only brought herself down to Laurel's level and she'd never do that.

With that thought foremost in her mind, she drew in a deep breath, stood up and walked towards the bathroom. She hesitated for a moment and looked back at her bed. It would be so easy to crawl back in, curl up and let the next few days pass by in a blur of tears…

'No! You will NOT do that!' she said out loud. 'You are stronger than this. Now get in that shower and clean yourself up!'

Using every iota of self-preservation she could muster, she pulled herself up straight, lifted her chin and walked into the bathroom. As the words of the song went, she was going to wash Maxwell Watkins out of her hair… and out of her life.

When the loud knock on the door came two hours later, Polly was deeply immersed in her latest book, curled up on the sofa under her throw and with Bailey snuggled up beside her. The noise jolted her out of the dark cave under the pyramids in Egypt and back onto her sofa in the Peak District.

'Huh? Wha—'

The knocking came again, this time more insistent.

'Okay, okay, I'm coming,' she muttered under her breath.

She opened the door and stepped back in shock when she saw who was standing on the doorstep, their hand raised to knock again.

'Helen?'

'Hi, Polly.'

'Er, what are you doing here? Is there a problem? Is everyone okay?'

'There's no problem and everyone is fine. Well... sort of!'

'What do you mean?'

'Um, can I come in? It's a bit nippy out here.'

'Oh, gosh, yes, I'm so sorry. Please, do come in.'

Polly moved to the side to allow Helen to enter but her mind was whirling as she closed the door. Of all the people she'd thought might be visiting her today, Helen was as far removed from the list as it was possible to be.

'Can I get you something? Tea? Coffee?'

'No, thank you, we don't have time.'

'Don't have time?'

Normally a rather patient person, Polly was beginning to feel that she might end up giving Helen a damn good shake if she didn't hurry up and get down to the reason for her being here.

'Marian is serving up her Christmas dinner just after one o'clock, so we need to get a move on to ensure we're back in time and you're all settled.'

With a sigh, Polly replied, 'Helen, I really don't have a clue what you're talking about.'

'Maxwell was supposed to ask you to join us for Christmas dinner today. When Marian found out that he hadn't, she went through him quicker than an extra-hot vindaloo curry. She is furious.'

'But… Laurel—'

'— is currently being airlifted out in a helicopter.'

'IS WHAT?'

'You heard! With all her shenanigans yesterday, she left her mobile phone in her cabin and missed a load of phone calls from her agent. She only found them this morning. It turns out a job has come up and she needs to be in St Lucia by the twenty-seventh. Some other model fell ill and they needed a replacement ASAP.'

'But… what about her declarations of love for Maxwell and all that? Isn't he supposed to be everything she needs and wants in her life?'

'Pfft! I think you and I both know that the only thing Laurel Devine needs and loves in her life is Laurel Devine! As soon as she heard this job was a Vogue shoot, she couldn't get out of the place quick enough. The agency somehow managed to sort out a helicopter – it's amazing what money can get you, even on Christmas Day – and as I was being instructed by Marian to come and find you, she was packing her stuff to leave. She should be long gone by the time we return.'

'Why didn't Maxwell tell me about the invite? Why didn't he come to pick me up?'

'Why Maxwell didn't tell you about the invite is something you'll need to find out from him. The reason he didn't come to get you is because Marian has given him the job of sorting out a cabin for you. She figured he was getting off too lightly if he'd been the one to pick you up so I offered to do so instead.'

'That's really kind of you, especially as I know you don't like me.'

'Don't like you? Where on earth did you get that idea?' Helen's face was a picture of incredulity.

'The day we were at the church, sorting the hampers, I caught you looking at me, as if you were sizing me up, and you didn't seem too happy with what you were seeing.'

'I was definitely trying to suss you out, you've got that right, but not for the reasons you might think. My kids had arrived home the previous weekend talking non-stop about this *cool* woman with the *cool* cat and *cool* television who was a *cool* baker and who'd made them a *cool* gingerbread house. I mean, come on! One "cool" is all it takes for a mother to feel inadequate – can you imagine what five of them were doing to me? I was trying to work out how genuine you really were.'

'Oh!'

There was nothing Polly could come back with on that so she gave a small shrug and said, 'If it helps, I can show you how to make a wonderful rabbit cake that will give you all the *cool* kudos at Easter...'

'Do you know, Polly,' Helen pulled her into a hug, 'I think you and I are going to be really good friends.'

Myriad feelings ran through her as she returned Helen's surprisingly lovely gesture of friendship. She couldn't ever recall having this many people care about her but here was Helen waiting to take her to the Christmas dinner Marian was insisting she be a part of. Monty and Andy had become dear friends, Alanna and Taylor thought she was "cool" and Ritchie, despite being many miles away in London, was still her pillar of strength whenever she needed him. She felt very blessed. The only person who didn't seem to be in her corner, right now, was Maxwell.

'Now then,' Helen stepped back, 'you need to go and

get your stuff together. Bring enough clothes for a couple of days.'

'Oh, but Bailey—'

'We've already thought of him. That's why Maxwell is sorting you out a cabin – so that Bailey can come along but where you have your own space and he won't be bothered by lots of strangers. Now, if you'll point me in the direction of where I can find his belongings, I'll sort him out while you sort yourself out. I've got Maxwell's pick-up, so there's plenty of space for litter boxes, scratching trees and so on.'

The tears were pricking at her eyes as she walked back over to Helen.

'Thank you so much for this, I... I... just thank you.'

Helen grasped her hands.

'Hey, it's fine. Now go, grab your gear otherwise Maxwell will think you're not coming and begin to panic... although, after what he's put you through, it would serve him right!'

She gave an evil little smile that had Polly chuckling out loud. Yup, Helen was right, it looked like they could be very good friends indeed.

After pointing Helen towards the kitchen and the adjoining utility room where she'd find most of Bailey's stuff, Polly ran up the stairs and was just walking along the gallery when Helen called up to her.

'Oh, Polly...'

'Yes?'

She looked down over the banister.

'Maxwell said don't forget the sexy underwear!'

<u>47</u>

'Hey, you came.'

Maxwell had been waiting at the door of the farmhouse as they pulled up in front of it. He ran down to help her out and was immediately followed by Taylor and Alanna.

'Polly! Polly! Have you brought Bailey? Can we see him? Please?'

'Let Polly get him settled in the cabin, you two. If you ask nicely, she might let you see him later.'

'Awwww, Muuuuum!'

'Look, if your mum is agreeable, you can help me put his stuff in the cabin. Your gran will be looking to serve dinner soon so I could do with your assistance.'

'Mummy, can we help? Please…'

'Oh, go on then!' Helen grinned at Polly and said, 'It had better be one hell of a rabbit cake, lady!'

They both burst out laughing and when Maxwell stood looking totally perplexed between them, they laughed even harder.

'Okay, Maxwell, where's this cabin you're putting me up in? I don't want Bailey getting too stressed in his basket.'

'I'll take you there. It'll be easier to drive the truck up to the door.'

He jumped in behind the steering wheel and let out a curse as his legs clattered against it.

'Helen!' he yelled, 'how many times have I asked you to put the seat back when you're finished?'

'Oops, did I forget,' she replied sweetly, 'sorry.'

As she turned away towards the farmhouse, she gave Polly a little side wink which set them both off again.

'Oh, bloody hell! I can see I'm going to have to keep you two apart.'

'Daddy! You swore!'

Polly turned around to see Alanna and Taylor on the back seat, one on each side of Bailey who'd now decided to take a vow of silence. Something he hadn't thought worth doing on the ten-minute journey from her house to here.

The drive round to the cabin was less than two minutes and Polly was glad the children were present. She wasn't ready for getting into a deep discussion with Maxwell right now over why his mother's invitation hadn't been extended.

It didn't take long for the four of them to empty her belongings and Bailey's out of the pick-up and into the pretty cabin. She didn't have time for a proper look around but the front door led into an open-plan kitchen, diner and lounge with doors at the far end that led onto a wooden veranda. There was also a downstairs cloakroom under the stairs and she opted to put Bailey's litter tray in there.

An open, wooden staircase led up to a large double-bedroom with a high, sloping roof and an ensuite bathroom. She dropped her carry-bag at the foot of the bed, laid her rucksack with her toiletries by the bathroom door, admired the view from the window for a brief second and by the time she'd returned downstairs, the children had spread Bailey's throw over the sofa and put some food and water in his bowls.

'Does he need anything else?' Alanna asked, poking her fingers through the gaps in his carry basket and gently stroking his nose.

'No, thank you. If you could just give me a few minutes alone with him while I let him out and get him settled.'

'That's not a problem. I'll park the truck over at mine and pick you up on the way back. I'll be a few minutes.'

'Thanks, Maxwell. That would be great.'

By the time the gentle knock came on the door, Bailey had sniffed about, found his food bowl and now had his nose in the trough! Polly figured he'd be okay on his own. She'd had a quick look about and couldn't see anything that might be a hazard to him.

'Are you ready to face a Watkins Christmas dinner? I warn you now – it's not for the faint-hearted.'

'I'm game! Now, if you could kindly take these bags for me, we'd better get a move on or Marian will be having a fit.'

They walked along the gravelled track that had been cleared of snow although the mounds at the side had small gaps and holes where little hands had gathered up snow for snowball throwing. When they reached the front door of the farmhouse, the children ran inside, leaving the door open wide behind them.

Polly found herself grinding to a halt on the doormat as she looked down the hallway, hearing the sounds of laughter and Christmas music blaring. Marian's voice carried on the cinnamon-scented air towards her as she berated David for sneaking mince pies behind her back. Just for a moment, all the fear and terror returned as the very same memories from her childhood sprung out of the recesses in her mind. The scene before her was being replicated in households all around the world – some things never changed, only the people did.

'Hey, it'll be okay. I'm here. You can do this.' Maxwell gently rubbed her back before taking her hand and placing a soft kiss on it. 'If it gets too much, let me know and we can come out for a breather, okay?'

'Okay.'

She smiled at him before taking a deep breath and stepping over the threshold.

48

'Oh, Helen, thank you, it's gorgeous.'

Everyone was now sitting in the lounge opening their Christmas presents and Polly had been quite shocked to find there were several with her name on. She'd just opened a lovely midnight blue, silky pashmina from Helen that would look gorgeous with her grandmother's coat.

She laid it on the pile in front of her which consisted of a new red coat from Monty that was a replica of the one he'd lent her when they'd first met but this one had been custom-made just for her and Andy had given her a cashmere beret and leather gloves in the exact same shade of red. She suspected he may have had them dyed specially.

Marian had given her the latest recipe book from the woman on the television who featured in a highly popular baking show and David had gifted her a bottle of his favourite tipple, Wild Berry Moonshine, that she'd found rather delicious when he'd asked her opinion on it last week. The children gave her a beautifully decorated cake cover made of tin although upon seeing the Cath Kidston logo on the side, she suspected it had been Helen's pocket money that had bought it rather than Alanna's and Taylor's.

Her favourite present, however, was the little silver and diamond snowflake pendant with matching stud earrings, from Maxwell. They were so delicate, not at all chunky, and exactly what she would have chosen herself.

When it was his turn to open her gift, Polly found it almost impossible to breathe. What if he didn't like it? What if she'd been too presumptuous? After all, she'd barely known him a few days when she'd ordered it although she knew that even after twenty-four days of knowing him, she would still have bought him the same gift.

'Oh wow! That's beautiful.'

Everyone in the room exclaimed when he removed the polystyrene packaging to reveal the beautifully carved reindeer inside. Deric's skill had brought the wooden carving almost to life. She'd sent him some of the photographs she'd taken of the reindeer on their visit to the farm and he'd captured the likeness to perfection, right down to the cheeky little twinkle in its eye.

'Polly, this is absolutely gorgeous.'

She knew he was being genuine from the way he was running his hand over the smooth, polished wood and inspecting the carving.

'Deric has done a good job.'

'Deric? You asked Deric to make this?'

'I most certainly did. I would say there's a good chance that the wood is one of the pieces you gave him.'

'They do say that things have a way of finding their way back to us…'

When everyone had finished opening their gifts and were talking over each other, creating a cacophony of sounds, Polly slipped quietly out of the room and was putting her coat on in the hallway when Maxwell appeared at her side.

'Not leaving already, are you?'

'I just want to go and check on Bailey – make sure he's alright.'

'I'll come with you. Just to make sure you do end up at the correct cabin.'

'I think I'll be able to find it.'

'I'll come anyway. Mum would not be happy if she thought I'd let you just wander off on your own. I'm still working my way back into her good books.'

He pulled on his thick, padded jacket and followed her outside.

They walked in silence for a moment or two, the stars glinting in the sky above. Old-fashioned style lampposts lit their way. A frost had come down and she could see her breath in the air as the gravel crunched under their feet. When Maxwell didn't say anything, Polly decided to get things out in the open.

'Maxwell, why didn't you tell me your mum had invited me to Christmas dinner? Surely you'd worked out I was going to be alone today. After all your efforts to make me love Christmas again, didn't you think this would have made a grand ending?'

'Oh, Polly,' he turned to face her, 'that was very much my plan. After the service last night, I was going to ask you to be my date for Christmas dinner today. I wanted to make it special, to make it really mean something. I'd hoped that by us being there as a couple, it would help to make the day easier for you. I understood that despite everything we'd done together this month, that Christmas Day was going to be the big one for you and I wanted to be with you to help you through it.'

'So… why—'

'Laurel! Bloody Laurel! You saw the way she was

behaving yesterday. She didn't give a damn about how she was affecting those around her – she only cared that she wasn't getting what she wanted and what she seemed to want was me!'

'But I saw you with her, out in the garden. You were sitting on the bench… you had your arm around her… you kissed her. That's what you do to people you care about.'

'It's also what you do when you're trying to pacify a narcissistic drunk so they won't ruin the party for everyone else.'

'And the invite from your mum?'

'I didn't want you having to witness Laurel fawning, flirting and draping herself over me all day long which is what she would have done. Messing with people's heads is one of her specialities – I know, I've been there. Today was going to be hard enough for you without adding her to the mix. I even thought about coming over to your place and it just being the two of us but the kids… and my parents… I honestly didn't know the best thing to do so I chose to do nothing. And hurt you into the bargain.'

He dropped his head and Polly felt her heart go out to him. He had been between a rock and a hard place. He was quite right in that the last thing she'd have wanted to see was Laurel going all out to claim him as hers. That would have hurt far more than being home alone without him.

'I understand. Laurel created an impossible situation for you. But she's gone now and we're still here, together.' She smiled at him. 'Were you really going to ask me to be your date?'

'I was.'

'You could still ask me…'

'To be my date?'

'Yes.'

'But… most of the day has gone.'

'But most of the night has not.'

He pulled her to him and she felt his warm breath on her face as his eyes shone from the streetlight behind her.

'Polly Snowflake, would you do me the honour of being my special Christmas date?'

'Maxwell Watkins, nothing would give me more pleasure than to be your Christmas date.'

'And what about New Year? Will you be my date for that too?'

'I will.'

'Can we sort out Valentine's Day while we're here?'

'I'll book it out just for you.'

'Now, how about Easter…'

Polly bit down on a giggle when she saw how serious he was. She looked up into his eyes and seeing all the feelings she held for him reflected back, her heart contracted tightly inside her. After all these lonely years, had she finally found a happy ending?

Was he her "Happy Ever After"?

It was too soon to tell but one thing she did know for sure – he was her "Happy Right Now" and that was a damn good place to start.

'Well? Will you be my date for Easter?'

'Bring me a Hotel Chocolat egg and I'll be all yours.'

'It's a deal!'

She briefly saw the smile on his face before his lips were on hers and he pulled her close to him, holding her tighter than he'd ever held her before, as though he never wanted to let her go.

His lips moved along her cheek, as he dotted soft kisses on her face. When he reached her ear, he nibbled the lobe ever so gently, causing an explosion of fireworks all around her body, before murmuring, 'Merry Christmas, my beautiful snowflake, Merry Christmas.'

ABOUT THE AUTHOR

Kiltie Jackson spent her childhood years growing up in Scotland. Most of these early years were spent in and around Glasgow although for a short period of time, she wreaked havoc at a boarding school in the Highlands.

By the age of seventeen, she had her own flat which she shared with a couple of cats for a few years while working as a waitress in a cocktail bar (she's sure there's a song in there somewhere!) and serving customers in a fashionable clothing outlet before moving down to London to chalk up a plethora of experience which is now finding its way into her writing.

Once she'd wrung the last bit of fun out of the smoky capital, she moved up to the Midlands and now lives in Staffordshire with one grumpy husband and another six feisty felines.

Her little home is known as Moggy Towers even though, despite having plenty of moggies, there are no towers! The cats kindly allow her and Mr Mogs to share their home as long as the mortgage continues to be paid.

Since the age of three, Kiltie has been an avid reader although it was many years later before she decided to put pen to paper – or fingers to keyboard – to begin giving life to the stories in her head. Her debut novel was released in September 2017 and her fourth book was a US Amazon bestseller in Time Travel Romance.

Kiltie loves to write fiery and feisty female characters and puts the blame for this firmly on the doorsteps of Anne

Shirley from Anne of Green Gables and George Kirrin from The Famous Five.

When asked what her best memories are, Kiltie will tell you:

1. Queuing up overnight outside the Glasgow Apollo to buy her Live-Aid ticket.
2. Being at Live-Aid.
3. Winning an MTV competition to meet Bon Jovi in Sweden.

(Although, if Mr Mogs is in earshot, the latter is changed to her wedding day.)

Her main motto in life used to be "Old enough to know better, young enough not to care!" but that has since been replaced with "Too many stories, not a fast enough typist!"

Printed in Great Britain
by Amazon